L E A V I N G ◆ M O N T A N A

THOMAS WHALEY

SAKURA PUBLISHING
Hermitage, Pennsylvania
USA

LEAVING MONTANA

THOMAS WHALEY

LEAVING MONTANA

Sakura Publishing
PO BOX 1681
Hermitage, PA 16148
www.sakura-publishing.com

ORDERING INFORMATION:

Quantity sales: Special discounts are available on quantity purchases by corporations, associations, and others. For details, contact the publisher at the address above. Orders by U.S. trade bookstores and wholesalers. Please contact Sakura Publishing:

Tel: (330) 360-5131; or visit
www.sakura-publishing.com.

Edited by Quentin Whitfield
Designed by Rania Meng
Photography by Tyler Cervantez, Shutterbird Photography

First Edition
Printed in the United States of America

ISBN-10: 0991180771
ISBN-13: 978-0-9911807-7-6

THIS BOOK IS DEDICATED
TO CARL, MY ROCKSTAR
HUSBAND, FOR MAKING
ME REALIZE I DON'T HAVE
TO RAISE MY VOICE TO BE
HEARD, AND FOR ANDREW
AND LUKE, MY AMAZING
SONS, WHO NEGATE THAT.

CHAPTER ONE

◆

M Y BAGS WERE ALREADY PACKED. I had made sure to put them in the car the night before, so I wouldn't disturb anyone. The alarm was set for three in the morning, but I had already woken up. I shut it off. Waking up before the alarm was something that happened to me often, especially when it was an important day. Growing up, it was always the first day of school, or my birthday, but as I aged, it became quite common.

I enjoyed lying in the darkness, listening to all the subtle sounds a sleeping house makes. It was soothing, but these were also the moments when I thought too much. And, I already had a lot on my mind.

My partner and two daughters were fast asleep, as I quietly prepared for the monumental day in the soft light coming from the master bedroom. I had been waiting almost two years for the day to arrive. Making these particular plans come to fruition had not been easy—especially for someone who was used to being quick and efficient. It was the day I opened the door, and emptied "*it*" out. Well, almost. It would be another day or two before I had the chance to empty "*it*" in its entirety, but the door was ajar. That was the most exciting part.

Having already showered the night before, I quickly rinsed myself off and fumbled around the bathroom, getting ready. The master bathroom was tight to begin with, and trying to be quiet made it seem even smaller. Our shower was the stand-up kind. It was like being in a test tube, and my elbows kept hitting the oversized shampoo bin, suctioned cupped to the side. Every drawer I opened, and each item I placed on the counter, made a louder noise than usual, but I wanted to make sure I looked perfect for the trip.

I slipped on my favorite pair of broken-in jeans, a maroon hoodie that I had gotten on a family trip to Maine a few years prior, my running shoes, and a ball cap. I had already laid out everything on the ironing board before I went to bed. It was going to be a long day of travel, and comfort was key.

I made sure not to dig too deep in my massive, walk-in closet. Only the things that I found easily came with me. This proved to be a very difficult process. Being a certified clothes whore *(and proud of it, I may add),* made it extremely hard to decide what to pack. Would I need something dressy, in case we went out to a nice restaurant? Did I need a classy sweater? Do I pack a pair of dress shoes just in case? A matching belt? This caused me stress every time I traveled, but this time, not having to dress like a professional made me happy, and somehow, it was easier to turn down all the accessories calling my name.

Faint, distant beeps from the coffee maker invited me from down the hall, into the kitchen. I inhaled the potent Columbian fragrance like a pothead inhales dope. The intense aroma always made me smile, but today, it needed to be especially strong— something that would keep me alert. Focused. Calm. Saying I had a severe addiction to coffee was an understatement. It had been a staple in my maternal grandparents' house, where I spent most of my time growing up. Memories of my grandfather, encouraging me to sip espresso from his tiny cup, as I sat on his heroic lap, came to mind each time I experienced a really good cup of Joe. By the age of nine—I was hooked. And straight up too. Never a drop of milk, and always unsweetened. What I like to call a "real" coffee drinker. Naturally, I was not allowed to drink it in front of my parents at such a young age, but like any child, I was a great sneak.

Last time I drank too much coffee on the way to the airport, I was forced to get out of my car and pee in the middle of traffic, so I made sure to hit the bathroom one last time before leaving.

It was a bitter, December morning, so I enjoyed a cup while my car warmed up. It had been an especially cold winter, and we'd already had well over 36 inches of snowfall on Long Island. A blizzard had dumped nearly 20 inches two weeks prior, so our house still had tall snow walls along the walkway to our front door, *and* the edge of the driveway. Underneath all that snow and ice were my hibernating English-style gardens. Knowing I would nurture and appreciate them sometime soon was the only thing that got me through the winters.

Gardening is one of my passions. Dirt calms my nerves, and whenever I felt anxiety rising, I would head straight to the local nursery. My gardens are the gifts that kept on giving, like my children. From the very beginning—when they are fragile and new, you get to nurture and shape them, hoping they eventually grow to be strong and independent.

A green thumb was one of the very few positive things that I had inherited from my paternal side. My paternal grandfather loved gardening. From as far back as I can remember, his gardens were the most exquisite. Blooms of all shapes and sizes, bursting with sweetness, and attracting a multitude of bees and butterflies. I would sit and stare. I often wished I could live inside one of his gardens. It was quiet there. When he passed away, his gardens died along with him. I would like to believe I am his apprentice, but to this day, I still cannot grow peonies the way he could.

It was not that cold on Long Island—not compared to where I was heading. That was the *only* downside to the journey. I despise snow. I loathe it. And the cold? Unless it is a cold shower, or a refreshing pool on a ninety-degree day, I am not interested. Layers, chapped lips, and wet, cold, wrinkly-gloved hands are not for me.

I am a summer kind of guy. Give me a lawn chair, a cold six-pack, the roaring sun, and by four in the afternoon, I'm a new nationality, ready to sport a crisp white pair of shorts to show off my bronzed skin and great calves. Although cold weather and bulky layers bothered me, I was more than willing to wear three layers for the occasion.

I was already running late. I couldn't procrastinate any longer—especially since it was the only flight of the day that could get me to my final destination. Although I was traveling within "The States," not many New Yorkers had reasons to travel to where I was going. *But I did.* The trip required precise planning, and there was a connection. So if I missed the first flight, I was screwed. Needless to say, I picked up my backpack and added my dirty coffee cup to

"Clutter Island" in the center of my kitchen, rather than putting it into the sink only steps away. Laughing to myself, I made my way down the hall and walked out the front door, gladly forgetting about the mess.

The car ride was tranquil. Hardly anyone on the highway. No questioning children in the backseat, and the sounds of *Simon and Garfunkel,* and *The Carpenters* playing from the radio. I had put those CD's in the car stereo a few days earlier, and now I was truly appreciating that I did. Both had number one hits in 1970. I didn't exist yet, and everyone was still *clean* back then.

I loved music from the 70's. All the songs somehow had lyrics you could relate to. I knew exactly which singers from the 70's to listen to at specific times. *Barry White,* for the times when I liked what I saw staring back at me in the mirror. For summer BBQ's, and trips to Fire Island—*Donna Summer* was a must. *Pink Floyd,* for when I felt the need to drown myself in booze, or lock myself in a dark room. Whatever the emotion—I had the 70's to run to. I truly believed that anyone who was born in the 1970's was conceived in lust, rather than love.

I know I was.

By the way, let me formally introduce myself. I am Benjamin Sean Quinn. Forty. Confidently handsome. Sexy, as I've frequently been told. And a damn good advertising executive. I have a fantastic, caring and supportive partner of 14 years. My home belongs in a Pottery Barn catalog. We live in a prestigious neighborhood, and our two adopted daughters are perfect in every way…but there's one *small* problem.

I am angry as hell.

Angry to the core.

Most people would question, *"How could someone with such a pleasant and obviously privileged life be so angry?"* Most people would, in turn, firmly state, *"What an arrogantly pompous, self-appreciating, douche bag!"* especially based on the way I just described my life, and myself. It is all true. I admit that whole-heartedly. But, I deserve to be. Now, you may think that no one deserves to be so self-appreciating, but I beg to differ. Growing up in a toxic environment that you have no control over forces you to make a choice: adopt that pattern and sink to the bottom, or swim like a motherfucker. I chose the latter. I am an *awesome* swimmer. I wonder if ALL of us have experienced toxicity in our youth—the kind that leaves us branded. But unlike cattle, being scarred with a symbol from a branding iron, it leaves a word on our foreheads that only certain people can see: SHALLOW, VAIN, NAÏVE, SLUT.

Personality traits we try to scrub away, or cover up when they surface. Isn't there at least *one* undesirable personal trait you blame your parents for? I believe you can. If you are someone who has not internally blamed your parents, or at least one of them, for one, or more of your shortcomings, then you must have grown up in a utopia.

It is natural to blame your parents. Everyone does it. It is an unavoidable cycle. We are timid, because our mothers were too overprotective. We have anger and abandonment issues, because our fathers were unloving and never available. We have issues with commitment, because their marriage was a bad one. Who knows what the reasons are. But they are there, lurking deep within.

Blaming my parents for ruining my childhood, and branding me POMPOUS, ARROGANT, SARCASTIC, and God knows what else, is an understatement. I often overhear people complaining about the ridiculous things their biological breeders have done to them, and I laugh inside. *"Big deal,"* I'd say under my breath, hoping they'd hear. *"Come on! You're still upset with your mom for not letting you go to prom with what's-his-name?"* Put that petty shit away already. Let it go. It doesn't matter anymore. Not to mention, it is trifling. Believe me, I know. When you have accumulated the amount of emotional baggage that I have, and yes, I DO blame my parents for it all, then you really can't just forget it. You cannot *let it go*. You *store* it.

This is why I like walk-in-closets.

I LOVE my walk-in-closet. It has *plenty* of storage.

Lined with spacious shelves, deep drawers, shallow drawers, hanging poles of various lengths, and tiered shoe racks—it truly rocks my world. When I stand inside and look around, I see my entire life before me. So many things from my past, yet ample space for my future. It is conceited.

I am a walk-in closet.

I am polished, refined and perfectly coordinated. A private clothing boutique on Fifth Avenue, with Italian cashmere sweaters. I am Calm. Collected. Confident. But in an instant, one thought from my childhood can transform me. I am Disorganized. Wrinkled. Torn.

I am dirty clothes twisted among clean. A confusing jumble of belts, shoes, pants and hats on the floor. Socks stuck in sleeves, ties still knotted, and things inside out. Scattered feelings, and emotions that cannot be sorted out, picked up, washed, or turned right side in.

I am a walk in closet—and just like a walk in closet, when your poles begin to bend, and drawers cannot close—we realize that we have accumulated way too much.

Listen closely, friend…. there comes a time in everyone's life when we hit a crossroads, faced with some of the most difficult decisions we ever have to make. Do we open our closet up and finally clean it out? Or do you close the door and pretend it isn't a total mess? I wanted to open mine. Carmella and Sean chose to close the door and ignore it. I chose to board a plane. When I left the house, I did not close the door. Anyone could peek inside. The effect could cause an emotional catastrophe. But I chose not to care anymore.

———————◆———————

Finding a parking spot at JFK was a pain in the ass, even at five o'clock on a Thursday morning. I lowered the radio, as if that was going to interfere with finding a parking spot. Do you ever notice yourself doing that? Randomly lowering the volume for no apparent reason? I do it all the time.

I focused on all the makes and models of the cars and trucks. It was truly astounding. When you live in a neighborhood full of Range Rovers, Mercedes, BMWs and Saabs, you forget the variety. There was a perfect match for everyone. Imagining what the owners of the vehicles looked like, and where they went, proved to be a humorous way to pass the time while searching for a spot.

Did any of them resemble their cars? You know—the way dogs and their owners eventually morph into one? I slowly approached a brown, oversized, slightly beat-up Yukon, which practically took up two spaces. I noticed that a piece of the side view mirror was missing. *Evander Holyfield*? Maybe just a coincidence, but uncanny none the less. There was also a meek, bullied Toyota next to it. It was missing a hubcap, which in my opinion, is the most unattractive thing about older cars. Hubcaps. Dented, rusted, MISSING. Replace the damn thing! If your shoe falls off, do you just walk around wearing one? Precisely.

Green*ish*. I stared at it for a second. I guess you would call it teal. No automobile should ever be teal. Ever. Or light yellow. Anyhow, after getting slightly annoyed and distracted by the hubcap, I noticed it had a *Reba McIntyre* license plate cover on the front. Obviously, this *car* had much bigger issues.

I stared at it. A concert souvenir, no doubt. The car immediately transformed into the owner. A pear shaped, tall, amazon-like woman, in her mid to late fifties. She was stuck in the 80's—with big, blown out, Ronald McDonald colored hair. She had split ends, but her friends were too nervous to tell her. She was probably on her way to some "I Am Woman, Hear Me Roar" convention. I began to frown, and when I looked into the rearview mirror, I noticed that my head was gently moving side to side in disgust. This very reaction happened to me quite often. I am shocked that it hasn't brought me any bodily harm yet. This caused me to laugh out loud and drip some coffee on my seat.

I quickly pulled over and got out of my car to wipe the coffee off my seat, before I ended up looking like I shit myself. I was still laughing. It felt good. It was the first time I had genuinely laughed recently. Feeling nervous was foreign to me. And although I was very excited about the trip, the unknown was still frightening. Things didn't usually bother me; my skin was thick as a rhino's. Inherited, I guess. Earned? Absolutely.

White lights. Someone was leaving. A flashy new, black Escalade dripping in chrome, was now backing out. It resembled a drug lord's ride. I was immediately intrigued. *True* Long Islanders are drawn to shiny, black Escalades like moths to a flame. "*Thank you!"* I mouthed to the mysterious driver with my thumb up. Again, similar to turning down the volume on a car radio for no reason, I wondered why I was "mouthing" to my hero—speaking through the glass without volume. I do that often too, and I never quite know why.

My mysterious parking spot friend was a gorgeous well-dressed Latino man. I had one word. YUM. His hair was long, wavy and slicked back. Although it was still dark out, he was wearing sunglasses. His shirt— white and crisp. I was impressed. Impressing me was hard to do. I also noticed the sparkle of his diamond cuff links. This sparked a fire. He was *pure* cocaine.

I hope his trip to Columbia was as enjoyable as my coffee.

◆

When I get to an airport, there are three things I look forward to doing: Browsing the magazine shops in search of some *quality* literature, getting myself a large cup of coffee, of course, and finding the right seat to people watch. It is one of the best places to truly appreciate the art of people watching. Airports and malls. Ample seating. Perfect for shallow, self-absorbed people to judge.

Upon finding the perfect spot, I made myself comfortable. To my dismay, there was a lack of interesting people, so I decided to enjoy my coffee and quality literature. *Men's Health, Vanity Fair,* and *GQ.* What did you expect? Shallow. *Need I keep reminding you?* These magazines kept my stomach flat, my wardrobe up to date, and my sex life smoldering. A gay man's guide to a perfect life.

My backpack had all the essentials for a day of travel, and my magazines were only a portion of them. The most important thing in my backpack was my crossword puzzle. I was addicted, especially to the one in the back of The New Yorker. To this day, I am still not sure why *that* particular crossword from *that* particular magazine brought me the most joy, but it did. I don't even read the content. It would require too much concentration. Sitting down with a pen, and having the uninterrupted time to work on one is better than jerking off to any *DNA* magazine photo spread. And yes, pen. Would someone as overconfident as I use a pencil? I think not.

It was time to board. 12D, an aisle seat. This was the only way to fly. To be crunched between two fat asses would make anyone cry, and I needed legroom. Plus, with the amount of coffee I had already consumed, a bathroom needed to be easily accessible.

As instructed by Flight Attendant Barbie, I placed my perfectly worn, leather carry-on bag in the overhead bin, and then I organized my array of quality literature in the seat pocket in front of me. After fumbling with my overstretched, tangled seatbelt—from the oversized passenger that had been on the flight before me, I tested out my pen, by scribbling a mini-tornado on the cheesy, airline mall magazine.

While Barbie informed us that our flight was going to be leaving soon, I caught myself humming *The Carpenters*. I bet my parents, Carmella and Sean, heard *We've Only Just Begun* by The Carpenters on their way to Montana—just as I had on my way to the airport. Although there was a forty year span between our visits, we all personally connected with that song during that moment in time. Carmella and Sean had only just begun their lives together. With each mile closer to Montana, Sean's control began to gain power and momentum. As for me, I had only just begun finding closure.

The stewardess began reciting her script, her voice reminding me of the schoolteacher in *Charlie Brown*. I looked around. No one was paying attention. Oxygen. Flotation devices. Blah. Blah. Blah. We all knew that if we went down, that shit wouldn't work. Picking up my crossword, I noticed my ink tornado on the cover. I smiled.

That tiny tornado was me.

Welcome to Montana!
The key is in the mailbox.
The entrance to your
apartment is around the back,
through the gate.
I will be back shortly.

      — Lilly

CHAPTER TWO

◆

CARMELLA ANNE RUSSO AND SEAN THOMAS QUINN met and fell in love during the spring of 1969. Their courtship was quick, lustful, and chaotic. Tumultuous, rushed, and spontaneous. An overwhelming match that neither family approved of. Very much like Romeo and Juliet, but without the fortune and nobility. Many cursed it from the very beginning, and from what I have heard, Carmella and Sean really enjoyed the attention. No matter how much you mature, I guess some things never change.

Sean grew up in a stoic, strict, Irish Catholic household. There was nothing warm and comforting about it. The eldest of four, his mother expected him to be a kind and considerate, church-going altar boy, a well-behaved and respectful student, and a responsible big brother for his younger siblings—who often got themselves into trouble. His painful youth was cluttered by nuns, rules, expectations, and hardship. Throughout his childhood, he longed for the positive attention and love only a mother could give. She never had the time, often busy working, or donating her free time to the church rather than her children.

By the time Sean reached early manhood, he couldn't wait to join the military. It meant freedom. An opportunity to escape his starchy prison. Freedom from the bleach-like, unloving environment that stripped away his ability to show affection.

Church incense was practically imbedded in his skin, but from the amount of *Marlboro Reds* he smoked, you couldn't tell. He'd taken up the habit by age twelve. Cigarettes were always available. His father smoked three packs a day, and he never noticed when Sean pilfered a few packs from the cartons he hid in the bottom of the china cabinet.

Sean's breath often reeked of whiskey. Booze and smokes helped him cope with his lack of self-confidence and the absence of emotional support from his parents. By the time he was a teenager, he'd become rebellious to his mother's unattainable expectations, and the harsh scolding from the old, bitter nuns at St. Agnes Catholic School. It wasn't uncommon for him to go to school with a flask of whiskey in his pocket, and on more than one occasion, he was suspended for locking a nun in the coat closet, before she bloodied his knuckles for being a sinner. Being holy wasn't all it was cracked up to be. Force-fed prayers and commandments transformed him into one of the best sinners in town. Sean couldn't wait to graduate, and be free of his parochial hell. His life had bi-polar written all over it, and his badass reputation gained momentum with each passing year.

Sean was exceptionally handsome. Besides his natural intelligence, it was the one thing he really had going for him. He realized this asset early on—*abusing* it to his benefit. Just over six feet tall, he had crystal blue eyes, a dirty blonde pompadour, and a bad attitude. He lived simply: drinking, smoking, fucking, and fighting. Sean loved to fight, and for no apparent reason. Fights always seemed to "find" him. It gave him a reputation—attention that he lapped up and used to fuel his ego. He enjoyed the control. People feared him. He liked that too. Any decent psychiatrist would recognize that his love of negative attention masked his desperate need of affection from his mother. Especially when he was a child.

Girls were drawn to Sean. Why wouldn't they be? He slept with many women, pretending to be committed to each and every one of them, but whenever something better came along, he easily tossed them aside. No regrets. No empathy. Although he had a reputation of being a cheating Casanova, women were still attracted to him, hoping to be the one that he would choose and settle down with. The woman who "tamed" him. Fact was, Sean didn't want to be tamed, and he enjoyed being the man that all the mothers and fathers warned their daughters about.

That is, until he met Carmella. She was a *challenge*, unlike the women that threw themselves at him. She was new territory. He had to work hard to impress her, and that didn't come easy. Sean did whatever he had to do to win this challenge. He gave up on all the other women. Well, at least in the beginning. Carmella's childhood experiences were much different than Sean's. She was a full-blooded Italian. Her home was never cold and uneventful. It was large, loud, loving, dramatic, and overbearing. She had three older, over-protective brothers, and a much younger, morbidly obese sister named Connie, who was cursed by tradition to care for her entire family—the curse bestowed upon the youngest daughters of all Italian, Latin, and Greek heritage.

Carmella's parents, Josephine and Pellegrino, were hardworking, second generation Italian Americans from Naples, who loved each of their children *unconditionally*. She grew up in a secure, loving environment, where no one had privacy and everyone was involved in each other's business.

From early childhood, Carmella was *spicy*. She liked to challenge her mother, and she often got in trouble for being sassy and sarcastic. She was a tomboy, and Josephine fought tooth and nail to get Carmella to wear dresses, put bows in her hair, and play with her baby sister rather than with her older brothers. Josephine wanted a proper daughter, who spoke softly and was well groomed to be a loyal Italian wife, but her temperament was fiery and argumentative. She desired independence. Being someone's housewife, cooking and cleaning all day—was not what she strived for. Besides, her sister Connie was already being groomed for that.

Carmella had a nice group of girlfriends, but she kept her love interests a secret. No Roman-Catholic Italian girl was supposed to be courting anyone except Jesus. Besides, her brothers always knew everyone in the neighborhood, and they had spies who watched her every move. If she even spoke with a guy, they knew about it before she got home. Although Carmella said her prayers and kept her legs closed, she was less than holy. She dated. She teased. She just never committed. Like Sean, she had no desire to be "tamed."

Carmella was just shy of five feet tall. Long, wavy black hair cascaded down her back. Although she came from a heavy family, her curves were in all the right places. Her clothes always accentuated her godly gifts. She enjoyed being the life of the party—the one with the loudest laugh, and the one with the best dance moves. Any social event was better than staying at home, and she always jumped at the chance to seek attention. Men were intrigued, but she never went too far. Just like Sean, she knew how to work a room.

Carmella Russo and Sean Quinn were a perfect match. Elvis Presley and Sophia Loren. But when two people who demand such attention merge—it ultimately becomes a competition. One night, at a local military dance, Carmella entered the ballroom, wearing a short attention-seeking, turquoise blue spaghetti strapped dress, and canary yellow stilettos. Sean noticed. The love song from Romeo and Juliet by *Henry Mancini* was playing.

The competition began.

◆

Being stationed in Billings, Montana was not what Carmella had in mind after marrying Sean. Although it was quite common for young, newly married military couples to be relocated early on, being a military gypsy-wife was not part of her original plan. Carmella had entered the marriage knowing it was a possibility, just not so soon. Besides, Sean had promised that he'd do anything he could to keep her as close to her family as possible.

New York made the blood pump in Carmella's veins. Brooklyn and Queens were lined with shops and restaurants. Smells and noises. And unlike the small population in Billings, there were people. Lots of them. New York made women independent. Polished. Confident. Right out of high school, she landed a good job and worked very hard. It allowed her the material things she'd longed for as a teenager, but her parents couldn't afford. Nice clothes, new cars, the ability to travel, and trips to the local beauty salon to have her hair long-ironed, just like in the magazines. Carmella had lived at home with her parents until she married Sean, and up until then, she answered to no one. She did what she wanted, and never asked for approval. But she was married now. Good Catholic-Italian wives were loyal and obedient to their husbands. It felt confining. Claustrophobic. When she married her military man, she slowly relinquished the independence she had fought so hard to obtain.

Sean didn't like women who were *too* independent. He believed independence was earned. Unbeknownst to Carmella, Sean had planned an escape all along. He *wanted* a transfer. As a matter of fact, he requested it over a month before the wedding date. Just three weeks after they were married, they were informed of his transfer to Billings, Montana. Sean acted surprised and consoled his new wife with the news that she would be leaving her family. Carmella cried on and off for days. She cried because she would desperately miss her family, but she also cried because she knew the reality—that she would now be dependent on Sean for everything.

Carmella was the first in her family and circle of friends to leave New York. The few who married before Carmella had remained close to home. This was quite common on Long Island, especially within the Italian-American community. No one left. Daughters took care of their parents, and sons were expected to communicate with and dote on their mothers more than their own wives. Many people were secretly jealous of Carmella. She gained freedom. Freedom from the unexpected visits and overwhelming expectations and responsibilities, that came with living so close to family.

When Carmella opened her eyes, she looked out the window and couldn't believe what she saw. More farmland. It was exactly what she fell asleep to. She thought she had been sleeping for a few hours, but she quickly realized that it had only been forty-five minutes. Each minute felt like an hour, and the thought of being cramped in the car any longer made her miserable. She stretched her legs and pushed her hands into her lumbar.

"Do you want to stop at least once along the way to sleep in a bed?" she asked.

Carmella was tired of trying to sleep on the hard vinyl seats. No matter how much she bunched up her jacket and formed it into a pillow, it was still uncomfortable, and all of her joints were stiff. All she wanted was a hot shower and a bed to stretch out on.

"I knew I should have brought a pillow. All of our things better be there when we arrive."

One of the perks of being in the military was that they covered the shipping expenses for the move. A few days before they hit the road, their boxes of clothing, bedding, and miscellaneous tchotchke were picked up outside the apartment, where Carmella and Sean were living after they got married. It was just a large studio, so there wasn't very much to pack—and it was furnished, like the apartment they were going to live in when they arrived in Billings. Not having furniture to move made the transfer easier, although Carmella looked forward to one day choosing new things for their permanent home.

Sean continued to drive, not paying much attention to her. Carmella repeated herself,

"So? What about stopping and staying overnight somewhere? I need to sleep the *right* way Sean. It's claustrophobic in here."

"I have to be on base by noon on Sunday. I don't need to be written up on the first day, Carmella. You knew it wouldn't be a comfortable ride, so stop complaining. Do you want to take a turn driving? My neck is killing me, and I've been driving since we left." As he spoke, Carmella stared out the window, still watching nothing go by.

"Fine. When we pull over and stop, just let me walk around a bit."

Carmella was not thrilled, but she knew that Sean needed to be there on time. He had already been written up twice for insubordination, and they couldn't afford him getting suspended without pay. The military used that as a scare tactic, to keep newbies like Sean in check. Although the military kept him focused, he did not like taking orders from anyone. It was the one thing he hadn't considered when enlisting.

Just ahead was a rest area, with two abandoned picnic tables, and a pay phone. They pulled over. They were right outside of Fergus Falls, Minnesota, on Interstate 94. You could see the heat rising from the hood of their white, two-door 1969 Chevrolet

Chevelle. They had been driving for ten hours, and the car needed a rest just as much as they did. It was Carmella's car. When she was an independent working girl, she would always get a new one every two years. Now, they only had one income, so Sean had to sell his truck. Besides, her vehicle was better on gas.

"Sean, can you get the small cooler from the trunk? Mom made us a few sandwiches, and I packed us soda. I'm going to make a quick call home to keep them posted of our whereabouts."

As Carmella walked over to the payphone, Sean did as he was told while he took off his white t-shirt. Although the car windows were open, the humidity caused Sean to perspire all the way up his back, under his armpits, and around his neck. He had considered driving shirtless, but realized quickly that the beating sun on black vinyl seats could burn his skin. Also, there were no trees around to park the car under, so he grabbed another tee and sat down to eat.

Carmella was disappointed to find out that the phone did not work. She wiped the beads of sweat from her forehead and pulled her hair back. Using the hair band on her wrist, she put her hair up to cool off her neck. She was wearing a pair of cut-off jean shorts, and a loose fitting Crush t-shirt, which belonged to Sean. After walking around a bit, she sat down to eat. The sun felt good on her naturally olive skin.

"It feels so good to stretch my legs," Carmella said, unwrapping the aluminum foil around her sandwich. Sean had already eaten half of his while Carmella walked around.

"So, do you know anything more about the place we will be staying? You spoke to the landlord yesterday, right?" The Human Resources department had made all the arrangements, so Carmella and Sean knew very little about their new apartment.

"Yeah. It's close enough to base." Sean took the last bite of his homemade pot roast sandwich. He crumpled the aluminum foil in his hand and tossed it into the field.

"That's it? I'm moving cross country, and that is all you know about our place?"

Sean paused for a minute before answering. He was facing her, but she wasn't sure if he was actually looking at her. His eyes were shielded by aviators. This often bothered her, because she couldn't gauge his emotions.

"What more do you want to know? It's a furnished place, and it's close to base. That is all we really need right now. Once we get there and settle in, we can figure things out."

Sean answered her with the same emptiness that Carmella witnessed between her in-laws and Sean's relatives at weddings, communions, holidays and impromptu get-togethers. Small talk and blank stares. It was painful.

Carmella continued to press the issue about their living arrangements. Pressing the issue, or *"pushing Sean's buttons,"* was something that came naturally. It was the only way she could shake up a conversation he was in full control of.

"What is the town like? Will there be any other wives around? Maybe I can make some friends." Each question quickly followed the next, lined with attitude and sarcasm. "I can trade recipes and organize coffee-clutches." She was almost antagonizing him.

He snapped back. "I have no fucking idea, Carmella!"

Finally! A reaction! Carmella thought to herself. She had his undivided attention again—control of Sean's emotions. Sean was red in the face. He took off his sunglasses and stared hard into Carmella's eyes.

"We have one car! I will be using it to go to the base. It is twenty below zero there, Carmella. Where would you want to go anyway?"

She looked at him with disgust. *One car in Billings and no friends,* Carmella thought to herself. But this was the life she chose. Her mother had made sure to repeat those exact words to Carmella every time she broke into tears while packing to leave. She had to roll with the punches and hope for the best. The long drive and lack of sound sleep had made them both irritable. She backed off. Carmella knew when to step back and stop egging Sean on.

"I'm sorry Sean. We are tired. Let's clean up and hit the road."

It was Carmella's turn to drive. After putting a towel on the seat of the car, so that her thighs would not stick to the vinyl, she repositioned the rearview and side view mirrors. She tried again to find music on the radio. Something to make the drive more bearable, the scenery more tolerable. After pushing every button, she remembered they were in the middle of nowhere, so she turned it off. She lowered the Jackie-O style sunglasses that had been resting in her hair over her eyes, and stepped on the gas. Their journey continued.

Carmella was concerned. Concerned about the uneasy feeling she couldn't seem to shake. She wanted to be supportive, but it proved hard. She wanted to be the perfect wife for Sean. Visions came to mind—of her preparing the same delicious meals her mother cooked for her father, and keeping their tiny apartment immaculate and homey. After long days on the base, Sean would come home to her. She would be patiently waiting, wearing one of the new negligees she got from her bridal shower. A few dabs of L'air du Temps on her neck and wrists, to entice him. He would come home and appreciate her. The adoring wife. The faithful husband.

As she drove, those fantasies danced around in her head. They made her feel happy and hopeful—like the day they got married. She glanced over at Sean. His head was cocked to one side, and although his sunglasses were still on, she could tell he was sleeping. He was peaceful. Masculine. Long pieces of dirty blonde hair were gently blowing around his face. Her eyes followed his jaw line and focused on his mouth.

She desired him.

The way she often did when he was quiet.

———————◆———————

Much to Carmella's surprise, Montana was quite beautiful. The air she inhaled was refreshing. It was cleaner. Lighter. Almost pure. Mountain ranges outlined the distance, the tops disappearing amongst the clouds. It took her breath away. As much as she wanted to share her initial appreciation, she kept those thoughts to herself. She wanted this to be a visit, not permanent. If she gave Sean any inkling of hope, her chances of escape could backfire. She watched Sean. He was in his glory. His entire demeanor changed the moment they crossed the Montana State line. He was in his element. His own Garden of Eden, free from the icy coldness of his family, and the control of Carmella's.

They arrived earlier than expected that brisk Saturday afternoon. When they pulled up to the small house at the end of Wanda Lane, their entire life was stacked outside the gate to the backyard. Six boxes. Their married life looked so small and inexperienced. As Carmella waited in the car, Sean walked up to the front door, where he found a handwritten note taped to the glass:

Welcome to Montana! The key is in the mailbox.
The entrance to your apartment is around the back,
through the gate. I will be back shortly.
- Lilly

After Sean found the key, he waved for Carmella to come out. They were happy to see their new place, and relieved that there was an outside entrance. The thought of having to invade someone else's space to get to theirs was unnerving. They each grabbed a box and walked around back, eager to see the apartment.

The apartment was small. Carmella was happy that she didn't have too much to keep clean. All of the walls had been recently painted white, and the smell still lingered in the air. The floors were covered in large black and white linoleum tiles, which made each room look like a large checkerboard. The furniture was dated, but in decent shape. Carmella knew that the right throw pillows would add some color, making it more livable and inviting.

As Sean brought down the boxes, Carmella unpacked. She enjoyed using the new, shiny chrome toaster and Farberware coffee pot. Placing the wedding gifts on the speckled Formica counter top made her feel closer to her family and friends. She began to unwrap, and place all of the other fragile decorative things on the small, round wooden kitchen table. Carmella cherished these things now, but eventually they would become annoying "dust-collectors" that she would pack up into boxes for donation to local thrift stores.

"Hello? Are you down there? It's Lilly," a shaky voice called from the top of the stairs.

"Yes. We are," Carmella responded, calling up the stairwell. "Welcome! Would you mind coming up here? My legs are a bit stiff today, and I don't want to risk the stairs."

Carmella and Sean walked up the stairs to meet her.

For a few moments they discussed the trip, and Lilly explained where the local market and shops were, so they could stock up on food and other necessities. Sean also knew they could use the store on base. They were given a monthly allowance to spend there, but it was closed on Saturday, so they needed some food to get them through the weekend.

Lilly was kind and motherly, with a soft demeanor that Carmella was immediately attracted to, like that of a grandmother. Lilly felt a connection to Carmella too. This was not the first time she had encountered a displaced, scared and nervous wife, far from her family. She recognized Carmella's "look"—like that of a doe in headlights. She would have to keep a close eye on her. Billings was a rough place to live, and Carmella was not used to that.

Throughout Carmella's life, her vulnerability rarely made an appearance. She masked it with that protective New York shell. Only those closest to her recognized it, but Sean could smell her vulnerability. The same way predators smelled the fear of their prey. Years of womanizing only enhanced this ability. And now, Carmella was far from home. Thousands of miles away from the security of her family, Sean knew he had control. Carmella was inexperienced and clueless, but Billings would force her to transform—to make choices that would change her forever.

The first few weeks in Billings were enjoyable for Sean. He easily acclimated. Carmella did her best to look on the bright side and adjust. Although settling into their new roles as husband and wife in a new state was unnerving at times, they both accepted the challenge.

They attended meet and greets on base, and soon they were invited to small apartment parties, where other newly transplanted couples got to know each other. Eventually, they formed some friendships and felt part of a group. It made both of them content, and helped to subdue the pressures they both felt to make each other happy. They held hands again, and never left each other's side. Things were finally falling into place.

Sean liked to drink, as did all of the other military men. It was one of the few pastimes Billings offered, besides bowling or poker. He fit right in. While the new husbands bonded over booze, poker and cigarettes, Carmella joined the eclectic group of misplaced wives, and sipped on cheap white-wine spritzers, talked about current unavailable fashions, doted on their husbands, and taught themselves how to smoke. Everyone in Billings seemed to do it, even if they didn't like to. Carmella was bored, so she easily took up the habit. Carmella and Sean were having *fun*, and enjoying the time out of their tiny apartment, mingling with their new friends.

This did not last long.

Moving across country was difficult enough, but having a beautiful wife that other men desired wasn't easy for Sean to swallow. Carmella was the most attractive of all the wives, and most of the other women had slowly transformed into the "local" look—bulky, unflattering clothes with no makeup and diminishing sex appeal. Carmella was not ready to throw away her beauty. It was the one thing that made her feel good when she looked in the mirror.

Although Sean was confident in his manhood and new military role, he was insecure as Carmella's husband. And all the second glances and long stares he observed, only enhanced that insecurity.

Sean wasn't always the jealous type. Or at least, he didn't know he was. Growing up, "relationships" with women were short and effortless. They were his conquests, easily replaceable. He knew he could have any girl he wanted, and all of his friends kept their girls close by. Sean was a womanizer. Women were jealous of *him*, until Carmella came along. But he knew that Carmella was stunning. Sean knew it would be challenging to walk around with her on his arm. Her clothes were still meticulously tailored, and she never left the house without her hair coiffed and her eyes smoky. He found her alluring. Provocative. What originally caused many a sleepless night for her parents was now Sean's cross to bear. His friends stared a bit too long. Their wives noticed and began to distance themselves from Carmella.

Sean noticed. His blood boiled inside.

His jealousy turned into anger.

Anger he felt towards Carmella.

The party was officially over.

◆

"Where the fuck are the keys?"

Carmella was frantically rummaging through her purse again. Nothing. She headed to the junk drawer to the left of the kitchen sink. Again, nothing. It was the third time in two weeks that Carmella "lost" her keys. She felt like she was losing her mind. The last two times she tried calling Sean on base to see if he accidentally took them, he was "busy." She would leave urgent messages. They were never returned. *"I didn't get the message,"* became his typical response. She believed it the *first* time. He never seemed to have them, but the keys would always show up in a bizarre place after he got home. And *Sean* always found them in places that keys would never end up. The bathroom vanity drawer. Her robe pocket. The milk-glass bowl on the top shelf of the hutch, which Carmella was too short to reach without a stool.

A few weeks earlier, one of Sean's friends overheard Carmella complaining to his wife about only having one car and feeling trapped inside all day. He offered to drive Sean a few days a week, because they worked the same shift. Sean was not pleased to relinquish his control over Carmella, but the offer came with witnesses and he did not want to reveal his true colors to the few friends they had left. Carmella now had a way to roam free while he was gone. This newfound freedom made Sean's jealousy of her intensify. Paranoia set in.

"Here they are, Carmella!" Sean yelled, as he threw the keys at her. She was standing in their tiny living room, just large enough for a couch, a side table, and a 15 inch console TV. The wall above the couch now had another new scrape across it.

The keys landed on the floor, behind the side table. Carmella leaned over the table to get the keys, knocking over the large picture of them on their wedding day. She left it on the floor, where it belonged.

"What the fuck is wrong with you?! Did you even think to check the jackets in the coat closet? I am getting tired of this shit!" He was a liar. She checked there. *Twice.*

"Fuck you, Sean!" She wanted to throw them back at him, but she knew better. They were her only chance to escape for a while. Sean ignored her, walking into the bedroom, and slamming the door. Carmella had become used to Sean's dirty mouth, but hers had evolved since moving to Montana.

FUCK THIS.

FUCK THAT.

Asshole.

Scumbag.

Luckily, she had her Rosary. Each night, she was cleansed.

She sat down on the gently worn, rust colored corduroy couch. Running her hand back and forth on the armrest, she stared at her wedding picture on the floor. A nauseous feeling came over her again. She was beginning to think that her marriage was a big mistake. Carmella got up, and pressed her lips to the bedroom door. She felt in control again, and she was done playing dumb in his games.

"I know that you're taking them with you to the base Sean. You are sick. I don't deserve this." He was asleep; he heard nothing. She went out, and had another set made. A few days later, the keys were missing again. She had it covered.

Having her set of secret keys made life more bearable for Carmella, and she enjoyed the freedom. Sean left for the base, and Carmella drove to places far from town and went shopping. She didn't want to bump into anyone who could tell Sean they saw her. There were several thrift stores in the outskirts, and she enjoyed wasting time, searching through all the racks and bins. It was mindless—and not having to feel sorry for herself, or angry with Sean for the things he was doing—made her feel human again.

She found clothes there too. Carmella did not like the fact that she had to shop for clothing at second-hand stores, but she had put on a considerable amount of weight since she was uprooted from New York, and money was tight. She needed clothes that were comfortable and roomy. All the months of being stuck inside watching soap operas, and snacking on bags of potato chips and pretzels, took its toll on her body. It was a part of her genetic makeup. Being overweight was something she'd always feared, but there was no reason to keep her figure in check. There were no discothèques, or fancy restaurants in Billings. Mountains and oil refineries. That was it. And now that her marriage was crumbling, she felt no need to maintain her sex appeal.

By now, Diane was Carmella's only "friend." Diane and her husband were transferred in from California, and they had settled in a few days before Carmella and Sean arrived. They had nothing in common, but she was the only woman who didn't get scared away, or feel threatened by Carmella's beauty and strong personality. Diane was quiet, proper, and what Carmella described to her friends back home as "cutesy." Also, her husband loved, respected and *trusted* her. Diane's husband always left the keys on the key rack by the front door. Carmella did not feel a lifelong connection with Diane, but she did enjoy the company, no matter how mundane the conversation. Besides, there was no one else. All the other wives and girlfriends of the men on base were locals, born and raised in Montana, and they paid her no attention. Carmella didn't care. She became comfortable with her loneliness. Montana was temporary, Sean was only stationed there until the fall of 1972. It was January of 1971. Five weeks before her 26th birthday.

◆

"My hours have changed, so I will need to use the car from now on." Sean made sure to look straight into Carmella's eyes when he said it. His eyes were ice cold. Calculated. Carmella had a pit in her stomach. She would be stranded at home. She wanted to scream at him. Slap him across the face for figuring out a way to strip her of her only freedom once again, but she didn't want to give him the satisfaction. Carmella chose to remain unaffected. This was her way of playing tug-o-war with Sean, and she knew it burned him up inside.

"Why did they change your hours? It has only been a couple of months." Although she tried hard not to reveal it, Sean could still sense desperation in her voice. It was exactly what he wanted. Her desperation satiated him, like a long swig from a hidden fifth of gin to an alcoholic. He wanted the control back. Sean explained to his superiors that changing his hours would make him more productive. He also said that his marriage was "strained," and he needed to be home to work on it. Sean was a liar. Carmella was his pawn.

"It is what it is. When they tell me to jump, I jump." Carmella wished he would jump. Jump off "The Rims," a set of tall cliffs overlooking Billings.

Sean got up and left the table, barely finishing his egg sandwich and coffee. He wasn't interested in an explanation. Sean's new hours meant that when Carmella woke up, Sean would have already left for the day. She would wake up alone, and go to sleep alone. The sad thing was, it really didn't matter. Even when he was home, she was *alone* anyway. The only difference now was that she had her own set of keys, but no car. She had to figure out another way to keep herself busy—to not fall into a depression. Walking was exactly what she needed to keep her mind clear and positive.

One morning, after reading the paper and having some coffee, Carmella decided to take another long walk. She was enjoying the new change in her routine, although it didn't give her as much freedom as the car. It was still bitter cold outside, but today, it was not as brutal. The fresh air and exercise felt good, especially since she had put on over thirty pounds since she settled in. When she stared in the mirror, she felt undesirable. Sexless. They were hardly having sex, but when they did, it felt like a chore. Her body image made it almost unbearable, and Sean's scent, once a turn on, now turned her stomach.

"*Where are my sneakers?*" She found herself rummaging through the coat closet by the door again. She knew she had put them in the coat closet after her walk the day before. It only took her a moment to realize that her sneakers were missing. She tore through every cupboard in the kitchen, looked under the sofa, and behind the table in the living room. Missing. Just like the keys. Her throat felt like it was closing up, and her heart pounded through her shirt. *"My boots!"* She rushed into the bedroom, and flung open the accordion closet door.

She froze.

Carmella took three steps back, and sat on the edge of the double bed. She picked up the large colorful blanket her mother had crocheted for her when she was a teenager. She held it close, and the tears began to roll down her cheeks. She stared into the closet. The entire shoetree was empty. Sean had taken all of her shoes with him.

———————◆———————

Lilly was a widow for 12 years and also a retired lunch lady. All of her children moved far from Billings, and all of her siblings had passed on. Being a landlady filled a void in her lonely life, but housing Carmella and Sean made her life much more interesting than all of her past tenants combined. It also made her feel needed. Lilly loved Carmella, and she felt that she was the only one that could reverse what she had already become. She watched Carmella quickly transform into someone sad and unrecognizable. Lilly knew it was time for action.

Lilly had a plan, and that plan was backed by one of the most important people in Carmella's life: her mother. Unbeknownst to Carmella, Lilly communicated with Josephine often. With each fight came an update. Lilly felt it was her duty to keep Carmella's parents informed, because Carmella was always too ashamed to admit the truth to her parents. Whenever Carmella called home, Josephine played along, waiting patiently for her daughter to share how controlling her husband had become, and how she felt like she had been kidnapped. But she never came clean. Instead, Josephine waited for Lilly to call, to alert her when the plan of escape was in motion.

The fights between Carmella and Sean escalated with each passing week, and so did the intensity. Carmella was already emotionally bruised, but now he had grown physical. He never laid a hand on Carmella, but his fist flew into anything that was close. Lilly knew it was only a matter of time before he turned his fist on Carmella.

Lilly had replaced doors and windows, and she had to re-sheetrock the wall behind Carmella and Sean's bed. She had to reinstall phones, torn from the wall with such force that the wires shredded the sheetrock along the kitchen wall. It was Sean's new favorite thing to do—destroy Carmella's lifeline to New York. To anywhere. No keys, no shoes, no phone. He assumed that her entire family knew everything. Sean wanted to make sure no one could talk her into leaving. But Carmella's family was not who Sean should have been concerned about, it was his landlady. Lilly remained hidden under his radar.

Lilly's plan was simple, and one morning, while some men fixed the wall in the kitchen, Lilly offered it to Carmella. Sean would get home around nine that night. He would be intoxicated, like usual. Sean celebrated his control and freedom at all the local bars. He had become a regular at most of them, and drinking after work became a part of his daily routine. It was fine with Carmella. She enjoyed being free of him. When he did finally walk in the door, Carmella would be *asleep* on the couch with the television on. She pretended to sleep, to avoid his drunken advances and foul breath. As soon as Sean was asleep, Carmella would lightly tap on the kitchen ceiling with her broom, which was directly under Lilly's bedroom. Lilly would know that Carmella was ready to admit the truth.

Lilly kept the spare car keys and small suitcase Carmella had given her in her coat closet. Inside were two days' worth of clothes, and her sneakers. That was it. No makeup or jewelry, except for her engagement ring and wedding band, which were too tight to take off. Carmella didn't want Sean to notice that the things she used the most were missing.

One night, after Sean came home drunk and instigated another fight, Lilly could hear Carmella crying through the floorboards. After Sean passed out, Lilly heard the thump.

It was Carmella's 26th birthday. Freedom would be the gift she gave herself.

I hate layovers. But when you can save over four hundred dollars, you suck it up. Having kids drastically alters your ability to spend frivolously. Five years earlier, I would have paid the extra money and bought myself a few *designer* flannel shirts for the trip. Do they even make designer flannel shirts?

When I landed in Denver, I called home to check in. It would be a quick phone call. I knew it would be chaotic with Max trying to get the girls ready for school and making it to work on time, but I wanted to hear their voices. I had uprooted our system and left him riding solo for the next few days. It was something we both dreaded, but he knew how important and life changing this trip was for me. He encouraged me to go. Max always encouraged me. We were a perfect fit, and I did everything in my power not to succumb to the *pattern* that my mind kept telling me to follow. I refused to give in.

Most people say that the formative years are from when we are born until we are young teens, but I beg to differ. Only until we escape them for good, do our formative years officially end. Believe me, I know from personal experience.

It is, and always will be a challenge for me. Being sane, that is.

I'm tainted.

Scarred.

Damaged goods.

Out of nowhere, waves of Carmella and Sean rush up and out of me like a volcano. I keep it held in. But if I someday erupt, everyone around me best run for cover.

CHAPTER THREE

◆

LIFE WAS GOOD. I had landed a cushy advertising job in Manhattan. Finding my first real job was easier than I had expected. The right haircut. A manicure. The fitted, crisp, navy blue suit, and white dress shirt. Eye-contact. A firm, confident handshake. And my uncanny ability to make anyone believe that I actually liked them. It was in the bag. I was confident that securing clients would come as easy as collecting friends.

Collecting people became a hobby of mine. Not intentionally. It just seemed to evolve on its own. The more "friends," the better. It made me feel wanted. More importantly, it made me feel loved. I enjoyed being surrounded by the large groups of people that I had accumulated. It filled those secret voids in my life, and helped mask the surmounting insecurities from my childhood. The more people in my inner social circle—the more important I must be.

Having such an abundance of friends was exhausting—then throwing a new boyfriend into the crock pot kept me extremely busy. It was just what I needed to keep my mind off of being disowned by Carmella and Sean again. The key word here is *again*. I had been thrown out of my parents' house four times during my teenage years. They had also disowned me several times for not living up to their expectations. I often had to live with my grandparents, but when I got older, I moved out and became independent of them. Carmella would write me off as if I never existed, for months at a time. It was her only way to control me. Like clockwork, she would come around, than expect me to forget it ever happened. My father would sneak in phone calls to make sure I was alright, but he always played Carmella's game.

The reason I was discarded this time? My gayness. All through middle and high school, as well as four promiscuous and drunken years at a small, private *Catholic* university, I played the game very well. I dated and easily slept with many women. It never felt like a chore. This was probably why Carmella had such a hard time with it. I was a good actor—but I put on my best performances for her. However, to the trained *gaydar* eye, all the signs were there.

All of my friends were girls. Well, not all. But it was a $^{90}/_{10}$ ratio. I tuned in to Oprah, and cranked up the volume for Madonna.

My prom dates were fat.

My high school jacket had Drama on the back.

Capisce?

Carmella was not buying it. She believed it was a phase. My way of trying to ruin their lives *again*. Yes, again. The older I got, the more she believed that I was going out of my way to embarrass them, humiliate them, and make their lives difficult. She prayed hard for my gayness to dissipate. She asked God to forgive me. To change me. To make it go away. I tried explaining that it couldn't be prayed away. That it was a part of who I was. When I spoke, she would look away, hiding her eyes from my devilish gaze. These were the moments I wanted to tell her "holier than thou" soul that I tried. In college, I joined Campus Ministries. I did the rosary every Wednesday. I made confession. I begged our newly appointed, young, handsome, energetic Father to make the gay go away—but even after sleeping with him several times, it was, of course, still there.

Carmella wrote me off for almost a year. When she came around, she explained how important it was for her to take the time to grieve the loss of me. The son she knew. As if I were trading in my designer jeans, classy button-down and V-neck Ralph Lauren sweater for ass-less chaps and a feather boa. It was all so dramatic, but I enjoyed the vacations.

At this point in their marriage, Sean didn't need to avoid embarrassment. He had no friends. Carmella had stripped him of that pleasure, along with his dignity and ability to be a father without her permission.

Carmella was alone. Free. She could feel the life she had been stripped of rushing back into her, as the distance between her and Montana grew. For months, she had longed for the comforts of New York, and the closeness of her family. She decided to drive straight through, caring little about the uncomfortable vinyl seats and achy back. It would take her over thirty hours, but her mind was focused.

On the way to Montana, she had begged Sean to stop overnight to watch some television and take a hot shower, but it was different this time. She was in a rush. Determined to reclaim the woman she left behind in New York, and abandon the one she allowed herself to become in Billings. Something was different about the return trip. The cornfields and nothingness were therapeutic. The cornstalks seemed to be pointing her in the right direction. She knew she would never go back. And she never did.

When Carmella arrived home, she cried for hours. All of the true emotions she had held back, every time she spoke with her mother on the phone, came pouring out of her. She begged her parents for forgiveness. For not listening, and trusting them from the beginning. Her parents and siblings welcomed her back with open arms, and no one spoke a word. All that mattered to everyone was that Carmella was home, and she needed to heal. They were all shocked with what they saw. A bloated shell of what once was. After a good cry, a small meal and a hot shower, it felt like she slept for days. And coming home made her realize how much she had taken advantage of her parents before she left.

After graduating high school, Carmella's behavior was difficult for her family. Disobeying rules, staying out late, and flaunting her independence caused anxiety for Josephine and Pellegrino. She took advantage of them, and because of this, Carmella felt that her failed marriage was a lesson from God. A punishment. She flaunted her handsome fiancé to her envious friends, ignored the advice from her parents, and then when she was far from home— realized that Sean was the devil himself. She wanted to repent and be forgiven for betraying her parents, and losing her own self-respect for a man. Carmella had realized all of this on the journey home, but despite everything, she also still loved him. It made her sick to her stomach, and she knew she had to keep it a secret.

As Carmella sped past the *Leaving South Dakota* sign, Sean realized something was wrong, although Carmella's things were still there. Like most women, he knew how attached she was to her things, especially her makeup bag and jewelry.

Every hour Sean sat around and waited, just made him more and more irate. The only person Sean tried calling was Carmella's friend, Diane.

"Hello?"

"Hey Diane, its Sean. Is Carm with you?" He acted calm. As if nothing was wrong. But inside he was hoping that she had some idea of Carmella's whereabouts.

"No. I tried calling her this morning to see if she wanted to come over to play Scrabble, but she didn't answer. She's probably shopping at the thrift stores, Sean."

Carmella had made sure not to mention anything to Diane. Sean was friends with her husband, and more importantly, she knew Diane could not keep a secret. In just the few short months she had lived in Billings, Carmella knew everything about Diane's marriage, sex life, and all of the dirty secrets that the other military wives had confided in Diane. Carmella knew that Diane was a gossiper from the onset of their "friendship," so she rarely shared anything personal.

"You're probably right, Diane. If she stops by, can you tell her to call home?"

"Sure thing." Diane hung up.

After waiting several hours, Sean realized that she was gone. He had no idea where she went, but he assumed she was some-where close—maybe at one of the many motels nearby.

Even though he was filled with rage, he knew that he needed to pull himself together. He had to be on base in two hours, and he couldn't let anyone find out that Carmella had left him. That only happened to pussies. Men who were controlled by their wives.

Sean knew a few of those men, and he had even taken part in bullying them on occasion.

Reputation was important, and any signs of weakness were ridiculed. Besides, he was Sean Quinn. No woman ever left him. She'd be back. He was sure of it.

Although they were practically strangers living under one roof, the thought of Carmella leaving him only made him want her more. She was *his* wife. It was about ownership.

◆

"I can't get this piece of shit off my finger." Carmella kept twisting and turning her wedding band and engagement ring over the pink bathroom sink. Her parent's home still had many features from the 1950's—including a pink and black tiled bathroom.

Considerable weight gain had caused her rings to become painful, and it was a permanent reminder of her failed marriage. Her skin bulged over the rings like dough. As Carmella kept trying to release her finger from bondage, her sister Connie kept watch, trying to keep her calm.

"Did you try olive oil? Mommy used that once to get hers off. And don't do it over the sink! The rings could go down the drain and Daddy is at work." Connie offered her advice in as soft a voice as possible, to show her support.

"I could care less! I can't believe this!" Carmella was pulling at her rings so hard that the edge of her wedding band dug into her skin.

Connie was shaking her head in disbelief. She couldn't believe what had come of her sister. She loved Carmella, but there was a side of her that secretly enjoyed watching her suffer, the way she did all those years. As much as Connie wanted to feel nothing but sadness for her sister, she couldn't.

Pure jealousy. It ran through Connie's veins from a very early age. She was always Carmella's shadow.

"Carmella is so beautiful."

"Carmella is always dressed to the nines. Look at her skin."

"That thick shiny head of hair."

"What a great figure."

She had listened to the rants and raves of family and friends as she grew up. No one ever noticed Connie. She was extremely heavy, and always helping Josephine in the kitchen during gatherings and holidays. She felt like a slave to her mother and siblings, but no one ever took the time to notice.

"Ugh, I hate to cook!" Carmella would say when she entered the cramped kitchen full of women, preparing massive amounts of food for whatever the celebration. She only helped bring the food to the table. Besides, Connie was the one who always did the dirty work, since Carmella never wanted to stain her clothes.

Carmella had no idea that her sister despised her on so many levels, but in Connie's eyes, they now shared a physical likeness and emotional void. She liked that.

After struggling with her rings some more, Carmella gave in and looked at herself in the mirror. "*Oh my God. Who am I?*" she thought to herself. She had transformed into the kind of woman she gossiped about with her friends—not the bride she worked so hard to be.

A few months earlier, Carmella had slipped into a size six, off-white, empire-waist wedding gown. It fit her body like a glove. It had twenty satin eye-hook buttons up the back, and sheer beaded sleeves. She felt like a princess. She could barely squeeze into a size 14 now, and although she knew the wedding dress was in her childhood closet upstairs, she still hadn't been able to take it out and look at it. It represented something pure and carefree.

Still staring in the mirror, Carmella closed her eyes and slowly opened them up again. A stunning bride was now staring back. She saw herself in the dress. Dark curls piled upon on her head, with just a few cascading down. Her grandmother's earrings, and just a touch of pink lipstick. She could feel the five inch satin heels on her feet. She would dance all night in them. She loved to dance.

A knock on the door brought Carmella back to reality.

"Carm? You ok? Carm, listen, I'm going to take you to our family jeweler. I called. He said he can cut your rings off."

With the bride no longer staring back at her, Carmella smiled at her reflection and answered Connie.

"What a great idea. I'll be right out."

Today, Carmella would be set free. After days of trying to pry her rings off, with all sort sorts of household lubricants—having them cut off was her only option. Connie was happy to take her, and Carmella was grateful that her sister made the arrangements.

◆

After checking in at home to make sure Max still had his sanity and our children were alive, I noticed I had a voicemail message on my cell phone. My flight was leaving in forty minutes, and I was going to have to shut down my phone. I did not recognize the number, so I decided to see who called.

The message was from my *new* therapist. She had called to confirm my appointment for the following week, asking if I wanted to make it a double session. She was expecting another meltdown. I could hear it in her voice. Another blaming, bitching session about Carmella and Sean, and how they ruined my life. I knew her concern by the tone of her voice. Remember, this was not my first time through the rodeo.

I chew up and spit out therapists. They work very hard for their money, trying to save me. They enjoy the initial challenge, always thinking they can fix my troubled soul, but most of the time they are left speechless. Defeated. I tell them I have no soul; they believe they can find it again. It's entertaining to say the very least. One time a friend recommended their therapist to me, and it totally backfired in my face. When I met my friend a month later for drinks, I could tell that she and her therapist friend had compared notes by the way she looked at me. So much for confidentiality. To avoid awkward feelings, I dumped the therapist, and disowned my friend.

Opening myself up, and embracing the help of others is not the issue for me. I have been accepting advice from others, whether it was good or bad, for a very long time, but as soon as someone says, "*You must learn to forgive and forget,*" or "*Time heals all wounds,*" I find myself cancelling the next session, and searching the internet for someone new. Listen, I can "forgive," I guess, but not forget. And *time* does not heal all wounds. I listened to the message again. Her tone was familiar. After deleting it, I canceled my appointment.

◆

The jeweler explained to Carmella that it was going to be painful. She laughed to herself. She couldn't believe how just a few months earlier these symbols to love, honor and cherish for eternity, slipped on her fingers so easily. Now they caused so much discomfort. It seemed appropriate. It was going to be painful, and uncomfortable…just like her marriage. She sat down, and placed her hand on the towel he laid out.

"Just cut the damn things off! They mean nothing to me." As the words came out of her mouth, her stomach ached, and she quickly rose. "Where is the bathroom? I am going to be sick!"

He pointed. Carmella ran. She had been sick a few times recently, but the vomiting was uncontrollable this time. She heaved. Connie rubbed her back, terrified. She had witnessed Carmella like this a few times since she came home, but they chalked it up to nerves. Carmella leaned over the toilet, as Connie put cool rags on the back of her neck. This time she felt different.

Although her finger was red and swollen, the rings would not come off that day. As Carmella tried to stand up, everything went dark.

Connie called 911.

CHAPTER FOUR

◆

SEAN GREW TO ENJOY HIS NEWFOUND FREEDOM. Although he missed his wife, he wasn't sure what he missed. He just knew he missed her presence. He hated being alone. But at this point in their marriage, even when they were physically in the same room, they were states apart emotionally. Keeping himself busy was not a problem. He picked up extra shifts on base, and slept when he got home. He had not heard from Carmella since she left, and all his attempts at communication were ignored.

Eventually, he was served divorce papers on base. He knew what was inside the bulky envelope, and it took him days before he actually opened it.

Rumors and gossip were inevitable. Sean was now the target. Some of the guys questioned him on base, at his weekly poker games, and in the local dives. It was easy for him to play along at first: she went home to help her mother; her sister was getting married, and she needed her there for a few weeks to plan; there was a death in the family. But his friends could tell. Sean was not the first to have his wife leave, and they knew by his edgy demeanor that she was gone.

It was time for him to move on. He hadn't had the affections of a woman since Carmella left. He signed the papers, and placed them on top of the fridge.

Luckily, Sean was still charismatic. He was single again, and the local ladies knew Carmella was gone. It didn't take long for Sean to find a replacement. He had seen her before, and now that he was a free agent, he knew what he wanted. Rosa.

Rosa was a young, thinner version of Carmella, but without the tough exterior. Her gentle ways and infectious smile drew him in. His good looks and bad-boy demeanor attracted her. She was 19.

They fell in love quickly. It was not chaotic or tumultuous. It was different. He felt different. He knew his marriage was over, and for the first time, he realized that Montana was home. They made love whenever they had the chance. It was passionate and intense. With each new release, Carmella was a distant memory. A learning experience. His future was here, with Rosa, the mountains and the military.

———————◆———————

Carmella opened her eyes. The lights were bright and blinding. As she began to focus, she could hear the beeps and sounds of machines. The smell of Clorox and latex floated through the air. Sterility surrounded her. So did her family.

All those present had faces heavy with concern. Concern for Carmella, but more importantly, concern for the consequences that could arise when they broke the news.

"Mom, what happened? Why am I here?" Josephine began to gently stroke the top of Carmella's hand. She looked down and noticed her rings were still on. She looked up at her father. His face was hard. It was obvious he was not happy, and his facial expressions made Carmella uneasy. Whatever she was going to find out was bad.

"Honey, you passed out at the jewelers. Carmella, sweetheart, you are pregnant." Pellegrino walked out of the room. Hearing his wife say it only intensified his anger. His daughter had a broken marriage at 26. She was living at home again, and pregnant. He loved his daughter, but dreaded the embarrassment of the situation.

Carmella sobbed. The IV didn't allow her to hide her face in both palms, so her tears were exposed. As people walked by, they glanced toward the loud sobs and cries coming from the room.

Carmella kept sobbing and repeating, "What will I do? What am I going to do? Oh Mom…"

It broke Josephine's heart. No mother wanted her daughter in that situation. Carmella was young, and now that she was free of Sean, she had a whole life ahead of her. There were many possible opportunities available, so she planned on guiding her daughter down a sinful path that would be frowned upon by anyone in their circle of friends and family. It would have to be kept secret, and Carmella would have to follow her mother's lead. In her eyes, Sean and Carmella were cursed, and this was just going to add fuel to that fire. A baby would chain the Russos to the Quinns forever. That would be a curse in of itself.

Connie watched as her sister's life continued to crumble. The sister she always envied, the one who escaped the cooking, the cleaning, and the caretaking—had self-destructed. It broke her heart, but it also opened her eyes. What originally made her jealous, now made her more focused. She didn't want to find a man to love her, she wanted to wait for the *right man* to fall in love with. And unlike Carmella's youthful marriage, Connie realized that she would take charge of her life, live it to the fullest and never settle. She did not want to be rescued.

Sometimes people have to make harsh decisions to move on. This was one of them. Abortion was the only option for Carmella, if she planned on divorcing Sean and starting a new life; there was no other choice.

——————◆——————

Rosa made Sean's favorite dessert for his 23rd birthday. Strawberry shortcake. By this time, Rosa had practically moved in with Sean, even though it wasn't official. Most of her clothes were there, but she still went home every day to spend time with her mother after work.

Just like Josephine, Rosa's mother disapproved of her relationship with Sean. Not because she didn't like Sean, but because he was still not divorced. They were also devout Catholics, and she disliked the idea of her daughter being involved with someone who was still married—whether or not his wife was living with him. Also, Theresa and Rosa were unaware of his demons. If they had ANY insight of why Carmella left him, Rosa would have never even given him a second glance.

Sean went out of his way to gain the trust of Rosa's mom, Theresa. He played an exceptionally good game. Even better than the one he played with Carmella's parents. Rosa was Theresa's youngest child, and she wanted only the best for her. Like a good mother, she *cautiously* celebrated her daughter's happiness.

Sean had turned over a new leaf. Rosa introduced him to a few couples she knew. Montana men loved to hunt, and now that he and Carmella were going to get divorced, he considered himself a permanent fixture. He learned how to use a shotgun with ease, and was hunting with his new friends within a few weeks.

Hunting became a passion. Sean could feel the blood pumping through his veins with each pull of the trigger. Hunting deer was like hunting naïve women. He enjoyed it, being stealth-like and smooth. Spying, following and capturing—the same strategy as luring women. Now that he had Rosa, hunting deer would be his outlet. A *positive* past time. Fortunately, this would prove beneficial in more ways than one.

After a delicious dinner and birthday cake, Sean and Rosa made love. They both lay in bed naked. She rested her head on his chest. He stroked her silky black hair.

"Happy birthday, my love", she said, staring into his eyes. Rosa meant it. She was soft and innocent. Rosa deserved this. She had prayed to God every night since childhood to fall in love with a man that would respect and love her forever.

Sean was her first, and she believed she made the right decision. The problem was that 19 year olds like Rosa, had no life experience to speak of. Rosa, like Carmella, entered into this love blindsided. The only difference was that Carmella had a family far away to run to.

The phone rang.

CHAPTER FIVE

WALKING INTO CHURCH USED TO BE comforting to Carmella, but this time she felt uneasy. Not only had she committed a mortal sin for leaving her husband and failing her marriage, but the abortion left her feeling like Jezebel. She was also a liar. Keeping a secret of this magnitude was going to be extremely challenging, especially when her emotions surfaced unexpectedly.

Crying was an everyday occurrence. One minute she felt fine, and then out of nowhere, her eyes would well up, and she would lose control. This is why she thought it was best to lay low. Since people caught wind of her being home, the phone was ringing off the hook—and there weren't many excuses left. Eventually, she would have to put on an act and spend time with friends and extended family.

The only people who knew about Carmella's "procedure" were her parents and sister. All four of them collectively agreed that Vito, Anthony and Michael—Carmella's brothers, and their families, should be kept in the dark.

Two of their wives were known for being "shit-stirrers," and tasty information like the abortion could end up being used as ammo. Especially towards Josephine.

Josephine disapproved of Anthony and Michael's wives, and made it a point to remind her sons of that every chance she got. They were lazy, or cold, or didn't have the same family values. Basically, they took away her sons. That was the Italian way. They could have come from *any* walk of life. Fact was, neither of those women ever had a chance in Hell.

Carmella's damning secret would be easy to keep from Michael, Anthony, and their bitter, revengeful wives, because they lived out of state. It was important that they did not find out. Both of her sister in-laws still despised Carmella for not choosing them to be in her wedding party.

St. Catherine's Church seemed tight and cramped. Every saint, statuette and Holy Roller seemed to be looking right at her, as if she were wearing the Scarlet Letter. The enormous Jesus on the cross overwhelmed her. Carmella felt like he was going to climb down and smack her across the face. She went up to the altar, knelt down and made the sign of the cross. Today, she would share her shameful secrets again. The confession line was short, and she sighed with relief as she sat and waited her turn.

Confession was never awkward for Carmella, but this time it was different. Only months earlier, she entered that very church wearing white. She was pure. She had said her vows, and promised to love, honor, and obey her new husband. Today, she entered scarred, scared, and broken. She was shrouded in sin, and Carmella was eager to finally confess them. Sadly, even after the confession, she would still be lying to those around her. It was a bitter cycle of shame.

Aborting a child was one of the worst things a woman could do in the eyes of the Lord. Carmella ended a life. She was a murderer. A mortal sinner. Crucified each and every time she caught her parents or sister looking at her. Even though it didn't show on their faces, she could feel their disgust. Of course, that was not the case. They were happy it was over, they tucked that family secret in their own walk-in closet and moved on.

Confessing about the failed marriage was easy. She didn't have to use the word divorce, because the lawyer had told her earlier that week that the papers hadn't arrived in the mail yet from Sean. But explaining why she felt guilty was barbaric! See, Carmella didn't feel guilt and shame about ending the life of her unborn child. It was quite the opposite. She was relieved. Happy it was gone. It was her last tie to Sean, and she was rid of it. It was hard to say, but once Carmella opened her mouth, the confession spilled out. Purification.

After many Hail Mary's and Our Father's, she kissed the cross on her Rosary, and proudly walked out a saved woman.

The phone continued to ring in the kitchen. It was obvious that whoever was calling was going to keep trying.

"Are you going to answer that?" Rosa sat up, ready to head into the kitchen to get it.

"Nah, I'll get it. You just lay here and look pretty. I'll be right back."

Sean rolled over and gave Rosa a quick kiss, then got up. He was still naked. As he walked past Rosa, she leaned forward on the bed and smacked him on the ass. He looked at her and smiled. He was happy.

Sean shouldn't have answered the phone. He should have just lay there and enjoyed his birthday bliss. But that was not in the cards. His future changed the moment he lifted the avocado colored phone receiver.

"Hello? Sean?" Scratching his scalp, he softly muttered a "yup," which the caller obviously did not hear.

"Sean?"

"Yeah, this is Sean. Who's this?" He was louder now, and annoyed. He had no desire to be talking on the phone.

"Sean, its Sue. Sue Mason. Catherine's friend."

Catherine was Sean's sister. Sue was an intern at Fairview Memorial Hospital in New York.

"Oh yeah. Hey. How are you? Is Catherine ok?" He was confused by the call. He hardly knew her, but obviously Catherine gave her his number. Also, Catherine had drug addiction issues in the past, and the first thing that crossed his mind was a possible relapse, especially since Sue was practicing to become an RN.

"Oh, yeah, she's fine. Had dinner and drinks with her last night. She met a new guy. His name is Jimmy. Nice guy. Could be the one." She kept rambling on, and Sean zoned out for most of the conversation. Not to mention that Rosa was now standing in front of him, naked, dancing around and being silly. He was ready for round two.

"Sean! Sean? Are you there?"

"Oh sorry, Sue. I got distracted," he winked at Rosa, and motioned for her to go back to the bedroom. "What's up?"

"Listen Sean. This is uncomfortable for me to say, but I have some really awkward news. I told Catherine to call you, but she didn't want to. She said she didn't want to get involved in your personal problems."

"Ok…" He hesitated. She sounded uneasy, and he knew it was going to be bad news from her tone. "What is it, Sue?"

"Well, you know I am interning for my RN, right? Well, the other day I was at Fairview Memorial Hospital and…God, Sean… this is really hard…" The long pauses irritated him.

"Jesus Christ, Sue! What the FUCK is it already? Are my parents ok?"

"Hey don't snap at me, asshole! Fine! Carmella was there."

Hearing her name was like getting kicked in the balls. His stomach ached. He didn't like where this conversation was going.

"Yeah, so what?" He put his hand on his forehead, and leaned on the cold white Formica countertop, speckled with gold.

He acted as if he could care less, but the fact was he did. He had blocked out and covered up any emotions he still felt for her—but now that he was hearing that she was at Fairview, it alarmed him. He was concerned. Being concerned made him angry, and Sean had no ability to control anger. He was like a champagne bottle that was shaken too much.

"Sean, Carmella had an abortion."

Sean was silent. He couldn't speak, but his hand was shaking.

"I am so sorry to call you with this news, but we all thought that you—"

Sean hung up the phone. He felt paralyzed and hot. Without any forewarning, Sean's cork popped. His anger erupted. He picked up the coffee pot, and threw it against the bedroom door. It was still half full from the morning, and brown water and coffee grounds decorated the wall where his wedding picture used to be. Whatever was within reach became airborne. Within seconds, the small apartment was littered with chards of glass, and upturned furniture.

From within the bedroom, Rosa could hear Sean's tantrum, but she was too scared to open the door. Rosa only witnessed this side of him once before, but it had been a drunken bar altercation.

She opened the door a crack, and peeked through. He was crazy. Punching the walls and doors, leaving holes and bloody smears. There were splinters of wood stuck in his fists, but he was so deep in rage that he was oblivious to the pain.

"SEAN!! OH MY GOD! WHAT'S THE MATTER?" Rosa was now screaming through the crack of the door. She was petrified by what she saw.

"I'M SCARED SEAN!!!" He did not hear her. Sean was in his own mental place, as he continued to destroy the apartment and scream out his wife's name.

She closed the door, and locked herself in. As quickly as she could, Rosa got dressed and opened up the window. It was a small basement apartment window, but luckily she was only about 100 pounds. She crawled out and ran. Scared, and devastated by his fury, she didn't even realize it was snowing, and she wasn't wearing shoes.

Rosa ran. She ran as fast as she could, all the way home. Rosa was 19 and naïve, but not dumb. It was over.

CHAPTER SIX

◆

BOARDING THE "HOME STRETCH" FLIGHT from Denver to Billings, my excitement began to turn to anxiety. I found my seat and repeated the same magazine and crossword ritual from earlier that morning, only this time, my hand shook as I scribbled my childhood doodle onto the airline magazine. My nerves were beginning to kick in, but being scared and backing out of my plans was not an option.

I tried to convince myself. "*It's Denver.*" I could always get off the plane, and hit the slopes for a few days. Smoke some really good weed. I could *tell* everyone what a great experience it was to see the sights of Montana, meet those who were expecting me to visit, and fabricate how it changed my life.

I sat down and buckled my seat belt. I had upgraded to business class. For thirty bucks extra, I treated myself to extra leg room, complimentary beer, wine and champagne. I immediately ordered two Heinekens. I asked the stewardess if I could drink one before the plane even started for the runway. She saw that I was "*off.*" She approached me.

"Worried about something?" she whispered.

Before I could explain, she walked away and quickly came back. She gave me a beer, and motioned for me to down it. I felt better. Calm again.

While sitting and waiting, I noticed that there was a little curtain on the flimsy rod directly behind my seat. I got up and examined it. This older woman, who reeked of religion, was on the other side of the curtain—facing me. She stared at me. She wore gaudy clip-on earrings, and heavy church lady lipstick. She had that "look." Legs so close together they were practically one limb. The stiff, polyester blend pants suit. Her eyes followed me up and down. She looked as if she had just smelled something God awful. I wondered if she always had that look on her face, or if she could smell the gay. *Those* ladies have that gift, you know. Carmella was destined to become one.

I was surrounded by them my entire childhood. Every Sunday, I was whisked away to church, never quite sure what was going on around me—but they were everywhere! Pinching my cheeks, and congratulating me for coming to God's house. Some were much younger, but they still had that look. And that smell. Heavy perfumes. I was so young—and after I got home, their presence lingered on my skin and clothes for a long time.

I stared back. Stoic. Cold. I waited for just the right moment. Slowly, I pulled the curtain closed while staring right into her periwinkle blue-shadowed eyes. Just as it was about to separate us, I winked at her and pursed my lips. Since I was old enough to understand what these women represented, I had always wanted to do that to them. Shield myself from their evil, non-verbal, judgment. This was my chance. I laughed and returned to my seat. I was back to *normal* again. It felt good.

◆

After calming himself down, Sean thought about his conversation with Sue. One thing kept bothering him. The word "*all*." She said "We *all* thought you…" right before he hung up.

This wasn't a secret. New York knew, and what pissed him off the most was that he was the last to know. He knew what he had to do.

After a brief discussion with his superior, Sean was granted a two week family emergency leave. Two days after his request, Sean was on his way to New York. He had people to confront, and loose ends to tie. He liked his new life, and if going back to New York to make sure there were no more surprises was what it was going to take, he was willing to do just that.

Time was of the essence. Especially if he wanted to win back the love of Rosa. After she ran, she refused to communicate with Sean. She was damaged, and the thought of her giving him her virginity, made her weak. After many attempts, Theresa had told him to stop calling. Sean did not take no for an answer.

The day before he was to leave for New York, Sean showed up on Rosa's doorstep, yelling out for her. As he was banging on the door, Theresa opened it. She greeted him with a loaded shotgun. Slowly, Sean moved back, eventually standing in the middle of the walkway. Calmly, Theresa explained to him that she knew Montana like the back of her hand. There were acres of forest and mountains that no one had ever examined. If she had to use the shotgun, she would. Sean would "disappear," and never be missed. After Theresa spoke, she closed the door. But Sean still loved Rosa, and Theresa knew that most likely, he would continue to try.

Sean knew that the longer it took for him to get to New York and tie up loose ends, the harder it would be to win Rosa back.

◆

"Carmella! Get up. You need to come downstairs now!" She was being summoned by her sister Connie. She would have ignored her any other day, but it sounded urgent.

"What's the problem, Connie?" Carmella was still in a fog and exhausted too. She tossed and turned all night. "Ugh, I could hardly sleep last night. Is coffee made?"

"Yeah, there's coffee, but you better get your ass in gear and get downstairs. Mommy and Daddy want to talk with you." Connie headed back downstairs.

Carmella had been unmotivated since she came home. She hadn't looked for a job, and she hardly left the house. She assumed today was the day for the long parental speech: "*You need to get out more! Why aren't you reconnecting with your friends? When are you going to get a job?*" As Carmella brushed her teeth, combed her hair and threw on her robe, she played the conversation in her head.

Eventually, she made her way down the steep staircase of the modest black and white cape by the lake. She had lived there since she was five. It was small, but every square inch of space was useable, and Pellegrino had finished the basement. It was used for family functions when there were too many people for the dining room. It even had a small kitchenette, so it could be used as an apartment. Josephine often spoke of having a tenant downstairs for extra cash, but neither of them wanted the headache of being a landlord. Still, that apartment would prove to come in handy.

When Carmella entered the kitchen, she could see her parents, sister, and brother, Vito, sitting at the table.

"Vito!! You're home!" Carmella ran into her brother's arms. Vito was her favorite of the three. He was seven years older than her, and as a young impressionable girl, he watched out for her the most.

Rather than spend most of his time out with his friends, he would stay home and play records for her. They would dance and laugh. Carmella was an amazing dancer, and he was the main reason why she was so good at the Lindy.

"Are you home for good?" She touched his face. It had been two years since she had laid eyes on him. He couldn't even be at her wedding, which was painful for her. Out of anyone in her life, he was her hero and protector. His advice was always well thought out, and she trusted his guidance.

Then Carmella realized that so much had happened in her life while he was stationed in Germany. It made her feel sick inside, because she did not want her brother to look at her any differently.

"Wow Vito. So much has happened since I last saw you," she said, with one eye on her parents and one on her brother. She continued: "Life has been crazy here Vito. My marriage…" He put his finger up to her mouth. She paused.

"He knows *everything*, sis." Connie emphasized the word everything, so that Carm didn't feel the pressure to explain. Carmella was glad she did. She didn't have to revisit the pain, and more importantly, she didn't have to lie to the one person she respected the most.

Vito and Carmella sat down at the table. As usual, the table was adorned with several delicious options. Food was never scarce in the Russo home. Josephine was always in the kitchen, and everything was homemade. Earlier that morning, Vito and Pellegrino bought pastries up the block. Connie had already opened the box, and was sifting through her options.

Carmella's emotions caused her appetite to fade. Since she fled, she had lost about twenty pounds, mostly due to her lack of appetite. Nonetheless, she was happy to look in the mirror, and it motivated her to put in more effort when getting ready for the day.

This was not going to be a "welcome home" breakfast. She could feel it. There was business to attend to. And the business, was about her. As Carmella sat down, she braced herself. Josephine immediately chimed in.

"Carm, I got a call from Lilly. She found a packet containing the divorce papers in Sean's apartment. I thought you told us the papers were filed."

Lying was no longer an option. Besides, she was not a good liar. Being far away made it easy to lie, but Carmella had the farthest thing from a poker face. She decided to be upfront and honest, especially after purging herself of the sins and secrets already. She vowed to never accumulate a pile that big again.

She became nervous and uneasy. She was on trial again. Without even realizing it, she began to play with her rings. She looked down and realized they were still there. And now they were loose, easily able to come off. She flexed out her fingers and examined her hand. It was youthful and delicate again. She slid her rings on and off. No one spoke. Carmella knew her rings could come off. She knew all along, just like she knew Sean hadn't returned the divorce papers.

There was a knock at the door. No one seemed surprised. All eyes were on her, and no one was getting up to answer it.

...Slowly, he walked toward him, and then he stopped at the doorway. He was hesitant to walk past him into the house.

He felt like an intruder now.

CHAPTER SEVEN

◆

THE FLIGHT FROM DENVER TO BILLINGS WAS PLEASANT. It was void of crying babies, suspicious odors and heavy traffic to the lavatory that was only four rows away.

More importantly, the stewardess was paying extra special attention to me, since I slipped her a twenty for that first nerve calming libation.

Her name was Nancy. I enjoyed watching her work. She only worked business class, and since business class on our flight was only ten aisles, I could keep my eye on her the entire time. Watching her glide around the cabin was like watching a TV reality show. Besides, the movie that was playing was outdated, and the earplugs never seemed to fit quite right in my ear canals.

You could tell that her job meant a lot to her. It was her entire life. I noticed she did not have a wedding ring on, and there was no sign of a ring tan line. But who knows, she could have had them cut off.

She was flawless, both in dress and productivity. Every one of us was happy, and she bounced around, glad to be doing her job. I wondered if it was all a cover up. An act. Was she really that happy to be serving us in business class? Was her life really fulfilled blasting off from one state to another, making sure that all the overhead bins were secure? Or was she an air princess by day, with a bad reputation off duty—a lover in each city she landed in? Someone's mistress in another no-name airport motel room?

Inventing stories for strangers made the time go by. I was good at doing that. I would stare, examine, observe and mentally outline their lives when, honestly, I should have been trying to figure out my own. Pure escapism. Brutal self-avoidance. Her life was easier to break down than mine was.

Nancy worked hard to get where she was. She grew up in a poor town, and by the time she was 14, she was a seasoned shoplifter, easily walking out of the local Wal-Mart with anything she desired. Her father left when she was three, and her mother was her mentor. One fine day, as she was stealing Tylenol from the town pharmacy, Nancy realized she wanted more in life. She ran away from her tormented childhood home, changed her name, and forgot about her past. Now Nancy was a stewardess, with a polished look and a good reputation. But what we learn during our childhood is difficult to escape. What the appreciative travelers in the business section cabin didn't know, was that Nancy still did the same thing. After checking into their fancy hotels, they would find things missing from their carry-on luggage. But no one expected the stewardess. Nancy had a good reputation, and catered to your every need. Service with a smile!

By the way, she has your watch.

As I was tearing apart her very being, she kindly brought me another beer and told me that we were scheduled to land earlier than expected. I was delighted to hear it.

◆

Sean wasn't quite sure of what he was going to say as he stood outside the door. There were two small, frosted, diamond shaped windows at eye level, and he could see a figure coming towards the door. He could tell by the height and shape that it had to be Carmella. He didn't like the way he felt. He had been angry upon leaving Montana, but his anger had been replaced with feelings that he was no longer accustomed to when it came to Carmella.

Although nervous, he was also excited.

The day before, Sean was surprised that Josephine and Pellegrino actually took his call, but he was shocked and overwhelmed that they had invited him to come into their home. It confused him, but he truly believed it was because they knew he would soon be out of their lives forever. A non-threat. But they had their own reasons to invite him in. A good plan was laid out. One that would force Sean into a corner that he wouldn't be able to escape.

Carmella's house was always the place to be. The smells, the laughter, and the love, enveloped anyone who entered. It was contagious. There were always neighbors over for coffee and cake, and masses of cousins coming and going. This was how Italian families were. Everyone lived close, and they all knew each other's business. Hugs and kisses were abundant and judgment happened behind closed doors.

Sean had always wanted that with his own family. Although Carmella's parents did not approve of their relationship, engagement and marriage, they had still treated both of them with love and respect along the way. And since Josephine and Pellegrino did, everyone else was *allowed* to. Everyone knew that Sean came from a different kind of upbringing, and Josephine and Pellegrino felt badly for him. They saw that he was different from the rest of the Quinn's—even though he was a "bad" choice for their Carmella. At the beginning, they told him their door was always open for him, and now here he was, standing in front of her door again, just like the first time she had invited him over for dinner. But the circumstances were very different now.

It had come full circle.

As Carmella crossed through the living room and approached the front door, she glanced out the bay window. The beautiful, large, Japanese Red Maple blocked most of the view, but she could make out the front end of a blue Impala, with New York plates. Her heart stopped. It belonged to her in-laws: Margaret and William Quinn. What the hell were they doing here?

From the very beginning, she hated them more than words could express. They were always cold and distant from her. Never accepting. She was an Italian. Not Irish. The thought of them made her feel like she was standing out in the cold naked.

Carmella looked through the frosted glass.

"What is Sean doing here? Mom! Dad! Sean is at the front door!" No one answered, so Carmella ran back into the dining room.

"Carmella," Josephine said. "He called last night while you were out. You both need to sit down and talk, Carmella. He knows about your situation. Someone must have called him."

Josephine was kind and reassuring when she spoke this time. She knew that if they were both going to move on, a sit down was necessary. And just in case it unraveled differently, she had a backup plan.

Carmella felt weak and vulnerable again. But she wasn't scared. She was home, and her family made her secure. It was something that she was not expecting, but she wanted to open the door. She looked at herself in the dining room mirror. She wanted to see him, but not this way. She needed to look put together. Strong and confident, not tired and sloppy. Carmella wanted Sean to see that she had put her life back together again. She did not want him to have the satisfaction of seeing her broken.

"I need to get dressed. Let him in. I'll be down in a minute."

Sean could see the commotion behind the frosted glass. He knew she ran back in, and no one else was coming towards the door. He turned around, and started to walk down the steps of the enormous concrete patio, that he had helped construct with Pellegrino and Vito a year earlier. In front of him stood a twenty-foot tall hydrangea tree. It cascaded with light green and white snowballs, ready to bloom. It was the backdrop of all their wedding party pictures. He smiled to himself as he walked past it.

"Sean! Hey!" Sean turned around. It was Pellegrino. He stood in the front entrance waving him in.

"Come in. Carmella just went upstairs to change. Come, have some breakfast."

Sean loved his father-in-law. But he feared him even more. Slowly, he walked toward him, and then he stopped at the doorway. He was hesitant to walk past him into the house. He felt like an intruder now. A devil. Sean had treated his daughter so badly. Sean extended his hand. Pellegrino accepted his offer. They looked at each other for a few seconds and Sean's eyes began to well up. His father-in-law put his hand on Sean's shoulder and guided him in.

Pellegrino understood Sean in a way that only an older, experienced man could. Sean was young, but he could teach him the way. Sean needed a solid family to guide him. He recognized the goodness Sean had, the *potential*, but when you were raised without love, compassion and guidance, what can you expect to become?

Sean was crying as Pellegrino closed the door.

———————◆———————

After Sean's outrage, Rosa stayed in her bedroom and had cried herself to sleep for days. She didn't cry because of what she witnessed, but because days after Sean's violent outburst, she realized she still felt the same about him. It made her feel crazy. How could she love someone with such violence hidden deep inside him? Her love was still real, and she needed closure. She was ashamed to feel the way she did.

Growing up, Rosa saw the consequences of getting involved with men like Sean. Men who took out their frustration on the women they "loved." Women walking around town with facial bruises that make-up could not hide. Sunglasses masking sadness and shame. Scared to leave. Her mother made sure to point that out to her. To warn her. Theresa's motherly advice told her to run, but her heart still ached for Sean. Besides, she had something important to tell him. Something that he needed to know.

Sean had been staying with his parents and called to speak to Rosa several times after leaving so abruptly, but Theresa always answered the phone and hung up. Rosa was unaware that Theresa had threatened his life before he left for New York.

One day, when Theresa was out food shopping, Rosa answered. It was the day before he was to go over to Carmella's house to tie up loose ends. Sean expressed his love to Rosa, but over the phone, he could tell she was damaged from the experience.

"Rosa. I am sorry I flipped out like that, it will never happen again, I promise." Sean spoke calmly, reassuring her. He pleaded with Rosa on the phone to believe him.

"I am not sure Sean. You scared me, and my mother really hates you right now."

He wasn't in front of her. Rosa liked eye contact. It was the true way of knowing if someone was being sincere. She also knew that Sean was a smooth talker. She knew that before they had even begun dating, but she was attracted to him and that didn't matter at the time.

"Sean, listen. I still have feelings for you, but I am not sure if I can forget the way you acted. Shit like that doesn't only happen once. My mother told me that men who abuse the ones they love once, will do it again. Besides, I think you are still in love with Carmella."

"What the fuck are you talking about?" His voice shifted. It was rigid and defensive. "I didn't hit you! What is your mother talking about?" He began to turn red. Rosa didn't need to be in his presence to feel the heat through the telephone lines.

Rosa did not answer. The quick change in his tone spoke volumes and only confirmed her suspicions.

"Ro. Are you still there? I am coming home soon. I just have a few things I need to get in order here. I'll be back to normal once I get things in order. Please believe me. I love you."

She found his pleas pathetic. Typical of those men she was warned about. In that very moment, she no longer felt sadness for loving someone like Sean, she felt regret. She decided that what she needed to share with Sean could wait. He was coming back to Montana anyhow, so why bother telling him over the phone when he was already agitated?

"I need to go Sean. Fix whatever it is you need to fix. I'll be here when you get back. I make no promises, but we'll talk then." She hung up. The dial tone was deafening.

It would be the last time he spoke to Rosa in almost 40 years.

CHAPTER EIGHT

◆

SINCE CARMELLA'S "SURPRISE" ARRIVAL HOME, Josephine, Pellegrino, and Connie could sense gossip brewing. Carmella avoided the people in her neighborhood that she grew up with. And her constant excuses for not being able to meet them only made the rumor cauldron bubble over.

It was difficult to go anywhere without bumping into someone who wanted information. The local bakery, supermarket and church proved the most difficult, and all the Russos did their best to keep the secrets intact.

Connie continued to do a great job of protecting Carmella. She was good at putting people in their place, and no one ever wanted to step on Connie's toes. She had grown into a young woman who could care less what other people thought. She was tough as nails. Connie always made sure to answer questions and concerns with a tone, telling them to "back off."

Needless to say, Connie was tired of dodging, and it was getting harder to come up with excuses.

Josephine and Pellegrino didn't want it to go any further either. Today would be the perfect opportunity to erase the recent events and tragedies in their daughter's life. Today, the future would unfold in one of two ways for the new, but failing marriage between Carmella and Sean. It was time to clean up.

Sean sat at the dining room table. Almost immediately, Josephine was pushing food on him, and Pellegrino had given him a cup of espresso. Sean felt awkward. So many bad things had happened, and it was no secret that he was to blame. So, why the open arms? Whatever the motive, and no matter how awkward he felt, he enjoyed sitting at that table again.

"Carm is upstairs. She'll be down in a minute. How was your flight? When do you need to go back?" Josephine began probing. She sat directly across the table from him.

Sean sat in the chair closest to the corner of the room. That was where he was "placed." Anyone who sat there couldn't just get up and leave. Sean would have to walk around everyone to get out. His placement made him uneasy. Vito and Pellegrino sat at the table in silence. Vito's stare was sharp, and precise as a hunting knife.

Sean felt like he was on trial. He came there to tie up loose ends. His nerves were shot, and now he needed to explain that his visit was going to be brief. He had booked the red-eye for Billings the following night. His purpose for the visit was specific. He would apologize for the failed marriage, make peace with Carmella and her family, and then make sure she was okay after having to make such a life-altering decision. But the moment he entered the front door, he could smell a plan. He knew that their kindness was masking a motive. Sean hesitated when he spoke.

"The flight was fine. Much better than driving. I don't think I will ever drive that distance again." As Sean was speaking, he knew what he was saying would strike a nerve, and he wasn't surprised at the reaction.

"No shit, asshole! *MY SISTER* had to drive the whole fucking way by herself because her new husband was treating her like shit!" Vito stood up, and slammed his hands on the table. He was angry, and although he had all intentions of remaining calm for his parents during this encounter, his temper had already flared at the sight of Sean.

Sean's espresso spilled over. As he got up to grab a napkin, Vito continued—his pointer finger inches away from Sean's face.

"Sit down!! Who the fuck do you—" At that very moment, Vito was interrupted as Carmella entered the dining room. Vito did not want to upset his sister. Naturally, he wanted to protect her from Sean, but he also needed to obey his parents. *They* called this meeting. He was under *their* roof. But in Vito's mind, Sean stripped Carmella of everything he wanted for her.

Carmella stood in the entrance of the dining room.

Vito left through the back door of the kitchen. He knew it would be best for his parents and Carmella if he wasn't present during the discussion. He did not trust Sean, and he didn't like what his parents had up their sleeves. His opinion was simple: Carmella and Sean did not belong together. They were toxic for each other. Carmella could tell by the way Vito slammed the screen door that he was sending her that message.

"What's going on here? Is everyone alright?"

As Carmella stood in the entryway, the light from the bay window was cascading around her. In a pale blue dress with small yellow flowers on the sleeves and around the hem, Sean admired her beauty again. Her longer hair was gently pinned up upon her head. She was softer. More youthful again. The hardness of Montana was gone. The lines on her face, and the dark circles from sleepless nights were gone too. He had become accustomed to her Montana face—full of regret and sadness. He had forgotten how beautiful she actually was.

Carmella stood there, allowing him to gaze at her. He stared at her the same way he did when they first started dating in the summer of 1969. She stared back at him. He was clean shaven and put together. The way he always was when he entered her childhood home. Carmella and Sean recognized each other again. Josephine and Pellegrino looked at each other and knew which road to take, and they were not surprised in the least.

"Sit down Carm. We all need to have a talk."

Court was in session.

Now only four people sat around the large oval table. It made Sean feel small. It made Carmella uneasy. Each player sat on one side of the table. Each placement seemed appropriate.

Josephine placed down a bowl of frezzelles—hard Italian bread biscuits, a freshly brewed pot of espresso, four delicate white demitasse cups rimmed with gold, and a large bottle of Anisette. They were all placed in the center of the courtroom table. It was time to get down to business.

Pellegrino had a presence. He was just shy of five foot eight, but his stature made him appear taller. His whole body was thick. His neck, shoulders and arms proudly displayed decades of heavy lifting. His hands were calloused and rough, and he had a perfect silver streak amongst his wavy black hair. Together, all of his attributes made him stand out in a crowd.

People who first met him feared him. Those who knew him loved him.

Despite his presence, however, Josephine was the judge *and* the jury of her courtroom. This was the case in every Italian household. The women ruled the roost. The men brought home the bacon. In this courtroom, Pellegrino was only the Bailiff. He made sure his family was well taken care of, and that everyone abided by JoJo's rules. That is what he called her in front of others. JoJo. Behind closed doors, she was his "bundle of joy." And she was. She ran his castle. JoJo was his queen.

From the very first moment Pellegrino saw Josephine, he loved her with his whole heart, but getting Josephine to love him back required a lot of time, energy and work. At first, she was not romantically interested. Pellegrino's father died before he was born, and by the time he was six, he was shoe shining to make extra money for his mother and three sisters. He was already physically *worn* by the age of 21. Hard work made him rough around the edges. Josephine was polished. Although she did not come from money, her father was a tailor, so she and her six sisters always looked beautiful.

Pellegrino worked hard to impress her. He was patient. She smoothed his rough edges. He allowed her to. Josephine was the reason he was gentle and kind. It took three years of courtship for her to love him with her whole heart, and their marriage became a fruitful one.

Throughout their marriage, JoJo and Pellegrino wanted what was best for their children. They wanted each child to be patient, and to find a love that would last forever. It took *them* three years, and they wanted to see if Sean and Carmella could start anew and learn from their example. Family came first, and they believed that was the biggest downfall of Carmella and Sean's failing marriage. Being far away from family.

I had never been away from Max and the girls for more than an overnight. I could feel the pit in my stomach, knowing that I could not physically touch them for the next few days. Nancy saw it on my face.

"Here is *another* Heineken, Mr. Quinn."

I graciously accepted it, but this time I felt like a recovering alcoholic who fell off the wagon. Was it me, or did she actually stress the word "another"? Maybe she did. After thinking too hard about it, I chose not to care.

This would be my fifth, and I had no plans on stopping anytime soon. I wasn't driving, and a taxi would be waiting for me when I landed in Billings. Just like any other good parent, being able to drink excessively without responsibility was a luxury. I was going to take advantage to the fullest.

Maybe I am a bit of an alcoholic. But aren't we all?

The aerial view was breathtaking! Crop circles of all sizes. Different shades of greens, tans and browns. It reminded me of this comforter our friends had at their Montauk estate. It was from Restoration Hardware. I never really knew much about crop circles. However, it always seemed to be a topic on the cover of those bad gossip magazines in the checkout line. *Aliens Make Crop Circles in South Dakota!* Other than that, I had never really thought about them, but to see them from so far up was astounding!

In the distance, they appeared. The familiar majestic mountain ranges I saw in those forbidden black and white pictures I found during my childhood. I had to catch my breath. Those images were real to *me* now. It was Montana. I said it softly to myself. *Montana.* My mouth *needed* to say it. It was a long time coming.

There she was.

Josephine's plan was simple: Sean was to leave the Air Force and return home to New York with all of their belongings. Carmella and he would move into the basement apartment of Josephine and

Pellegrino's home, and Pellegrino would have a job lined up for him at the produce warehouse that he worked for. More importantly, it would be "leaked" that Carmella had a miscarriage. *This* would eradicate all the rumor and gossip.

It was a solid and well thought out plan, but it was not a conversation at first. It was a lecture. Void of any emotion, Josephine laid out all the cards perfectly on the table. Step by step.

Carmella and Sean were not allowed to speak. She made that clear from the very beginning. They were to sit and listen. Carmella and Sean needed to understand that this plan was a *gift,* that both she and Pellegrino were offering them. At no point did Pellegrino interject. He sat in his place, and occasionally nodded. His head was tilted down, as if he were studying the gold rim around his demitasse cup. He strategically avoided eye contact with either of them. Josephine was precise and straightforward, and he always agreed. Like two elementary aged students, Carmella and Sean sat quietly as their teacher spoke. Neither of them interrupted. Other than an occasional glance and sip of espresso, they listened. The plate of pastries and frezzelles sat untouched. For the first time in the Russo home, no one had an appetite.

Listening proved difficult. Having to hear others talk about your weaknesses proves difficult for anyone, and Josephine was throwing criticisms at both of them. However, it did allow each of them the opportunity to see things through someone else's eyes, and with a different perspective. Although they did not agree with everything Josephine said, hearing her suggestions and advice was therapeutic. Her plan made sense.

Carmella and Sean both knew that they needed a fresh start as individuals. That was why Carmella left Montana. That was why Sean came to New York. What they didn't expect was that both of them leaving Montana, for completely different reasons, would end up being a fresh start for them as a married couple.

CHAPTER NINE

◆

A FTER A TOTAL OF SEVEN HEINEKENS, I was abruptly woken from my boozy slumber by Nancy, my kleptomaniac flight attendant. Her hand was gently placed on my shoulder.

"Mr. Quinn. Mr. Quinn? We are about to land. You need to put your seat in the upright position and stow away your snack tray."

I had stretched myself out across the two seats and propped my jacket behind my head. Quickly, I sat up and looked out the window. For a brief moment, I had forgotten why I was on the plane, and where I was headed. I could see Billings' airport in the near distance. It was small. Probably the smallest airport I had ever flown into, except for the one in the Dominican Republic, when Max and I took a vacation there before the girls came along. Now that was small! Max and I still laughed when we reminisced about that trip.

Security actually pulled me out of line and questioned me for a few minutes. They asked me if I was in the mafia. The funny thing was that the line was filled with so many people, who were obviously more interesting. By the looks of Billings' Airport, I expected to stand out just as much.

Getting off the plane, finding the baggage terminal, and getting a taxi took all of twenty minutes. It was the most pleasurable airport experience I had ever had. Way better than the airports in New York City, where it can take over an hour to get through security.

Immediately stepping outside, I stopped and breathed in the air. The air was different. It was crisper. Cleaner. Faint trails of petroleum came and went, but it gave the air character. I remember learning somewhere that one of Montana's biggest exports was petroleum, so it made complete sense to me. It didn't bother me at all. It was fitting, just like the air on the Long Island coastline, which smelled of salt water.

On the way to the motel, the gravel and sand road edged along a cliff. I couldn't see how far down it dropped, but I was drawn to this spot. I quickly asked the taxi driver to pull over. Before getting out, I reached into my jacket pocket and pulled out a folded white envelope, which contained three black and white Polaroid pictures from 1970. I stepped out of the car. I recognized the design that the massive boulders in front of me made. There was a shale walkway leading up to it, which disappeared to the left of it, obviously wrapping around the humongous structure. It was a path to somewhere familiar. I walked back to the car and asked the taxi driver to wait for a few minutes. The pathway was steep and worn. Many people had stopped and visited there. Now, it was my turn. I walked up and around, and when I reached the top, right behind the boulders, I felt as though I were looking through her eyes.

It was picturesque. Right off of a postcard. Below were a small town, and a deserted military base. Mountains of grays, slate blues, and off whites back dropped the scene like a painting. I was speechless.

I pulled out the pictures, and flipped through them. There it was. Carmella, standing in front of the same painting.

She wore a military bomber jacket. For a brief second, I felt the connection between us. The only difference was that I was smiling.

The taxi ride to the motel was fast and convenient. Too short, in fact. A longer ride would have given me the opportunity to take in the scenery, and absorb some of the local flair. My motel was right off the "main" highway, so I didn't get the chance to see anything interesting. By "main," I mean *only*. It seemed as if everything led off of this main road, and from the view off the cliff, I could see the road leading straight through the small town.

Once checked in, I planned on taking a hot shower, calling home, checking my emails, and crashing. A bit of anxiety about lacking internet access or cell phone service set in as the taxi pulled up to the motel, but to my relief, I saw a Wi-Fi sign in the lobby window.

It was like *Bates Motel*. There were many rooms in a row, making the shape of an L, all with outside entrances. But, there was a small casino next door. As a matter of fact, on the short drive to the motel, we must have passed about a dozen small casinos and BBQ/Slot Machine businesses. What a great idea! You leave there with the worst case of acid reflux and the runs, but then you're too broke to buy antacids.

Although I loved to drive, and I usually did when Max, the girls, and I went anywhere, I enjoyed being a passenger. It gave me time to relax, and take in the sights. I especially enjoyed examining all the different styles of homes. So many shapes, sizes and yard designs. You always wondered who was inside. *Did the way the house was decorated match the person you pictured in your mind?* Guessing what the homeowners looked like based on the curb appeal, was just as entertaining as trying to match drivers to their vehicles.

Growing up, I used to take a lot of road trips with my grandparents, Josephine and Pellegrino. I referred to them as Nana and Poppa. They went everywhere and were invited to everything. Weddings, christenings, communions, confirmations, you name it. Mostly religious events, with the occasional high school graduation, or Sweet 16 thrown into the mix. They always took me along. It was my escape. I would sit at the bay window of my house for what seemed like days, waiting to be rescued. I knew the blue Buick would pull up sooner or later, but I was always ready, hours before their arrival.

"Benny! Nana and Poppa aren't going to be here for another two hours. Why not go outside and play with your friends for a little while?" Carmella would repeat herself several times, but I usually did not answer, or I would just shake my head. I always thought that if they didn't see me in the window, they would leave.

I loved those trips. I longed for them. When they would call and ask Carmella and Sean if they could take me, I knew it meant a weekend stay. They lived about an hour from my parents, so it was easier for them to keep me for the rest of the weekend, until they came over for Sunday dinner to pick me up.

My favorite visits were to Astoria, Queens. Queens had the best houses, and we had lots of extended family there.

All of the houses were connected, but painted all sorts of different colors. One color more harsh and over the top than the next. Salmon, pink, lime green, you name it, someone painted it. Each owner made sure to display his or her own personal style—mostly people of Italian or Greek decent. One concrete yard seemed to roll right into the next. As a child, I never quite knew where one "yard" started and ended. Each house had a steep brick staircase to the front entrance. Property lines were divided by wrought iron gates, and cement urn-like planters—some overflowing with real red or pink geraniums, or faded plastic flowers. The *one* flowerbed each place had was impacted with overgrown azalea bushes, bursting and intertwined with the colors of Easter. I swear if you looked hard enough, you'd find a family of PEEPS living in them.

Fountains, gaudy Roman statues that had no pupils in their eyes, and plastic flamingos, as far as the eye could see. Outdoor "patios" (or as my Nana and Poppa called them—breezeways) strung with hanging tiki lights, floating above folding chairs of all shapes and sizes. Everyone seemed to own a Cadillac that was as over the top as their home. I loved it then, and in my memory, I still do.

I didn't see any of this on my trip to the motel. The few homes I saw were small. Grey, tan or brown. No statues, or flamingos, and certainly no Cadillacs. Trucks. Lots of them. And flannel. Trucks and flannel for miles.

After checking in, I called home to check in on Max and the girls. I missed them terribly already. Tonight I would go to bed without gentle kisses from my babies. I looked forward to those every night, and after a quick phone call, I let Max get back to getting them ready for bed. Immediately, I got naked, and took a long well-deserved shower. The warm water felt nice, and it washed away the flight germs, and the remaining buzz from drinking. Although I was physically exhausted, I was too wound-up with the excitement about the following day to fall asleep.

I turned on the television and put on the local news. I wanted to check the weather for the next few days. I logged on to the internet and went to Google: *"What is a crop circle?"*

Before I had a chance to find out anything about them, I fell fast asleep.

———————◆———————

"Housekeeping!"

I could hear keys jingling outside my door. Her voice was muffled, and I thought I was still dreaming. *Obviously* she must have said it several times before I actually heard her, and I must have forgotten to place the *Do Not Disturb* sign on the door. Before I even had a chance to react to the opening door, there she stood. Only a few feet away from the foot of my bed—the shocked and embarrassed cleaning lady. She was no more than five foot tall—a sweet older woman with a wiry black and gray bun on her head. I was completely humiliated—well, at least for a minute I was.

"Oh my! I am so sorry." She had dropped the white dusting rag on the floor, in order to cover both her eyes. She turned away and the door slammed. The poor thing was mortified. I just sat there and rubbed my eyes, still laughing to myself. I was sure that when she opened the door, the last thing she was expecting to see was a fully exposed man, legs spread wide open, lying on his back in the bed right in front of her. I am sure my dick shouting "Good Morning, Montana!" made it even worse.

It was going to be a good day.

I would've been embarrassed myself, but I really have no shame, and besides, I knew it would give her something new and exciting to chat about with the other housekeepers. Come on…I'm eye candy. Shit like that doesn't happen to women like her every day.

Lying on the floor next to the bed were the same clothes from the day before. I picked them up and got dressed. I was sure that there was no need to impress anyone during continental breakfast. After stumbling into the lobby and getting myself a few cups of coffee and a muffin, I made my way back to my room. On the way, I could see the housekeeper entering another room a few doors down. I wanted to apologize to her, but I actually looked better naked than in my wrinkly clothes and uncombed hair. I didn't want to destroy her memory of me.

Back in my room, I took out the array of "Welcome to Montana" pamphlets and tourist guides from the airport, and I began to plan out my day. Originally, my main goal for the day was to retrace the steps of Carmella and Sean from so many decades earlier. I wanted to see if I could feel them there. To stand in the exact spots they did such a long time ago. I had a collection of addresses and names that took me months of research and investigating to accumulate. What I planned to do on the first full day in Montana would take balls. I thought I had a pretty decent set, but now that I was actually there, I was beginning to feel like a swimmer entering the ice cold Atlantic.

Do I walk up to random doors and knock?

Do I say, "Hello, I am sorry to bother you, but did you ever know Carmella and Sean Quinn?"

The very idea of what the reactions *could* be put a pit in my stomach. I wasn't sure if I was ready for that. The address and name book went back into my backpack, and I decided to look through the pamphlets some more. Today, I would find *some* culture in Billings.

The Fun Express Bus. Now, I am not one for bus trips, never was, but my options were limited, especially without a car. I chose not to rent one, especially since the people I was visiting planned on picking me up the following day. The Fun Express Bus pamphlet caught my eye, and I couldn't resist the temptation.

"Board the climate controlled Fun Express Bus, and enjoy an unforgettable, fun filled, educational tour of Billings. This white bus with wide viewing windows and cushioned seats offers a one-hour tour of Wild and Wicked Billings, and a one-hour tour of the Historic Moss Mansion. Travel to Boothill and view the city and the Yellowstone River from the Rimrocks. The historical and cultural passport to the legendary West begins with stories of opium dens, ladies of negotiable virtue, Calamity Jane, rumrunners, the notorious underground tunnels, Billing's only lynching, and a few ghosts."

Opium dens, underground tunnels *and* "ladies of negotiable virtue" were exactly what the doctor ordered. Reservations were necessary, but when I called up, they had room. What a surprise! I was so sure it would be a booked excursion!

The tour lasted about two hours and ended up at Jake's, a luncheonette on Main Street. Now, coming from New York, "Main Street" means an assortment of unique shops—usually expensive restaurants, bars, art galleries, and privately owned clothing stores. That was certainly not the case in Billings. This was refreshing. It was easy to take in the sights, and I really embraced that.

There were a few small bars and shops, and places to buy ammo. The largest place to go on Main Street was no surprise—a casino. And it was packed. By far, I observed the most people going into that casino compared to any other place around. But considering how bitter cold it was, with snow already steadily falling, it didn't really take much to draw you in—at least you could sit in front of a slot machine for a few hours, nice and warm.

Idle chitchat with some of the elderly Fun Bus riders, and a Swiss burger with fries kept me busy until the tour was over. In no time, we returned to the place the tour bus picked us up. Luckily, the pickup spot was only a quarter mile away, so I was able to walk to and from the motel. My conversations throughout the day were light and airy, and every single person on the tour lived in or around town. Many times the thought crossed my mind, *I wonder if anyone on this bus knew my parents?* But I decided that today was all about me.

I was the only stranger with a funny accent. And even though I wore clothes that I deemed appropriate, they did not come from Cabela's, so I still felt like I stuck out. All day long, I observed the locals—both young and old, and when I got back to the motel, I examined myself, which was something I did quite often. It was very important for me to belong—to have the people I was going to meet to like me.

I stared at myself in the full length mirror screwed to the wall. Staring back at me was a well-groomed poser, looking to fit in. I had played that part many times throughout my short, intense life. Portraying someone who did not exist. I began to self-destruct again.

An Abercrombie flannel. Not the oversized, large patterned, lumpy kind, but a fitted one—tucked in neatly, with a glimpse of the new white Calvin Klein tee underneath. It was perfectly wrinkled. Like I was out in the woods hunting moose. Sleeves cuffed for that "casual" look.

Banana Republic jeans. Tattered. Not torn from being a bad-ass hunter and gatherer, or stained from changing the oil in my over-sized truck, but by a machine and tumbler at the jean factory somewhere. My inseam high and tight—not at my knees.

Cole Haan boots and belt. Matching color and distressed.

Rolex.

Aviators. Like a tiara, neatly resting in my hair, which looked perfectly "sloppy" with a pea-size drop of product.

I stared at myself.

"Who the FUCK do you think you are?"

"Who are you trying to be?"

"You are a BRAND – not a person!"

I traveled across the country to have an experience that would change my life forever, and I was ashamed to begin the journey playing a role. Facades came easy to me, and they were always a way of protecting myself from pain and ridicule. This protective exoskeleton of clothing was like a scab. When it began to come off, I was pink and vulnerable. At that very moment, I made a decision. It would be the first time in my entire life that I would finally be myself from the very start. No fancy exoskeleton to protect me. No subtle deepening of the voice when meeting someone new.

I was going to be me. Take it, or leave it.

CHAPTER TEN

◆

I T WAS RARELY QUIET in the house that Carmella grew up in. Whether it was the banging of pots and pans in the kitchen, or *Connie Francis* playing on the record player in the living room, there was always something going on. But today, the silence was deafening. Carmella and Sean sat at the dining room table, staring at Josephine and Pellegrino, speechless and confused.

"Do either of you want any more espresso?" Josephine asked. She had gotten up and begun cleaning off the table. Sean and Carmella both declined, not because they weren't thirsty, but because they both still despised the taste. Espresso and anisette was a staple in the Russo home, and JoJo always made it, even though most of her children didn't drink it. Pellegrino closed the pastry box and picked it up, holding it out towards Josephine.

"JoJo, do you want to bring these to Vicki and Dom's?"

"Sure. Listen, your father and I are going to visit our friends in Glen Cove. We will be back around dinner time. Do not leave this house. You both have a lot to talk about." Before Carmella and Sean had the chance to speak, Josephine and Pellegrino were getting their jackets out of the hall coat closet.

Carmella and Sean got up and walked towards them to kiss them goodbye.

"Mom, Dad," Carmella tried to speak, but Josephine interrupted her.

"Listen Carm, your father and I are always here for you, but the ball is in your court now. You have options, just like you did *before* you married Sean, and moved to Montana." She turned to Sean. "Sean, we are giving you a second chance to prove yourself to our entire family. You both need to talk this out. No one will be around today, and Connie is working until seven, so you have plenty of alone time. Use it wisely."

Hugs and kisses were exchanged, and before either of them could respond, Carmella's parents were out the front door. Both Carmella and Sean knew they had a lot to sort out, and it would take time to talk through it all. There was so much to say.

For the first few minutes, it was awkward for both of them. It was much more comforting when others were in the house—it was sort of a buffer. They really hadn't needed to interact with each other during the three-hour lecture, but now their reality set in. The one thing they both enjoyed was finally getting to stand up and stretch.

Sean walked into the dining room and over to the corner chair, to grab his khaki green military bomber. He fumbled through the pockets and took out his pack of Winstons and his engraved Flip lighter.

"I'm going to head out back for a smoke. You want?" He held out his pack. One cigarette was sticking further out than the rest. It was tempting. Very tempting. Carmella had quit once she left Montana. She never really liked the taste, so it was easy to stop. Besides, she only started smoking in order to "fit in" with the other wives in Montana, when there was nothing else to do. This time was different. Her mixed emotions made her crave one, so she reached for it.

"Why not? My nerves are shot."

They both sat across from each other on the maroon-stained back deck off of the kitchen. It was cold out, but the fresh air was inviting. The backyard was lined with more hydrangea trees and purple lilac bushes. Both the cigarettes and the sweet scent from the blooms were calming, and they enjoyed the silence. They both knew it would be a long afternoon.

"Let's go in. I'll make a fresh pot of *real* coffee." Carmella laughed as she walked in the back door. "I can't believe she still makes espresso. Daddy and Vito are the only ones who drink it."

Sean twisted the tip of his smoke off and flicked his filter out onto the grass.

"I know. I could've really used a cup or two during *that* talk."

After the coffee was ready, they both decided to sit and talk in the living room. They were back to square one. Figuring out if the road mapped out for them by Josephine was one they were each willing to travel on again. The one thing that Carmella knew for sure was that Montana was no longer an option.

"Sean, listen. I have had lots of time to think things through since leaving Montana. You ruined me. Montana ruined me. I can never go back there, but I know that I still love you. I love the man I fell in love with here in New York. But it can only work here."

Carmella continued to explain that she wanted family close by. Sunday dinners, impromptu gatherings with family and friends. She wanted advice offered over coffee rather than a phone line.

Sean sat, and *really* listened to her for the first time since they got married. He looked upon her as his wife, and not a possession, and while she spoke, he knew that these were the things he wanted most too. Sadly, from the conversations with his mother and sister days earlier, he knew that his own family still did not like Carmella, but as long as he had the love of the Russos, this new beginning could work.

"Carm. I am so sorry for everything." Sean choked as he began to apologize for all the pain and suffering he had put her through. Tears gently rolled down her cheeks as she listened. It was never easy for Sean to express his feelings. Having the ability to express feelings was something learned, and showing emotion was never an option in the Quinn home. This was all new to him, but it felt good to truly express himself. It was no longer a sign of weakness. He opened up and let it all out.

"Honey, I need to tell you something. Something that happened after you left Montana." Sean was scared to tell Carmella of his infidelity. He still felt love for Rosa, but he knew that his reputation in Billings was less than desirable. Who would he have there? Everyone knew his business.

"I already know about Rosa, Sean." Her voice was monotone and stiff. Carmella sat up and faced him. The facial expressions he had become so used to seeing in Montana, were back in that instant. Hard and bitter. He didn't know what to say, which was perfect, because before he could speak, Carmella finished.

"Lilly called and told me. I've known all along. Sean, I left you for good. I had no idea you would be sitting in front of me again. This plan was a shock to me too, but all things happen for a reason. God brought us together again. Montana is *my* past. *Our past.* I never want you to speak her name again. You are *my* husband, not *her* boyfriend."

Although her voice was stern, and he knew she had put him in his place, Sean felt free. She didn't ask him to talk about it, and she *forgave* him without any explanation. This was the very beginning of their role reversal. She had control now. The very man who took her across country and stripped away all of her confidence was now back in her life. He was on her territory. Things would be different.

After several hours of crying, explaining, forgiving, forgetting, smoking and drinking coffee, both Carmella and Sean were emotionally spent. With a decision made, they sat on the green velour couch holding each other. Eventually, they fell asleep.

Pretending things never happened comes easily to some people. Or at least pretending to "pretend." Carmella and Sean's re-transition as a happy, New York, newlywed couple went flawlessly. Fractured friendships rekindled. Carmella's family members welcomed Sean again with open arms, and no one ever spoke of, or alluded to their "*past.*" No questions were asked, but most people were still skeptical and concerned about Carmella and Sean's future together.

Sean worked in the warehouse with his father-in-law. Pellegrino had made sure Sean worked long hours so that they could be financially secure after losing all of the military benefits. Health insurance was expensive, so Sean worked as a fulltime employee, pulling 14 hour shifts. Full-timers had full benefits, and with Carmella being pregnant again, it couldn't have happened at a better time.

Benjamin Sean Quinn. A brown-eyed, bouncing baby boy, was born to Carmella and Sean in the spring of 1972. I completed their flawless transition, and Carmella loved *me* more than anyone in her life from the moment she first laid eyes on me—including Sean.

"He is my gift from God. Perfect in every way!" From the very beginning, she told everyone I was her gift from God. From the very beginning, Sean really had nothing to do with it.

The moment Carmella recovered from her C-section, she began taking me to church. With a little cross pinned to my lapel, the power duo went to Monday Rosary, Wednesday confession and Sunday mass, which usually lasted over an hour. From infancy, I was surrounded by incense, the chiming of bells, and God.

GOD. GOD. JESUS. THE LORD. MARY. ST. JUDE. CHRIST ALMIGHTY. HAIL MARY. LORD. MARY, MOTHER OF GOD.

Forgive my blasphemy.

Saying Carmella had become engrossed in her religion was an understatement. It had become an addiction. Her saved marriage and my birth were the beginning of a love affair with Jesus. The more time she devoted herself to God and the church, the less sinful she felt about her past. Although the past was the past, it still haunted her. Fortunately, she had her baby now. I kept her busy, and thinking about the past happens less when you're busy. (*This is the main reason why I've kept myself VERY busy throughout my life.*)

I was a gift from God. She reminded me of this many times during my childhood.

"*I remember the day you were born. The first time you stared into my eyes. My life had new meaning. You looked right at me and smiled. It was precious. My beautiful baby boy!*"

As a young child, I loved hearing those words. People often talk about how deep a connection some mothers have with their sons, but from as early as I could remember, Carmella was my everything. She was my mother. My angel and protector. She could do no wrong, and when I was with her, I felt shielded. She kept me safe from all danger around me. Safe from those in the shadows, waiting to get you.

She was clueless. I was clueless. I was young. She was selfish. Children love what they *know*. And I was always too young to understand. If I knew then what I know now, the first time we met would have translated very differently.

I am sure my first word would not have been ball, but rather help.

◆

The first eight years of my childhood were good. My parents worked hard, and did whatever they could to provide me with all that an only child could want. We were a "normal" family.

After years of saving money, they moved out of Josephine and Pellegrino's basement apartment and had a small house built for us. It was just enough space to live comfortably in, with a nice sized yard, and an excellent school district. Dad worked nights, and Mom worked during the days, while I was at school. Carmella and Sean hardly saw each other, and when they did, I was their main focus. Thinking back, this was probably the main reason why their marriage "worked." And like many other happy households, they lost interest in each other to make sure their children were cared for properly.

For the first three years of elementary school, I was a typical boy. Physically fit and healthy. Forts, cars, army men, tag. My neighborhood friends and I played for hours after we did our homework, and I even had a "girlfriend" down the block named Stacy. There were birthday parties at McDonald's, late night Fourth of July block parties, and all the neighborhood moms walked us to the bus stop to see us off. Carmella and Sean did a good job. Well, most of the time they did.

From time to time, I recall waking up in the middle of the night to heated arguments that I was not supposed to hear. They frightened me. I would creep down the hall, hide behind the love-seat, and listen to them say mean things to each other. I had no idea what they were saying, but I could tell that the words were bad. I always made it back to my bed without being heard or seen. Sneaking around came easy, and I was really good at keeping secrets—two things that would prove both beneficial and catastrophic to my very being.

On several occasions, I would hear Carmella tell Sean that she hated being married to him. That she didn't trust him. That getting back with him was the biggest mistake she ever made. Once, I found my mother's engagement and wedding rings sitting on the counter. She often took them off when she was cooking. They sparkled on her finger like pieces of rock candy on a stick. Without hesitation, I snatched them off the counter and smashed them with a hammer in the basement. Based on what I had heard her telling him, it *seemed* like the right thing to do. I was six. My instincts were already kicking in. I was trying to protect my mother.

Aside from the late night arguments I would eavesdrop on, I loved this time in my life. It was innocent. Spinning around barefoot on my front lawn until I was too dizzy to stand. Staring up into the sky and squinting to keep out the rays from the sun. The cool grass underneath me. I was carefree and clean. Life was good.

Then I turned eight.

◆

Since Sean had worked long hours from the time I was born, Carmella wanted us to spend more time together. She often expressed her concerns that the reason why I had a difficult time bonding with him was because of his work schedule. He was usually tired or sleeping during the day, but she explained that if he didn't show more initiative early on, I may never connect with him. She wanted him to introduce me to fishing and hunting. Sean's two favorite things to do.

Carmella was right. By the time I was eight, I had no functional relationship with my father. He was a stranger who left me surprises on the kitchen table. Surprises that I found when I woke in the morning, and he was sleeping. The tall handsome man I called Dad. He had a handlebar mustache and he dressed like a police officer. I thought he was awesome, and even though he was only a nightshift security guard, in my eyes he was as important as a policeman. Leaving the warehouse was difficult, but the pay and benefits were substantially better. Also, he had every other weekend off, which gave him more time with Carmella and me.

My whole young life was dictated and orchestrated by three strong minded women: my mother, my aunt and my grandmother. What I ate. The way I dressed, and the things I liked to do. As an adult, I like to refer to them as *"The Three Sisters."*

According to Iroquois legend, corn, beans, and squash were three inseparable "sisters," who only grew and thrived when they were together. Obviously not of Native American decent, I thought of my three "sisters" as ricotta, parmesan and mozzarella cheeses. Together they made a mean ziti or lasagna, but when apart, something just wasn't right.

Of course, Josephine, my Nana, was the parmesan. The strongest and sharpest of the three cheeses. The two other sisters followed her chain of command. Constance (or Connie), my aunt and chosen Godmother, was the mozzarella. She had a sense of entitlement. Her lonely childhood and early lack of self-esteem had drastically changed. She was now strong, confident, and an egocentric. Mozzarella. The cheese that could transform. Carmella, my doting mother, was the weakest of the three. The ricotta cheese. Without the guidance of the other two, she became loose and shapeless without purpose. The Three Sisters all agreed. Sean needed to step up to the plate, and have more quality "father-son" time. Being off on the weekends made it easier to follow their commands on how to be a good father.

Parmesan and Mozzarella told Ricotta to have Sean take me to work with him one night. I couldn't wait! I was an eight year old boy. A nightshift with my mysterious cop-like Dad? I remember that day vividly.

I was in third grade. That day, my friend and classmate John had brought in a record. Our teacher played it for us a few times that afternoon and allowed us to dance around the classroom. It was *"Nine to Five"* by *Dolly Parton*. We had no idea that it was a top-grossing movie at the time, but on that day, 25 eight year olds turned the classroom into a disco. That song still makes me smile.

I walked in the front door in a great mood that day. My mother was sitting directly across from the door on the sofa. She was parked there every afternoon when I came home from school. On this particular day—the day I would begin bonding with my father, she seemed nervous. Next to her was a bushel sized bag of sun-flower seeds. She spoke to me, while nervously fumbling with her seeds and keeping one eye on *General Hospital*. *General Hospital* was her escape. I never quite knew why she was so engrossed in that soap opera, but now I understand completely. For one whole hour each day, Carmella could focus on the drama in Luke and Laura's lives, rather than her own.

"Benny, guess what? You're going to work tonight with Dad!"

"Really, am I sleeping there?" I was confused. He worked the overnight shift, and I had never stayed up later than nine o'clock, unless it was a holiday or someone's wedding.

"Dad is really excited to take you to work with him. Since you have no school tomorrow, it won't matter that you'll be up late. You'll have fun!"

She was really promoting this special event, because my facial expressions not only showed excitement, but apprehensiveness. My mother continued to explain how I would be able to see what Dad did at work, and how important his job was, but the entire time she spoke, I could tell that she was desperate for time alone. Time to think.

In recent weeks, Sean had become distant, more removed than usual, and Carmella had become suspicious. She could not put her finger on it, but he acted different when he got home. Conversations were shorter, and after a quick shower, he went straight to bed. And there were flowers. Lots of them. Sean used to give her flowers in Montana after one of their fights. Flowers meant guilt. She was getting them weekly.

With each bouquet of flowers, she ate a bag of potato chips.

More flowers = pretzels. A dozen roses = a tray of anything.

She was big. The biggest she had ever been. Carmella ate her emotions, and by the look of her, she was troubled. Today, it was another bag of salty sunflower seeds.

"Fine. Can I bring some books and stuff?" By stuff, I meant artistic things. As a child, I became engrossed in the Arts. I loved to sketch and color. This followed me all through high school, and at one point it expanded into the Dramatic Arts. The Arts became a passion. And the day I went with my Dad to work was probably the reason why I became so good at acting. I was eight. And I could have won an Academy Award for the performances shortly to come.

I gathered my things, and when Dad was done showering and ready for work, off we went. He had recently bought a new sporty blue firebird, and since it was only 1980, I could sit in the front.

CHAPTER ELEVEN

◆

S HE STARED AT ME. Her lips didn't move, and her ice-blue eyes felt like daggers. Her skin was sun-kissed. She just stared.

I felt uncomfortable. So did she.

Her hair was a beautiful bouquet of ambers and reds, like there was a pile of flames upon her head. It was long and wavy. I didn't know it then, but now that I think back, she was definitely going for the *Farrah Fawcett* look. Tight blue, Gloria Vanderbilt jeans and very high boots. She was thick, but firm. Those were the details that I noticed. Those are the things I can still remember.

"Your father will be back in a few minutes. He has to make his rounds." She sounded like a robot. Monotone. The total opposite of my third grade teacher, Ms. Murray. I felt special when I was with her. She was approachable. Now, I felt like an intruder. Children can feel when they are "in the way." She made it obvious that I was.

I sat in the tall swivel chair, as instructed by the cold stranger, and gazed out into the large parking lot that wrapped itself around a warehouse. Probably similar to the one dad worked at before he changed jobs. There were dozens of parking lot lights, and they all reached up into the sky like fists. Clusters of moths and other insects flew about, mesmerized by the beauty of the light. I kept watching the moths, fluttering as I spun around in my makeshift carnival ride. I spun and waited with nothing to say.

In the distance, we saw the headlights of a golf cart getting brighter as it approached.

"Here he comes!" Her demeanor changed in an instant. The cold, monotonous stranger became a bubbly, vivacious teenage girl running to the door. I got up and ran next to her. She felt my presence and moved over a step. She smiled at me for a brief second.

I smiled back. We were both acting. My skills were beginning to blossom. Her name was Heather, and she was jealous of me.

For about three months, I went with my dad to work one night every two weeks, and he would let me ride around in the golf cart with him on rounds. He would get me a hot chocolate, and sometimes I was able to drive. I'd wear his leather jacket with the security badge on it, and for once, I felt important to him. Heather would be there writing things on her clipboard and doing paperwork. When I was bored, I would draw her some pictures. She hung them up, but the next time I came to visit they would be gone. I guess they reminded her of *the boy in her way*.

One night, when I went with him to work, a black man replaced the company of the fiery redheaded woman. Heather had moved to a smaller office inside the warehouse and was now in charge of doing rounds with Sean. I looked forward to having my Dad all to myself, but within minutes of arriving, Sean and Heather would grab their clipboards and off they'd go. Sometimes they were back quickly, but most of the time there were "issues" with one of the loading docks, so I'd spend most of the time bonding with Spades.

Spades was awesome. It was his nickname. Thinking back now, it must have been a poker term, because otherwise, it was just plain wrong. And Spades *had* come to our home often for Carmella and Sean's infamous poker parties. My father enjoyed working with him, and they became close friends almost immediately after starting his new job.

Spades was huge. At least six-foot-four, and extremely muscular. He could pick me up and place me on his shoulders without even bending over. His arms seemed to get longer all by themselves on command. He reminded me of a Harlem Globe Trotter. I called him my super hero. Spades would bring me sandwiches, and share his Oreo cookies with me. Funny. Oreos. This memory makes me laugh. Our friendship was like an Oreo. My new male role model was a big black man names Spades who shared his Oreos and liverwurst sandwiches with me. You can't make this shit up.

Carmella and Sean continued acting odd around each other, and as more time went by, the three of us together became rarer. It was awkward. When I was alone with either of them, they asked me a lot questions. Some were about school and friends, but most of them were about each other. She asked questions about my time with Sean. Carmella wanted details.

"So, honey, what did you do at work with Dad?"

"Where did you guys go?"

"Who was there?"

"Meet anyone new?"

My answers were always age appropriate. "Not much," "It was ok," or "Just Spades."

After a few months, Heather wasn't at the warehouse anymore. I overheard my father telling Spades that she was transferred to a different location. She was out of the picture, and I would no longer have to fight for his attention. Don't get me wrong, he did try to make me happy when I was with him, but donuts, hot chocolate, and watching the feeds from the security monitor screens around the facility were getting old. Still, there was one thing that I enjoyed the most: driving the golf carts, and collecting small frogs around the warehouse. And now that she was gone, I was back to doing the rounds with my Dad.

When Sean took his rounds with Heather, Spades taught me how to drive a golf cart. There were several of them. The security guards would have to circulate the facility and make sure there were no trespassers on site. Also, they had to check the security points, specific spots around the facility that had these red flashing lights. These were motion sensors. If one of the lights was not flashing, it needed to be reset. Spades would take me. After a while, he let me sit on his lap, and I was allowed to steer. It was such a thrill! I felt like a badass. And there were hundreds of little frogs everywhere! It was as if they were falling from the sky. A sign from God? Looking back now, I think it very well may have been.

I would collect as many as I could catch, bring them back to the small glass security house, and play with them for hours. After a while, I would set them free on the last drive around. This would be the last night I could go to work with him. His hours were changing, and it would interfere with my Boy Scout meetings.

That last night, driving around and collecting frogs with him was amazing. He has his coffee, I had my hot chocolate. I drove.

"Hey, Benny. You want to go to the beach tomorrow? We can get bagels on the way. Just you and me."

"Sure!" I was thrilled. I loved going to the beach. We hadn't gone in such a long time, and I was hoping he would help me find change in the picnic area, and sea glass on the beach. I had a small pile of sea glass in my bedroom that he had given me, and I loved looking at it when he wasn't home.

"Great. I'll let mom know when we get home. It is supposed to be nice tomorrow. I'll show you how to use my metal detector."

I loved his metal detector. I always felt like a pirate searching for treasure. Even if it was a bottle cap, or just a penny, it didn't matter. Dad loved me. When he asked me to go, I felt happy and secure, and I couldn't wait to go to bed and have the morning arrive as soon as possible.

"Benny! Time to wake up. Come have breakfast," Mom called me from down the hall. She was in the kitchen filling up a small Igloo cooler for the beach.

"I'm so glad that you and Daddy are going to the beach together today." Carmella was genuine. I could sense it in her tone.

"Mom, what are you doing today? Why don't you come with us?"

"Aww, honey I can't. Aunt Connie is coming over, and then we are going out to lunch."

It was a perfect beach day. When I looked out the window he was right—the weather was just perfect. The three of us hadn't done anything fun together recently, and I hoped she would come, but today I knew I would find treasure. I would be able to start my own treasure box like Dad's.

Sean kept a large wooden box in our kitchen hutch. It was heavy, and I was not allowed to touch it, but every now and again he would take it out. On the rug he would create small piles, and I would get to observe them.

Old spoons, forks, costume jewelry and buttons. Ragged and worn. The salt water had eaten away their youth, but replaced it with character. Each piece had history. A story and owner. In a small tan felt pouch was his secret stash of gold, silver and gemstones. This was my favorite bag. Old high school and college rings. Piles of lonely earrings—each one longing for their mate. Bracelets and necklaces. Everything was shiny. Sean polished them as he found them.

"One day I am going to melt all of this down and make something," he would say. I wondered if it would be for me.

I would grow up and call this Ghetto Gold one day, but for now, it was my dad's treasure. That day, I had hoped to find something I could add to his little felt bag. I'd be important. Just like his gold. I'd be his treasure.

Masses of seagulls swarmed around our car as we pulled into the parking lot of the beach close to home. I always feared we'd run some over, but it was as if they had little turbo engines attached to their wings. Occasionally, I would see one dead in the parking lot. Its feathers gently blowing in the salty breeze. It was alone. The other seagulls avoided going near that one—as if it was a bad omen.

"Aw Shit!!"

"What's wrong Dad?"

"I forgot the damned metal detector! I must have left it on the front porch, when I grabbed our cooler from Mommy. I'm sorry, Benny. Next time. Let's find some seashells."

Today, I would not find any treasure.

Walking through the tunnel under the dunes was fun, especially for an eight year old. Everything you said would echo. I'd yell things as loud as I could. No one was there, so I could listen to my own voice reverberate through the tunnel, as if it were calling back to me. But today was different. Someone's voice echoed back from the other end of the tunnel.

It was her. Her fiery red hair gently blowing around her face. She wasn't alone. A woman with darker hair was with her. They each had a bag. I held onto Sean's hand tighter, stopped and stared up at him. Dad let go of my hand and kept walking, leaving me behind.

They walked quickly, and talked as I tried to keep up. I was scared.

"This is Donna." That is what *she* said. She wasn't my mother. She was a trespasser.

"Donna wants to take you for a walk on the beach," she said. "She likes to collect seashells. Don't you?" When she spoke to me, she towered over me. She never knelt down. I felt like I was in trouble. I was in trouble.

Sean did not speak. He just stood there. He motioned for me to go. I kept thinking, *where is he going? When is he coming back?* My mouth could not open to speak. Donna took my hand, and I followed along. Off Sean and Heather went, disappearing into the dunes. Neither of them turned around. I was a child. I had no sense of time, but watching my Dad walk away felt like an eternity.

Donna didn't want to find seashells. I lost my innocence that day—along with my soul. Sean meant nothing now. He was just a shell. So was I. The only two we brought back home from the beach that day.

Two years. I was burdened with my dad's dirty secret for two years. Playing an adult game that I was way too young to understand.

It was like a dark shadow. For my entire life, my secret would always be lurking around me, constantly reminding me of how innocent I once was.

I became a defeated secret keeper without a soul.

A mother betrayer.

An actor.

A victim.

A liar.

His metal detector was still in the back seat of his car.

CHAPTER TWELVE

◆

BEFORE GOING TO BED the night before, I had remembered to put the *Do Not Disturb* sign on the door. I did not want to scar any more housekeepers, and I wanted to sleep in. Sleeping in was a commodity hard to come by! I was up at four in the morning every weekday. If I slept any later, I would miss the express train to Penn Station, which ultimately made me bitter, stressed and unapproachable by the time I walked into the office. Also, being a father of two small children, Max and I were up by 7:30 on the weekends. Even though the girls would tip-toe in "unheard," they would jump into the bed to wake us up.

Max and I would often take turns, letting the other sleep in for an extra hour or two after our two little tornadoes touched down, but unlike Max, I could never really fall back into a deep slumber. I would lay in bed and think about my life, or I would make a mental list of everything I needed to accomplish during the weekend. Today was exactly the same, but unlike home, I was not getting out of bed because I believed I was wasting value time, which could be used finishing laundry or yard work. No, I was nervous about my day in Billings. It would be life-changing, and I still wasn't sure if that was a good or bad thing.

I glanced over at the alarm clock. It was 8:22 Montana time, which meant that everyone would be up at home. I wanted to talk with my family. I needed to hear the sweet voices of my little angels, and the calming reassurance that Max had brought into my life from the very beginning. I needed it desperately—to bring me back to the mental place I needed to be. After calling the front desk to cancel my wake up call, I called Max's cell. Everyone we knew used their cells exclusively. We often wondered why we actually had a landline.

The phone rang several times, and I was about to hang up—but the sound of candy streamed through the phone, immediately reviving me.

"Daddy?" It was Ava. Our beautiful little girl, Ava Margaret. My heart melted every time she said the word *Daddy*. It was a word I never thought I would hear.

———————————◆———————————

Ava Margaret was our second born, but first to come home. Max and I knew from the very beginning of our relationship that we wanted children, and it was Max who sealed the deal for me. I was never quite sure if fatherhood was something I could handle. Having had a rough childhood, and very little respect for my own father, I thought it best to focus on myself, rather than risk continuing the cycle, and fucking up my own children. But the moment I met Max, I knew that he would bring out the best in me—both as an individual and parent. Adoption was our choice. Surrogacy was extremely expensive, and biology was not important to either of us.

We had gone up to Vermont and signed up with an agency that dealt with adoptions, both opened and closed, within the United States. It was also one of the only gay-friendly ones without some ridiculous religious affiliation. Unlike Carmella, my children would not be gifts from God, but rather birth mothers somewhere unknown. Max and I knew we wanted children from our own country, which was totally fine, since most other countries had banned us homosexuals from adopting any of the lonely, abandoned, children piling up in their orphanages. We also knew we wanted to be able to access the parents, if any of our children needed medical attention, such as a blood transfusion. Medical history was important. Knowing that we had a list of specifics, we expected it to take several years before we were chosen. It ended up being the complete opposite. Within fifteen months, we had two infant girls, seven months apart, and a yellow lab puppy named Scout. We like to call ourselves the "Insta-Family". Many called us insane.

Although Ava Margaret was the first to come home, she was not our firstborn. Her sister Charlotte Rae, or *Charlie*, was. She was also the first one Max and I met, held, and fell in love with through pictures and emails. She was in foster care across the country in California, and we met her for the first time during the Christmas holiday. Her biological parents were meth addicts, and it took time to terminate their parental rights—so although we were told that she would eventually be ours, we were cautious. We decided to keep ourselves active with the adoption agency we signed up with, just in case adopting Charlie fell through, which was often the case with foster children. As we continued our communication with the DHHS regarding Charlie, we were contacted by the adoption agency.

A woman, who was five months pregnant, was interested in Max and me. We were picked by her to adopt her unborn child, and Charlie's parents' rights were terminated two weeks after we brought Ava home. The rest is history.

Max, Ava and Charlie changed me forever. As each one of my saviors entered my life, I slowly transformed into the person I always admired from afar.

"Hey babe. How are you doing?" Although I loved both of my daughters very much, and the sound of their voices calmed my nerves, it was Max's voice that made me feel at ease. I would be getting picked up in a few hours, and I knew talking to him would make me feel more secure in my decision to fly to Montana in the first place. Max gave me the push I needed to make the journey, and he knew I needed to find closure and bring the peace into my life that I so desperately needed.

"I am nervous as hell, Max. I keep wondering if I made the right decision coming here." He could sense the anxiety in my voice.

"Listen Ben, you knew from the very beginning that this was something you had to do. It may have taken you two years to get there, but if you don't follow through, there would still be that void." I was quiet. This wasn't very common. I had a tendency to talk myself out of the things that made me feel isolated, or threatened. Being so far away from home, without someone by my side to look at or touch was alien to me. This was exactly how Carmella had felt so many decades earlier. Alone and unsure of what would happen next. I never quite understood how she felt, but on that day, I had compassion and empathy for her.

"You're right. But, I can't help but wonder what they will all think of me, you know?" I began to sob. I was vulnerable. My childhood had left me calloused, and I often had difficulty feeling anything when I was backed into a corner. It was as if I had a shut off valve. Crying was for the weak, and I had learned very early on that crying would not change circumstance. But still, when I heard Max's voice, the tears flowed.

"Ben. It will be fine. You can do this. You have to do this. Listen, bundle up and go for a run. You have some time. It'll do you good."

"That is a great idea. I'll blast some R.E.M. and reel myself back in. Ok, let me go, I'll touch base later. Kiss my girls." Max hung up. I was on my own. Just me. The cold wind around me, and R.E.M.

Getting ready to go running, in a place that I had never been was refreshing. Back home, my exercise routine was less than thrilling. Waiting my turn to squeeze in a few reps at some random machine, some isolated free weights, sit ups, and a run on the treadmill. I was a robot, like everyone else there. Sometimes I ran outside, but I often used the same route through our neighborhood. Having mountain ranges in the distance, and knowing that I would encounter all new scenery rejuvenated me. Since I was close to town, I decided to run to the place where it all began for Carmella and Sean—the military base. After dressing appropriately, I put on my iPod and pressed play.

Running to the military base had not been a part of my original agenda that day, but it seemed fitting. It was about two and a half miles away from the motel, so I kept a steady slow pace. In recent years, I noticed that my left knee felt weaker, so I could not alternate my running speed the way I had liked to. This was fine today. It allowed me to listen to the one song that made me feel stronger. More capable. I had listened to this song hundreds of times since high school, often playing it over and over again, singing the words on the top of my lungs where no one could hear me. Today I sang loud and I didn't care. Here, no one knew me. No one cared.

Green from R.E.M. What I believe to be the best album ever recorded. It was written for me. For people like me. Wounded, searching for pieces of themselves amongst the rubble—in shock and disbelief that they are still alive. Many times over, I listened to this album when I felt broken. It spoke to me, and kept me going, especially the song, *World Leader Pretend*. It was especially important for me to listen to it over and over again today—as a matter of fact—I listened to it constantly lately. Blasting it in my car on the way to the train station, as I ran on my boring route, even when I had no reason to.

Listening to the lyrics, I knew I couldn't have outlined my life any better with my own words—both then and now. To this day, I thank them for writing that song and keeping me whole. And as the old abandoned military base came into view, I sped up. I had the speed and agility of a twenty year old. There was no pain today. I focused, and realized I was here for a reason. I would no longer wage war on myself for the things I could not control. Carmella and Sean were the barricades that caused me to crumble inside. Today I demanded a rematch, and it was not *my* mistake to make good, but theirs that I needed to fix. The walls I put around me were for protection, but I no longer needed them. This was my world.

Do Not Trespass. I could hear the sounds of the past echoing through the run down brick buildings. I listened intently. There were no signs of them. Just like Carmella and Sean, the youth of the military base had been stripped away by the elements. The mortar had weakened. I stood before the abandoned site, and for the first time in a very long time—I felt free.

———————◆———————

My clothes were already laid out on the rented bed when I got back from my run. I felt lighter, both physically and mentally. My eyes slowly scanned the outfit, making sure that I kept the promise to myself that I had made the day prior—to avoid looking overstated and unnatural. My anxiety was gone. And I was no longer scared of where I was going and whom I was meeting. After a quick shower, I got dressed. I gazed at myself in the mirror again, and this time I was pleased at what I saw. My shirt was un-tucked with two buttons open, making me feel less constricted. I opted for my favorite pair of looser knock-around jeans, and although they had a few stains on the thighs and knees from various household chores, they were still presentable. Calm and casual, ready for the next step in my life.

Originally, I was supposed to be picked up at the motel around noon, but I had gotten a phone message asking to meet at the local Barnes & Noble around one o'clock. This was fine, since I hadn't eaten much before the run. Luckily, there was a small grocery store close by, what we would call a *bodega* back home. I got myself a cup of coffee and a roast beef and Swiss cheese sandwich. I enjoyed eating. Along with the run earlier, eating only made me feel more relaxed.

From very early on in my teens, I began a love/hate relationship with food. Like Carmella, and most of my maternal side of the family, I learned to both drown *and* celebrate my feelings with food. There was never a reason *not* to overindulge. I found myself gaining and losing 10 to 20 pounds every year or two, like a yo-yo. It wasn't until I reached young adulthood that I found harmony between feelings and food, which kept me in pretty decent shape. Being fat was not an option for me. I was much too vain for that.

The taxi ride to Barnes & Noble took about twenty minutes. Along the way, I noticed several small trailer park neighborhoods. Although they were clean and neat, they lacked personality. The personality that I was used to. There were no bright colors or shrubs. Just rows of trailers and mailboxes. Occasionally, I would see one trailer or home with an overabundance of "things" outside. Not trash or clutter, but decorative things. Wooden or metal signs that said something like "Welcome to Our Pad," tires turned inside out as flower pots, and plastic hanging plants. They were the rebels of the neighborhood.

I arrived about twenty minutes early, so I could look for a book or two for Ava and Charlotte. Hello Kitty was their flavor of the month, so I immediately found my way to the area of the children's books splattered with pink, purple and sparkly things. Our house was a treasure trove of sparkly girly things, and Max and I always had to make sure to scan the vacuum canister for lost beads, Barbie shoes, and other "important" items they would miss. On this day, I would add two cheaply-made pleather Hello Kitty pocket books, lined with pink fur (*that would fall off in chunks and end up in our vacuum*) and a copy of *Hello Kitty, A Little Book of Happiness* into the mix, totaling $26.89. Unbelievable. I should have wiped my ass with the money instead.

My Rolex read 1:10. I couldn't resist. It was a gift from Max and the girls for my fortieth birthday, and I wore it whenever I had the chance. I realized that I was ten minutes late, but it allowed me a chance to look from afar. Walking slowly towards the café inside the book store, I saw her. I stopped and breathed in as deeply as I could. Slowly exhaling, I walked towards her. She was focused on the people standing in line at the café, but as I got closer, I could see her eyes turn my way, looking at me peripherally. Her face aligned with her eyes. She smiled, stood up and walked over to me.

"Hello Ben." I was frozen.

She held her arms out and embraced me. It melted me. I lifted up my arms and embraced her back.

"Hello Rosa."

We sat down at the small café style table, and situated ourselves. She had come straight from work, having taken a half-day to meet me. Rosa must have had the same idea of arriving early, because she had some work spread out that she was now putting away.

"Thank you so much for being flexible today. I had an emergency staff meeting and we had to let someone go this morning. It was awful." Rosa spoke as she stuffed random papers into a *Penda flex.* She then placed it in her purple monogrammed *Eddie Bauer* canvas bag. She also wore a purple shirt, which made me assume it was her color of choice. It was my mother's favorite color as well. For a second that made me uneasy—like it was a sign from Carmella's God—letting me know that he was aware of my secret rendezvous with her past. And it didn't help that Rosa had the same characteristics.

Rosa was easy on the eyes, although father time had weathered her just as he had Carmella and Sean. Her shoulder length hair was a lighter shade of auburn, with scattered strands of silver throughout. It was held up in the back with a black banana clip, like the ones I remember girls wearing when I was in high school. She hardly wore any make-up, but you could tell that if she did, the structure of her face would hold it well. She had a mouth that when relaxed, still had that hint of a smile. Rosa made you feel relaxed without even speaking, and I had a feeling that was how most people felt when they met her.

"This is my favorite place. I just love reading. So many books to learn from, and never enough time to read them. Sometimes, I read two or three books a week. Do you like to read?" She was staring at the new release shelf, probably scoping out her newest adventure.

I laughed to myself, "Sadly enough, no. I hate to admit that to people, but I really don't like to read. Actually that isn't completely true. On occasion, if the first ten or fifteen pages grab me, I'll finish it in two days, but that rarely happens."

"Do you have a favorite genre?" She was interested, and ready to persuade me to read more, I could tell.

"That's the problem. I don't."

"I love mysteries and science fiction the most. They keep you guessing. But I usually figure them out before I finish the book. No one ever lets me join their book clubs!" Rosa began to laugh. So did I. We had broken the ice.

For about an hour we talked about our jobs and families. She was especially inquisitive about the adoption process, having wanted to adopt a child in her youth, but she already had three children and figured it would be difficult to raise another child considerably younger than the others. Gay marriage was another topic we touched upon; she seemed like someone who rolled with the punches, saying "If I had to be a lesbian, I'd choose Angelina Jolie." Who wouldn't?

Rosa was the first to initiate the real reason why we were sitting with each other. I guess she could sense my hesitation. She was a mother of two sons, 41 and 32 and a 35 year old daughter, so she had that motherly instinct.

"Ben, I am so glad you contacted me. I must say, I was shocked when you called. I hadn't heard your father's name in over 40 years. It threw me for a loop." She was playing with her hands now. I could see that some memories had flooded back. She continued. "You know, I loved your father very much back then. I was so very young. I had no idea what I was getting myself into, but Sean was my first love. I guess you seldom ever get over that. It stays with you, no matter how badly you want that feeling to go away."

I wasn't sure if I could say the same. As I listened to Rosa, I tried to think if I had a first love. The one that changed your life forever. I used the phrase "I Love You" in several long term relationships, but now that I think of it, I don't think I actually loved any of them—but rather loved the idea of having someone close to me. I realized that Max was my first *true* love.

"Rosa, I came here because I needed to make things right. When my father sat me down and told me everything, I knew I had to find you. *I* may have no relevance to your past with Sean, but *we* are connected in more ways than you can ever imagine. He broke your heart and abandoned you when you were hurting. There was no closure for you. I have been knocked down by him over and over again my entire life, and I realize now that you are the closure I needed."

Her eyes began to well up, "My god! I told myself I would not cry over that bastard ever again, and now look at me." She was searching through her tote for some tissues, but I got up and grabbed some napkins off the counter.

"Like I said, Ben, I was very young and impressionable. Your father was a womanizer. I knew that from the very beginning. Your father was a sweet talker. He knew exactly what to say, and what to do. He even cheated on me. If I would have known that Sean was going to go back to your mom, I wouldn't have—"

"—wouldn't have what? Fallen in love with him? Listen Rosa, Carmella left him for the things he was doing to her. She drove back to New York and filed for divorce. He thought it was over. He was 23 years old for God's sake! You were just kids." I was actually defending my father. I couldn't believe what was coming out of my mouth, but it was making total sense. For the very first time, I felt bad for him. He was a man. And men are weak. I asked myself, "*If Max were to leave me and drive off to California and never call or write, would I find someone new while I waited to get a divorce?*" I guess I would. It must be genetic.

"I knew it was wrong though," Rosa was looking down at her hands. "I did. My mother knew it was wrong, too. God, I wish I would have listened to her and my friends. Who the hell is an adult at 19 anyway?" She wasn't talking directly to me, but arguing with herself.

I responded with the first thing that came to mind,

"Well, whatever the case may be, both of you were together, and I am here getting to know you. Can't dwell on the past now, can we?" I winked at her. We laughed again. But when those words came out of my mouth, I realized that I still was. Dwelling on the past that is. Should I be offering someone advice that I was obviously not using myself? Rosa looked at her watch and got up,

"Wow. Time does fly. Listen, what do you say we start heading back to my place? Everyone is coming over around five for dinner. Do you need to make a quick stop at the motel on the way?"

"Nah, I'm fine. Unless it's black tie." I had a feeling my sarcasm would be reciprocated.

"By the way you're already dressed, I'm sure you really do have a tux back at the motel, don't you?"

As I put my hand on her shoulder, we walked out laughing. We were friends. Instantly connected. Not the type of friends that would communicate often, and take vacations together, but the type of friends that bonded through common history. And even though I had spent hours trying to pick out clothes that made me appear casual and relaxed, like a true friend, she saw right through me.

CHAPTER THIRTEEN

◆

SEAN WAS A WOMANIZER. As those words came out of Rosa's mouth, my poles began to bend. As a matter of fact, they almost snapped in two. Fact was, I knew that for two years, and I had kept it to myself. He had Heather, and for the first year of their relationship, I had a girlfriend of my very own, who taught me how to lie and conceal my emotions. Sean and I were each living two separate lives. He had a mistress and a wife he was betraying, and I…I had a twenty-something year old predator, and a mother I was betraying. I wasn't even ten years old.

All that would change with one phone call on a beautiful spring day in April.

I had just walked in the door, and my mother was sitting in the same spot. As I ran up to hug her, I hesitated, because I didn't want to interrupt her watching General Hospital, but then I realized the television was turned off. She was staring at me with an unfamiliar look. She had a smile on her face, but it was sad. The one you see on someone's face when you're about to find out that someone died, or your pet had to be put to sleep. Also, the lamp next to her was off. She had been sitting there alone in the shadows.

"Come here, baby." She was motioning for me to come closer. I put down my backpack, and sat down next to her on the sofa. I was scared to look her in the eyes. She seemed so sad, and I wondered if she knew my secrets. I avoided eye contact with her every time Sean and I came back from one of our *outings*. Although I was just a child, I could put away one emotion and replace it for another instantly. I loved my mother way too much to ever hurt her, even if it meant being used by Sean, Heather and Donna. She wrapped herself around me.

"Benny, you know that I love you very much, right?" She was facing me, I could see her through the corner of my eye, but I did not turn. I faced forward and nodded. She touched my chin with her trembling hand and guided my face towards hers. Tears gently rolled down her face, but she did not sob. We had the same eyes. I had heard this all my life. I hadn't ever noticed that until now.

"Listen, I want you to know that sometimes mommies have to make choices that can be hard. I love you more than…" the phone rang. Carmella got up and picked up the receiver without saying hello. It was not a surprise; she was expecting it to ring. I tried to eavesdrop, but the wall between the kitchen and living room muffled the whispers being exchanged between Carmella and the caller. For a few minutes she walked around the kitchen, whispering. The cord on the telephone was extremely long, and often got twisted together, not allowing you the freedom to roam, but today it was untangled.

"Hold on," she said into the receiver. She handed me a small bowl of pretzels and a glass of orange juice, then put on *The Brady Bunch* for me.

"I'm almost done, you ok?" Again, I nodded without eye contact. I focused on Cindy, and the funny way she talked. By the time she got off the phone, I had watched the entire episode.

After she hung up, she walked down the hall into the bedroom, and came back dragging two large black plastic bags, like the ones you would use to collect leaves. After placing them by the front door, she went into the kitchen and got her keys. I got up and sat in the bay window, watching her put both bags into the trunk of her old, brown Buick Century. The upholstered roof of the car had already ripped off, and the light brown vinyl seats could scald your thighs in the summer if a towel wasn't placed under you. It was "paid off," so my mother would not get rid of it. I ran back to my spot on the sofa, as she walked back towards the front door.

"Mommy? Are you donating clothes to poor people again?"

This time I looked directly at her, and *she* couldn't look back. Only now, as an adult, do I understand why. She knew what was coming, and the innocent question must have twisted her insides.

Outside, I heard a car door slam. I got up to see who it was, and Carmella ran over to me. Sean was walking up the driveway towards the house. His face was a hot shade of red. I knew that color. I saw that color when I snooped in on their late night quiet arguments.

"Benny, I want you to go outside and play." She had her hands on my shoulders. She looked into my eyes. She was no longer sad. She was petrified. Her pupils were large, practically covering all the tones of browns and gold that made her eyes so inviting. The front door flung open so hard I thought it would fly off the hinges. Rather than turn, she looked right into my eyes, she mustered up a soft motherly smile, the one that they used to show how much they care about you, and said "Go."

I turned, and walked past *him* out the front door.

◆

Growing up as a small child, I rarely witnessed the anger that ruled Sean. However, I could sense it. It was always there, just beneath his skin, waiting to surface. Everyone else had a taste. Rosa, Carmella, and also Heather. I witnessed his rage on Heather during one of our visits to a park close to my Grandparent's house. Although I was a distance away, with my girlfriend collecting salamanders, I heard it. The intensity of his voice caused me to turn and investigate. Donna made sure to keep me busy, but I knew from the sound of his voice, what he was truly capable of. On that particular day, the hellishness in his actions would shake the remaining hint of innocence right out of my boyish body, but oddly enough, it didn't surprise me in the least.

I sat on the driveway, next to his blue Firebird. All I could hear were the funny sounds coming from the engine as it cooled. Metallic twangs, echoing bings and something that sounded like paper bags being crumpled up. I sat there, holding my two newest Matchbox cars, given to me to keep silent, and waited. Although the screen doors were open, it was strangely quiet, and with the way he entered the front door, I was expecting noise. I slowly walked up the front stoop and sat under the kitchen windows. As

I approached, I could finally hear something. It came from down the hall somewhere, so I was able to stand up, and look through the screens. I saw my mother's burgundy leather pocket book on the table, and her keys lying next to it. There was a bulky address book sticking out of the largest pocket. The noise got louder and closer. I ducked. They were in the kitchen, right above me.

"I know all about her, Sean! She has been calling and hanging up!" Carmella's voice was strong and matter-of-fact. She was stating the obvious.

"What the fuck are you talking about? Who? I don't know what the hell you are talking about Carm!" His voice was tense and nervous. The intense sound of his heavy steel-toed work boots following her around still echoes in my mind. I could also hear the sound of papers rustling.

"Sean, I have the phone records. Who is Heather? She's the one from work, isn't she? She answers the phone there? I called the number, Sean. I recognized her voice." His silence was frightening. Sean was backed into a corner. He had nothing to say, and this alone confirmed the suspicions she had for over a year.

"I'M DONE!" She threw the phone records at him. I was standing now—staring in. They were too focused on each other to even notice the young eyes witnessing the collapse of their marriage. She walked towards the table and went to grab her pocketbook, but he pushed her aside and grabbed it first. As she fell to the floor, the color in his face returned, and his eyes were wide. So wide in fact that he didn't even seem to blink.

"Where the FUCK do you think you are going? Huh?! You think you can leave me AGAIN?" As she got up, he blocked the entryway.

"It's over Sean. You can have her. I'm done." Carmella walked over to the phone, but as she reached out to pick up the receiver, Sean hit the phone with the side of his hand. He was still holding on to her purse and keys. The phone tore out of the wall, and landed across the room. With full force, he pushed my mother to the floor. She looked up, seeing me. She tried to get up, but he grabbed a fistful of her hair. He saw her stare, and turned around. He saw me too, but it didn't matter. In that moment, what I was seeing didn't matter to him at all. Carmella was his property again, and he wasn't going to let it go.

"BENNY RUN!! RUN! Go to Nana and Poppa's! GO!!!" She was shrieking. Scared. Because of the beating that was to come. Mortified that her baby was witnessing her impending doom. She screamed out my name over and over again,

I turned and ran. The shrieks got further away. I fell and skinned my knees on the loose rocks from the buckling pavement. There was no pain as the blood ran down my legs. I could hear her screaming. Glass broke. Neighbors were gathering outside. Sobbing hysterically, I ran for *her* life.

Josephine and Pellegrino had moved a few houses down from us, the year prior to the collapse. Both were long retired, and living over an hour away from the remaining family seemed illogical. Josephine's body was aging quickly, making it difficult to travel as often as they liked to, and she knew being closer to her daughters would be the best for everyone.

Carmella and Connie were the only two left on Long Island. Over time, their brothers and families had moved out of state and rarely called or visited. Even though the family had become smaller, the drama had lessened considerably. Josephine's sons had become distant and uninterested. They were also jealous, and had been for many years. Jealous of the relationships she had with her two daughters, and the bond I had with both her and Pellegrino. Pellegrino and Jojo's other grandchildren were disinterested in having a bond with them, and had been taught to hate them by their mothers.

I was the apple of their eyes. Eventually, later in life, Connie would have a son too. Together, we would continue to make them beam with pride until they died, but the bond that I, alone, had with them, became stronger each time they saved me from Carmella and Sean's destruction. Today was just one of the many times they guarded me from being torn apart.

By the time I reached my Nana and Poppa's house, he was already waiting outside. A neighbor had called to let them know I was coming. Our street was tight, full of caring families with kids all around the same age. Josephine and Pellegrino had become the matriarchs of Mount Place, the street we lived on. All the young couples stopped by when they saw JoJo and Pelly sitting outside. Pelly became his nickname when they moved into the youthful and energetic neighborhood. The neighbors also knew of Sean's possible infidelities. Carm had shared her concerns with several other women she had become close to over the last few years. Her coffee clutch. They all silently watched, and waited for this day to come. Someone called to let my Nana and Poppa know that I was running, bleeding, and that Carmella was being held hostage in her home only a few houses away.

"Benny, come here! I want you to go inside with Nana." My grandfather pulled me gently to him by my arm. I held onto his waist, confused and numb. I wasn't crying anymore. I was in shock. As he guided me up the front stairs towards the door, the sounds of several cop cars startled me, and I turned around. Three of them quickly drove past, sirens blasting. They stopped in front of my childhood home. There were already two more there. Red, white, red, silver, red, silver, red, white. I focused on all the lights twirling. There was a sea of flashing lights that hypnotized everyone. Neighbors walked towards them like zombies from a horror movie. Pelly picked me up and brought me inside.

"JOJO?!"

"I'm in the back room! Bring him here; I don't want him looking out the front window!" My Nana was in the back bedroom, the farthest point from the fuckery occurring up the block. She sat in a large armchair, waiting. Her arthritis was extremely painful, so she couldn't get up to rush to me. He placed me in her arms like a newborn. Unable to communicate, and emotionally and physically fragile, she held me tight to her breast. She hummed softly into my ears. My Nana smelled like garlic and basil.

She had been prepping for Sunday.

"Can you stop at a liquor store so I can pick up a bottle or two of wine for dinner?"

Rosa turned to me, "No one drinks, but if you would like to have some, I can. There is a wine and spirits place right up the road."

"Yes! I totally need a glass of Pinot Noir tonight." We both laughed.

"Honestly, I haven't had a glass of wine in years, but I may just go ahead and enjoy a glass or two myself. Good idea!"

After stopping, and picking up two bottles of *Mark West* Pinot Noir, my new favorite, we drove to her house. When we pulled up, I noticed that her home was neither bland, nor overly decorated. It was tasteful and simply stated. Just like her. If I had passed by her place, not knowing who she was, I would have imagined her perfectly. There was a large porch, newly built, that ran along the entire side of her home. Although it was snowing and cold out, I could easily picture her on the deck, laughing and barbequing, surrounded by the family that loved her. The family I was going to meet.

There were two large trucks, and a small old Honda already parked along the street in front of her house. As we pulled into the driveway, I took her available hand into mine.

"Oh God, Rosa. I am nervous as hell." I looked at her. She had the same facial expression that I did.

"Me, too."

I picked up the two bottles of wine, which seemed like a shitty token of my appreciation for entering her home and meeting the family. How could two bottles of Pinot bring comfort to those from Rosa's past? Those that helped her pick up the pieces from the damage that Sean caused? I felt almost embarrassed, like it would have been better to show up with nothing but myself.

Rosa opened the door, and I stood directly behind her, holding my pathetic bag of peace offerings. I walked, face down, expecting to shield myself from the arrows and bullets of the mountain men I would meet, but when I looked up, everyone was smiling and sitting around the living room. Rosa immediately grabbed the bag from my hand and took it to her kitchen island a few feet away. It was organized, unlike mine. I stood alone, feeling vulnerable and studied. I slowly took off my jacket. A woman came up to me.

"Here, let me take that from you. I am Layla, Rosa's daughter. It is so nice to finally meet you." She took my jacket, and hung it on a hook next to the door. She was stunning. A younger version of her mother, with the same mannerisms. As she approached me, the rest of Rosa's family had gotten up. After she hung up my jacket, I moved forward, introducing myself to one of her sons. His name was Skye. The youngest of the three. Handsome and athletic, with the same inviting smile and facial structure as Rosa. His handshake was firm and sincere.

There was a woman standing next to Rosa that was staring at me. She looked at me with the same eyes Heather did when I was just a boy. She walked over to me, and I felt her contempt.

"Hello Ben. I am Rosa's sister, Esperanza. I have to say, at first I thought you were nuts for coming here, but I am glad to meet you." To Esperanza, I represented a part of her past that she did not want to remember. She had helped Rosa get back on her feet after Sean emotionally bruised her. She was tough as nails, and she didn't take shit from anyone—especially a man.

I turned and faced the remaining three before me. Her two teenage grandsons, Scott and Collin, and her eldest son, Brian. The boys stood behind their father, one to each side, like bowling pins. Collin's face was softer, more relaxed. Scott's, focused and cautious. They each had a strong presence, but very different styles, which I immediately admired.

Brian stood in front of his sons like a warrior. I felt small standing directly in front of his six-foot-two, three-hundred pound frame, but although he was the most intimidating, he felt the most approachable, like my grandfather. We stared at each other for a moment. His blue eyes were familiar.

I walked up to him and held out my hand. He grabbed it, and pulled me forward. In that instant, I was no longer an only child.

Brother. Uncle.

I had practiced saying those words over and over to myself, but they never felt real until today.

CHAPTER FOURTEEN

◆

I WOKE UP IN DARKNESS. The sounds of the evening news coming from down the hall. At first I thought I was in my own bed, but then realized that I was at my Nana and Poppa's house, still in the back room. To my surprise, my mother was lying next to me on the daybed. Her arm wrapped around me. The shock of what I had witnessed must have caused me to pass out cold from fear. When I drifted off in my grandmothers arms, I thought I would never see my mother's face again.

A few hours after the violent explosion between Carmella and Sean, cops were able to talk Sean into releasing his hostage. He had repeatedly threatened to kill Carmella, and been so irrational and psychotic that the police officers immediately handcuffed and arrested him for her safety. He "disappeared" for a few days. I wondered where he was, and if he would be showing up at my grandparent's house.

For the past two years, I had learned to *silently* hate him, pretending to be the good son, accumulating way too much of his baggage. Ignoring the things that made me feel scared, but ultimately numb. But now I didn't just hate him. I feared him. Would he come and try to kill my Mom? Me? Watching him attack my mother caused me to wake up drenched from nightmares, and to be deathly afraid of the dark. A fear that he would be lurking somewhere—waiting to harm us. He was the enemy.

Deciding that I no longer wanted a father came easily, especially since Carmella had a restraining order placed against him. The lack of physical contact, and never seeing his face, allowed me to erase him from my mind. Carmella and I were a team now. She had saved me from my father's bitch, but was clueless that she also rescued me from the whore that had stolen my innocence.

Carmella's job was to protect me and surround me only with people who really loved me—*her* family.

Transitioning into my *new* home was easy, unlike many other children going through a divorce. My old home—*as I would call it*—was only four houses away, and I had visited my grandparents almost every day anyways. So there were no feelings of displacement. Josephine and Pellegrino provided us with a "safe home."

Life continued as *normal*. Every day I got up and dressed for school. Nana would make me an omelet, and I got on the bus with the same group of friends. The only difference was that my mother didn't walk me out until the bus had stopped in front of the house and beeped. Like a bodyguard, she looked both ways before she walked off the property. The bus driver would nod and let me on. Carmella had created a security system just for me. Everywhere I went, there were spies. Watching. Making sure that the devil didn't emerge.

Sean was living down the block, in the house that Carmella told him he could keep. Over the course of two weeks, she was escorted by police into the home while Sean was at work, to gather our things. In obvious fits of rage, Sean had destroyed most of Carmella's belongings. A pile of clothes in the backyard burned by kerosene. Leather purses, shoes, and important documents floating in a tub full of water. Beautiful jewelry given to her either in love or guilt was now a twisted pile of metal on the kitchen table. In their bedroom, she noticed her closet door was open. Inside, she found that all of her scorched clothes had been replaced with those belonging to Heather. In the back of the closet was a long brown garment bag. She stared at it. She flung all of the whore's clothes aside in one swift motion, and opened it up. Staring back at her was her wedding gown. She tore it off the hanger and left. Sean had replaced her again. Carmella had won the first round, but this time, she allowed Sean's mistress to win.

Today, she would have a fire of her very own.

◆

When Carmella decided that she was going to file for divorce, she also felt it necessary to cut a small hole in one of my main arteries, and drain the Quinn out of me. It took months of hard work, but over time, even though I had no reason to, I decided that I disliked all of them and I began to feel ashamed to have such a sordid last name.

"You are nothing like the Quinns." This is what I was told. I knew my last name was Quinn, but it confused me that I was nothing like *them.* Carmella would say *"I can't wait to take my maiden name back!"* This is what I overheard. What did that mean? If she wasn't going to be a Quinn anymore, could I too make up a new last name for myself? I didn't want to live my life with a name that my own mother would despise. So I did what any confused child would do, I began to write Benny Russo on everything.

"Benny, can you come up to my desk please?" It was my fourth grade teacher. This was something I heard every day in class, and I already knew what it was about.

"Benny, listen, your name is Benny Quinn—not Benny Russo. You have to start writing your real last name on your papers. We talked about this before. I'm going to have to call your mother." He would show me my paper, and Russo was always crossed out in "teacher-red," and rewritten as Quinn. Red seemed appropriate. Like fire from hell. I could feel my face burning up from the inside, but I never gave in to my anger. That would make me just like him. Exactly like a Quinn.

Politely I would explain, "I have a new last name now. I am not like the Quinns. My Mom told me." I continued to politely do as I wished, and after a while, the desk visits subsided. I was allowed to pretend again. As a matter of fact, everyone let me pretend. Slowly—as the next two months passed, I rid myself of any signs of Quinn, and I adopted all of Carmella's opinions about my father and his family. Carmella had officially drained every last drop, and I gladly stitched myself up.

Sean moved on *again.* And just like Rosa a decade earlier, he had someone to fill Carmella's place in his destructive world. Sean played his new role just as he had with Rosa. He treated Heather like gold. He manipulated her and made sure that she was by his side at all times. Like Rosa, she was young and naïve, and Heather ignored all the signs of his emotional malfunction. She thought that she had won the man of her dreams and was ready to take on the new role of the future Mrs. Quinn. She even wore the engagement ring to prove it.

Sean could not be alone. He always needed to have someone by his side. To love, control and manipulate. It made him feel important. Now that he had Heather full time, he knew he needed to make sure she would stay. He worked hard at keeping her happy, and that alone made it difficult for him to realize what he had lost. This was the reason why it became so easy for Carmella and me to move on. Well, easy for *me*, that is. When the dust began to settle, Carmella began to mourn. Mourn the loss of the life she worked so hard to create.

Although Carmella surmised that Sean had a mistress, like me, she had learned to play pretend too. She had already been in this situation once before, but without a home, child and "history." When she left Sean in Montana, she knew that he had found someone new, but she also got him back. She controlled him. This was a private and personal triumph that she dared not share with anyone. A victory. Wife versus mistress. Wife prevails!

Although Sean was violent, she realized that she was beginning to feel the same way. She found herself wondering how she could let another woman step into her life and destroy it. Destroy everything that her parents helped her organize, take away her husband, and then live in her home? Carmella felt jealous. Not for Sean, but for the things that Heather was using that belonged to her. Connie could see it written all over Carmella's face.

Connie lived in the apartment downstairs from us. When Josephine and Pellegrino purchased the two-family home, Connie was eager to move in, and be close to her parents and sister. Carmella had learned to rely on her sister for emotional support and guidance. Connie knew she was weak. She could see it in her face again, the feeling of despair. The wife who lost everything to another woman. But unlike a decade earlier, Connie was not going to sit back and allow her sister to fall into the pattern again. Josephine and Pellegrino were older and tired. They did not have a plan this time. Connie knew that she had to do whatever she could to keep Carmella from feeling that divorcing Sean was a "loss." It was not as if Carmella was holding up the white flag in defeat—Sean was mentally sick. And she did not want her sister to get hurt again. Connie needed to talk with her.

◆

Carmella woke up to the sound of the telephone ringing in the kitchen down the hall. She stumbled down the hall, bumping into Pellegrino along the way as he came out of their room.

"I've got it, Dad." Carmella motioned for him to go back to bed, but he was too concerned about the call.

"Madonna Mia! Who's calling at this hour? I hope no one died." For some reason, Italians always assumed someone died if the phone rang in the middle of the night. Carmella got to the phone first and picked up the receiver, as her father sat down in one of the dining room chairs.

"Hello?" She could hear someone on the other line, but no one answered.

"Hello? Is anyone there?" The caller hung up.

"Who was it, Carm?"

"No one. No one answered me. They hung up. Probably the wrong number." She suddenly felt nauseous. She had gotten used to dozens of hang-ups, right before she confronted Sean about his affair.

Pellegrino sighed. "Damn. I won't be able to fall back asleep. I'm going to watch the news." As Carmella began walking down the hall, the phone began to ring again. This time Pellegrino picked it up.

"Hello? Hello, who is this?" Carmella watched as her father sat down. He was listening to someone speak. She could hear the muffling sounds of someone talking from the receiver. She walked over to him, but he quickly put his hand up for her not to come closer.

"Dad! Who is it? Is everything ok?" He ignored her. Carmella sat down, knowing who it was. She could see the anger in her father's face, which was something he rarely showed. Then the muffling stopped.

"Listen, I don't want to get angry, Sean. Everyone is sleeping here, including your son. Now is not the time to be calling. As a matter of fact, you are not supposed to call here at all. Good night." Pellegrino hung up. He sat for a second before he spoke, as if he were trying to collect his thoughts before he alarmed Carmella too much.

"Listen Carm. It was Sean. He was drunk, and asking to talk with you. I told him…well, you heard what I said." As he spoke, the phone began to ring again. This time he picked it up and did not say a word. Sean was on the other end yelling. Carmella could hear his words.

"Put that BITCH on the phone!!! Let me talk to my WIFE, she's still my wife! She's not going to divorce me!"

Pellegrino hung up the phone and disconnected the wire from the phone jack. He couldn't look at her. He spoke softly. Jojo had not been feeling well lately, and he did not want her to wake up in the middle of the night to the stress of what he knew was coming.

"Carm, this is not good."

From beneath their feet, they could hear a phone ringing, followed by the muffled sounds of a conversation. The door at the bottom of the staircase opened, and Connie called up.

"Dad? Carm? You there?"

"Connie? You ok?"

Connie came up. She was still startled from being woken up so suddenly.

"What's going on, sis? Sean called me. He was telling me that he tried calling, and Daddy wouldn't let him talk to you. I think he had been drinking."

"Was he angry? He was shouting to Daddy. Calling me a bitch, and that I was his wife. I'm nervous, Connie. What did you tell him?"

"I told him that he needed to move on, and that he couldn't call here anymore. He hung up after that. Oh, lord! You don't think he will come here, right? You have that order of protection still?"

Connie paced around the kitchen. She could hear her phone ringing downstairs.

"I'm going to heat up some of this coffee. You want?" Pellegrino held out the half-filled Mr. Coffee glass decanter. Connie and

Carmella nodded. The three sat at the kitchen table, listening to the phone ring, then stop, ring, then stop. No one said a word—until it stopped and never rang again.

After about an hour, everyone went back to sleep. Connie slept upstairs on the sofa and Pellegrino on the armchair by the front entrance. And although the three of them were glad the harassment was over, they each knew it was just the beginning of what was to come.

Four houses down, Heather sat in the dark bedroom, listening to Sean make the phone calls. She was scared. Scared that his drunken temper and threatening tone would be refocused on her.

The next day, Heather left Sean. Just like Rosa, she may have been young and naïve when she met him, but when she saw a small glimpse of Sean's demons peeking through, she knew her future would be no different than Carmella's. And just like Carmella, she packed up and left while he was at work, to avoid any of Sean's manipulations, or fits of rage. He came home, and found all of her stuff gone.

Once again, Sean was alone. He now had time to think about what he lost—and he blamed Carmella for Heather leaving. He blamed Carmella for why he had nothing. Sean wasn't capable of seeing things in a rational way anymore. His anger had reached the point of no return, and he wanted revenge.

———————◆———————

It was the day. The day that Sean decided to begin his reign of destruction. He hadn't slept a wink the entire night before, which added more fuel to his fire. As he sat and mapped out his day, he kept thinking to himself *"If I can't have her back, then no one can have her."* He got up and began pacing back and forth, thinking about how he could *make* her come home. This was always Sean's problem, even as a teenager. He thought he could threaten people back into his life, proving his love for them through anger and frustration. He couldn't stop himself from acting out. Everyone was helping Carmella and *his* son all the time, but no one was reaching out to him. It made him feel disposable. Not only did he believe that Carmella abandoned him, but she also took his fatherhood and tossed it in the trash—disposed of it, like a dirty paper plate.

My father believed I was his property, too. Even though he knew that his actions fucked me up, he did not like losing the things he owned.

Calling Connie or the Russos was obviously not going to work, so he decided to go to Carmella's job. It was a crowded place, and he knew that he could easily walk in without being noticed, but he also knew that his flashy, mid-life, Firebird was not the right car to use. It was easily spotted. If he needed to flee, he would be quickly found. He also wanted to try and talk with her calmly. This was something that Sean was able to do—change his emotional state in a heartbeat. He had become a Jekyll and Hyde. That scared everyone the most, including me. I had been trained by those around me to not trust him if he were ever to approach me. My mother, my grandparents, my aunt Connie, my teachers, you name it.

"Benny, listen to me carefully. If somehow, someday, Daddy comes up to you, and he is being nice to you, you need to scream and run. Do you understand? He is very angry with mommy, and I don't want him to hurt you, or take you."

I always nodded.

"Benny, if you see your Daddy in the bus loop, you have to tell us okay?"

I politely answered, "Ok."

"Benny, if you see your Dad outside the window, you have to come and tell Poppa, Me or DeDe Connie. Don't open the door either. Okay baby?"

I would always hug my Nana, and she would kiss me on the forehead. That's how we communicated. Although each person was only trying to protect me, it made me more nervous and paranoid. I had learned to only expect the worst from Sean.

Sean borrowed his youngest brother's car to pay Carmella a visit. It was a run down, unnoticeable Honda. Something that would blend well in the massive parking lot outside her workplace. On his way there, he found his happy place and put on a smile. He practiced his words as he looked in the rearview mirror: *Carmella,*

I am so sorry. I love you Carm! I want you and Benny back. I will do whatever you want me to. Please Carmella, give me a chance to talk to you. We can make this work. We did it once, we can do it again. Sean was happy with the words he chose, not because they sounded really good, but because it was what he truly felt. When Sean was calm, he did have genuine feelings. He was sensitive. But those moments were few and far between.

As he pulled into the parking lot, he immediately saw Carmella. The supermarket was a sea of windows, allowing anyone to see everyone. He parked close enough to watch her, but not close enough for people to see him. Sean sat and sipped at his large 7-11 coffee. He had a pair of aviators on. He sat back, observed, and waited for the right moment to enter the store. He knew that everyone in there was on guard. Carmella was a good worker, and since she left Sean, she had taken on a new role as front-end manager. She needed the money, and the extra hours kept her mind off of her current situation.

Sean saw her take off her smock. His eyes followed her as she walked over to the punch clock and lifted up her timecard. He sat up, put down his lukewarm coffee, and knew the time had come. She was going on her break, and he knew that the break room was upstairs, away from all the action. There were no cameras either. With the confidence of a star football player, and the emotional state of a psychiatric ward inmate, he entered the store and made his way down the produce aisle.

Carmella was tired. She slowly made her way up the two flights of stairs to the cold, isolated area that the employees called their break room. She placed her lunch bag and pocketbook on one of the four randomly placed, large, brown cafeteria-style tables. The scattered coffee cups and sandwich wrappers on the table next to her was evidence that other employees used the area that day. Not many people did. Most of the employees escaped the workplace to the pizza parlor or Chinese restaurant to eat their lunch. But it was raining, so some of the employees had already used the break room. Carmella grabbed her cosmetics bag from her purse and made her way to the ladies' room.

Carmella stared at herself long and hard. She looked at herself with the same eyes from a decade earlier, again not recognizing who stared back at her. She wiped away the stress from her eyes, and began to correct her smudged eyeliner and mascara, which did absolutely nothing to mask her sunken eyes.

She brushed her hair and grabbed her make-up off the sink counter. She didn't know what to do when it came to Sean. Should she walk away and start a new life as a single mother, struggling to make ends meet, or the twice-betrayed wife who fights to save her marriage and the vows she took? As she pondered her personal debate, she opened the door and looked up. There was Sean, sitting down at the cafeteria table across from her lunch bag. Frozen with fear, she stood there, waiting for him to come at her. It was the first time she was in his presence since that dreadful day.

"Hi Carm."

Sean spoke first. He was calm, just as he had practiced. He was fearful of her reaction, and concerned by the look on her face. He stood up, and it caused Carmella to take a sudden step back, now holding on to the bathroom door. She knew it dead bolted from the inside, and it would be the only way she could get away from him. The stairway was across the room, too far away for her escape.

"Carmella, listen, I am not going to hurt you. I promise. You can stay over there. I just have some things I need to say."

Carmella opened the door and stood halfway in. Her voice trembled as she opened her mouth to speak.

"Sean. You shouldn't be here. You need to go."

"Please Carm, please just hear me out." His voice was vulnerable and broken. He wanted to remain calm, and truly realize how much he missed her as she stood before him. Carmella saw the pain in his eyes, but she kept thinking of what Connie had told her just the night before, "*Sean's a manipulator,*" and it seemed to be exactly what he was trying to do.

"Ok Sean. I will listen, but when you are done, and I ask you to leave, you must leave." Although Sean was happy to be allowed to speak, the fact that he was *asking her permission* and being *allowed to,* made him feel inferior. Now he was "working" at being calm.

"I want you back, Carm! I miss you. I made a mistake, and I am sorry. Whatever you want me to do, I'll do. We can go to therapy, like you wanted to months ago." He waited, expecting her to get soft with emotion, like she did many years earlier when she saw him for the first time, after leaving Montana.

"Sean, you hurt me. You threatened to kill me, Sean. Our son fears you. I am scared of you too. I don't think…" Sean took a step forward, causing her to stop, extend her arm and hold out her pointer finger at him, "Go! Go, Sean. You need to get out of here."

Sean turned around and began to pace. It was not going the way he had hoped, and even though his heart was telling him to stay calm, his brain was demanding a reaction. Carmella saw his demeanor changing and remained calm. She knew she could scream and lock herself in.

"Sean, I don't want you to cause a scene here, and I don't want you to get arrested again. Just turn around and leave. I won't tell anyone, I promise." Carmella meant it. She was tired, and not emotionally capable of arguing.

Sean turned, and began walking towards the stairwell, but then he turned back.

"Do you think we can get back together? Can't we try and make it work again? I love you, Carmella. Do you still love me?"

She looked right at him and didn't break her stare. Straight into his crystal blue, bloodshot eyes. Now he was weak and at her mercy, just like she was when his hands were wrapped around her throat. And as she backed herself into the bathroom and put her fingers around the deadbolt, she answered in her *Quinn* voice:

"No."

It was a lie.

I made myself the diversion.

It allowed me to avoid topics that made me feel uncomfortable or fragile. Doing this too often eventually led me to feel uncomfortable if I wasn't the center of attention.

CHAPTER FIFTEEN

◆

Rosa's house smelled spicy and alive, fitting for a family of Spanish decent. She was full-blooded, just like Carmella. One woman of full Italian descent; one a full Spaniard. I found this quite amusing because it was evident that Sean had a "*type*" in his younger years. Shorter women with dark hair, dark eyes and beautiful smiles.

My brother, Brian, had decided to make his famous chili recipe, which explained the amazing smell that immediately made my stomach growl; chili was a favorite. Rosa's sister, Esperanza, brought a large aluminum tray of her homemade cornbread. Brian had taken the initiative to do something welcoming for me, something that he was known for here in Montana, long before he ever knew, or heard of me.

For about an hour, we sat around Rosa's living room engaging in small talk. There were several small conversations taking place— of which I knew I was the topic of choice. We were talking away that elephant in the room, which was totally fine, because it gave me time to adjust to my new surroundings. We eventually talked ourselves closer and closer to that "*comfort zone.*" That moment when everyone silently exhales and relaxes.

"So Ben, how were your flights? You had a layover in Denver, right?" Esperanza's voice had acquired a more genuine and kinder tone.

"They were long, but overall, fine. Nothing to write home about. My layover in Denver wasn't really long enough for me to leave the airport and walk around, but I *was* able to visit some of the shops and do a bit of reading. The airport is designed like a shopping mall."

Something I said caught my nephew Scott's attention. It was the first time he looked up. During small talk, he sat directly across from me, texting someone on his cell phone. For all I knew, it could have been his entire posse in one huge group text. I couldn't even begin to imagine what he was saying, but I was damned sure by his shit-eating grin and random giggles, that it was totally about me. How could I think anything different?

"Dude! My gay uncle that I never knew I had is visiting from New York. He is sitting right across from me! It's crazy shit, man!"

"NO WAY!!! Is he like, really gay? Ya know, like the ones on those TV shows?"

"Nah. Different. He has kids and a partner and shit. He seems cool, but it is so weird."

"Wow. I wish I had a gay uncle from New York." (I am sure this wasn't part of his original texting, but who wouldn't want an awesome gay uncle from New York?)

Please! I'd be blowing up so many cell phones with this talk-show craziness, I would end up developing carpal tunnel. But the fact that I had been *reading* something is what tore him away from his wireless conversation.

"I love to read. I practically live at Barnes and Noble. What are you reading right now? I just got done reading *The Four Agreements*, by *Don Miguel Ruiz*. A totally great read!"

I sat staring at Scott in both total amazement and personal embarrassment. He was intellectual, and well versed. As he continued to briefly describe what the book was about, I tried to figure out whether or not to divulge the quality of literature I read. My nephew, who moments earlier, was blowing up all of his friends' cell phones with gay uncle gossip, was also reading Toltec books on finding your own personal freedom and leading a better life. Shamefully, on my way to Montana, I had shallowly engrossed myself in magazine articles, dictating what to wear during your ski trips this winter, and the Top 10 ways to reduce facial razor burn. *What the fuck is wrong here?*

I was mortified, because I knew I had to answer honestly. It was a promise I made to myself when I stood in front of the mirror back at my no-tell motel. Be real. *Don't represent yourself as someone that others wish you to be for them.* And I wasn't going to lie to the nephew that I had just met and was already so proud of and impressed by.

"Unfortunately, I am embarrassed to say that most of the literature I read is printed either weekly or monthly."

"Magazines?" He didn't seem surprised, which at first made me feel less embarrassed, but then I also wondered if his aloofness about my reading fluff made him perceive me as shallow and self-centered.

"Yes. I often find myself too tired to even consider a book after working all day, and hanging out with my girls before bedtime." He appreciated my truthfulness. I could see it in his eyes.

"Well then, you need to read this one. I already read it, like, four times. If you want it, I'll give it to you tomorrow when I pick you up for coffee." He got up and walked into the kitchen to get himself a drink. I glanced over at Brian with a puzzled look.

"Did I miss something? Are we going out for coffee tomorrow?" I thought at some point everyone had agreed on plans for the following day, while I was in the bathroom or something.

"Yup. Scott is a coffee hound! Drinks it all day, man. That's why he is so high energy. Probably the reason why he can be so sensitive too; too much caffeine will fuck you up."

"I drink way too much coffee. It's an addiction. Doesn't he have school tomorrow?" I looked over at Collin, the quieter of my two nephews, "Don't you guys have school tomorrow?"

"Yeah, but Scott's not going. I probably won't either. If our grades are up, we are allowed take some days off here and there. As long as they don't interfere with our school work."

"Are you going with us to get coffee?" I directed my question to both my brother and Collin. Collin shook his head no.

"I'm sleeping in tomorrow, bro. And I need to go to work for an hour or so to check on a few things. It's all you."

Brian and Collin got up and walked into the kitchen, where the rest of the family had begun to gather. Rosa was beginning to ladle out huge bowls of chili. She had all kinds of different toppings on the table: chopped onions, shredded cheddar cheese, sour cream, you name it. The way everyone gathered reminded me of the Sunday pasta dinners at my Nana's house when I was young.

As I rose, Scott walked back into the living room area and headed towards the bathroom down the hall.

"Hey Scott, what time are we going for coffee tomorrow? I'm staying at a motel a few miles from here."

"I usually get up at seven, even if I don't want to. Can't sleep late. I'll pick you up by seven-thirty or eight."

After Scott told me when he would pick me up, he didn't even give me a chance to respond. He had a confidence about him that I recognized. As I sat down and enjoyed two bowls of the most amazing chili and cornbread I had ever eaten, I perseverated over the coffee date that I had the following morning with my uptight, caffeine-driven, confident, yet vulnerable, early-rising nephew. I basically had a coffee date with myself.

◆

Dinner talk was airy and light. We all ate way too much and continued polite conversations. We talked about jobs, shows, or movies we had recently watched, the weather and other non-political, non-religious topics. The one topic that never came up was Sean. I was glad. From the moment I had stepped into Rosa's house, knowing that I was going to see my brother and nephews face to face for the very first time, I dreaded that happening. Not because I was afraid to talk about him, but because I knew it would ignite different emotions for each person in the room—especially me.

It was too soon for me to lay down belly up. And from the way that everyone seemed to be carefully avoiding the topic, I was glad that no one wanted to visit *it* tonight. Although, I did have a suspicious feeling that Scott had a lot of questions. During dinner, I saw the wheels turning, the questions piling up. He was sorting through them, neatly stacking them in chronological order. I emotionally readied myself for several back to back cups the next day.

"Let's open up one of these!"

I was sitting on a long bench next to Rosa and Brian's younger brother. We all turned to find Layla holding up one of the bottles of red wine. I was glad to see someone decided to partake in my pathetic peace offering.

Immediately after dinner, Esperanza had left because she needed to get up early for work, so Rosa poured a glass of wine for me, Layla and herself. Brian got up and grabbed a beer from the fridge. "I can't drink wine. It gets me all crazy and shit!"

Rosa chimed in. "You can say *that* again. Brian is not a good drunk. He has a temper just like your dad."

Everyone got quiet and took a sip of whatever they were drinking. The ice had been broken, and nobody was sure if it was safe to walk on the pond. After taking a huge gulp of wine, I placed my glass down on the kitchen island. A mess had slowly accumulated, and I pushed a few things aside to make sure it wasn't too close to the edge. Scott got up from the table, walked over and picked it up. He brought it up to his lips.

"Scott, what do you think you're doing?"

"Relax, Nan. I just want a taste."

"You have to drive home! Put the glass down."

"I'm not drinking it, I am tasting it. God. Besides, we live around the corner, Nan. If I get drunk off of my *sip*, I'll walk home." He winked at her, making light of the situation.

Rosa smiled, "Smart ass."

"Ya know it!"

Scott put the glass down after his sip and walked into the living room. He sat on the sofa and put on the television. "Come on guys, let's see what's on."

He did it. Scott did exactly what he wanted to do; he diverted everyone's attention away from the awkwardness of Rosa's comment and redirected it onto himself. I admired it, because his ability to refocus an entire room was familiar to me.

For decades, I had diverted people from asking questions about my parents or life, by making myself the center of attention. I made myself the diversion. It allowed me to avoid topics that made me feel uncomfortable or fragile. Doing this too often eventually led me to feel uncomfortable if I *wasn't* the center of attention. Watching Scott's performance made me wonder if that was the case for him, too. It also made me realize how much of an egomaniac I had become—not because I wanted to be, but because I had to be.

After a while, Brian and Collin left. Brian also had to work the following day, and Collin wanted to go home and play video games for an hour or so before bed. That was his thing. His escape. Video games. That was all I really knew about him so far. He was still observing, deciding if I was worth his time. I didn't blame him in the least.

Scott had his own car, so he decided to stay a bit longer. Not because he wanted more conversation, but rather alone time with Rosa. She was his rock. Their bond was strong. They had the same closeness that I had with Josephine. I loved seeing that level of understanding before me, and I was curious to know how it evolved.

It was unspoken, but assumed at this point that I would be crashing in the spare bedroom. It was almost midnight; I had several glasses under my belt, and Rosa was exhausted from working a half day. She was drinking a glass herself.

Scott rose. "Ok Nana, I'm going to go home and hit the hay." He walked over to her, kissed her cheek, and hugged her hard. This hug was Scott's message, telling her it was all okay. I used to get and give hugs like that too. As I watched, I realized I desperately needed one of my own.

"Ok Unc. I'll see you bright and early." He came over and gave me one of those macho sporty half-hugs, which somehow gave me the exact same message.

"Sounds good. Hey Scott, can I borrow that book from you?"

"Sure thing. I'll bring it in the morning."

———————————◆———————————

I was never one for "quality" reading. A novel required too much concentration. It just didn't seem to fit my personality. Most of the time, my mind was too erratic, concerned about the things I needed to do tomorrow, next week, or even something I wanted to accomplish a year from now.

Over the years, I watched those around me, especially Max, read novel after novel, absorbing its contents like a sponge. Each character's journey added excitement and new perspective. It was like brain candy—an addiction. I found this very intriguing. How people could disappear inside a book. Often, when I would look over at Max, he had that look. Mesmerized. Focused. I could see his wheels turning, just as I had seen Scott's wheels turning during dinner. I often found myself jealous of those who could sit down and finish a really good book in two or three days. The way they would talk about it, share it, break down its components—like a really fantastic vacation.

This wasn't for me. For the few—VERY FEW—books that actually sucked me in, I had no desire to talk about them when I was finished. Book talks to me were like boring slide shows, or photo montages your friends and family *invited* you to watch after their Disney Cruises, or trips to Hershey Park. I'd rather repeatedly poke myself in the eye with the bendy straw from Ava's happy meal.

This is the reason why I like memoirs best. They are personal. You learn things about yourself from others who took similar journeys, and you'll often find that what you experienced, although traumatic, isn't half as damaging compared to others. Sad thing was, I found most of the memoirs I tried to read utterly boring. If I couldn't relate to the victims then I felt like it was a waste of my time and money. The memoirs I purchased were often like my therapists—easily shelved.

◆

To my surprise, both Rosa and I were early risers. Down the hall, I could hear her making coffee. It reminded me of home. Lying in bed, I would listen to Max wake up and shuffle his way down the hall, disappearing into the darkness. The gentle bubbling sound of water as it filled the carafe and splashed into the coffee-maker. I would stretch and smile, knowing that soon enough, he would bring a mug to me as I got out of bed.

I glanced over at the clock on the dresser and could barely make out 6:08. It was earlier than I wanted, but once awake, it was hard to fall back asleep. Besides, I wanted to have some alone time with Rosa again. I blinked and rubbed my eyes, trying to focus them, realizing that I had slept with my contacts in again. Unless I got up to rinse them, they would adhere to my eyes like glue, and Scott was going to be picking me up soon. I picked up my clothes from beside the bed, got dressed, and followed the bold Columbian smell.

"Up already?" She seemed genuinely shocked. She was already showered and dressed, sitting at the kitchen table.

"I was planning on waking you up at seven so you'd be ready for your *day* with Scott." A morning of coffee had transformed into a day, and she began to laugh after she stressed the word. She got up, poured a cup of coffee and handed it to me.

"Here you go. I assume you like it black?"

"Yup. How'd you guess?"

"Just a gut feeling. I have a toothbrush and towel laid out for you in the bathroom next to your room." She saw me rubbing at my eyes. "I also have some contact solution in the cabinet above the toilet—feel free to help yourself."

Rosa was a natural caretaker. Kind, motherly and unconditionally generous. My soul felt calm in her presence. Mind at ease. I joined her at the kitchen table, my hands warm around the mug.

"Thank you for letting me crash here last night. I enjoyed myself very much, although the wine is definitely fighting back this morning."

"My pleasure." Rosa sat directly across from me. I could see that she had questions. I recognized her body language all too well, and I wanted to answer all of them for her without sending myself into a tailspin. I wanted her to feel at ease.

"So, need I be afraid of my day? Scott seems like an intense young man."

"Ah, yes, my Scottie. He is such a great boy. Smart, sensitive, and yes, intense was a good choice. You are going to have a great day with him. He has been looking forward to meeting you. His life hasn't been easy at times. Scott carries the world on his shoulders, like you do. I can tell. Scott has questions. We all do."

She was right. I did carry the world on my shoulders. A world of anger, sorrow and regret. For years, it accumulated and grew heavier and I was often amazed by how much I could carry without stumbling to my knees. Only someone experienced can recognize that burden. Every person has had to hide battle wounds from others, suffering behind closed doors, licking their wounds while smiling to the world. Most heal without being noticed. Some do not. Those people, like Carmella, Rosa and me, have noticeable scars that most people would rather ignore than inquire.

Sean's wrath connected us. I wanted her to know what my life had been like. What it still was like. What she avoided by cutting him loose, like the wild animal he was. And although most would think this a betrayal to Sean and Carmella, I knew it was the closure that Rosa needed. I didn't want her to feel like a pile of clean laundry mixed among the dirty. She worked hard all her life to be right side out, and Brian was the reminder of Sean that occasionally turned her inside out. I wanted to erase that.

I sat across from her. She was ready to ask. I was ready to talk.

"What was it like? Your childhood with your father? I am sorry for being so upfront, but I often wondered what type of father he would've been to Brian. He reminds me so much of Sean. It was so tough at first with Brian. He was such a great child, but he often wondered why he didn't have a dad around. Was Sean a good dad when you were little?"

The question was direct. My answer was too.

"No. He was too young and irrational to be a father."

Rosa sighed, and looked out the window next to the table. It was beginning to snow outside. I watched the flakes fall steadily and accumulate on the trees in her neighbor's yard as we spoke. They gently floated and swirled in the brisk cold air, soothing us as we shared our painful memories.

Rosa openly shared the hardship and struggles of being so young, and raising a blonde, blue-eyed son in a town of mainly dark skinned people. Although she had a family that stood by her side, she still felt abandoned. Rosa expressed forty years of anger and frustration for Sean never trying to contact her when she was pregnant, or reaching out as Brian grew up into a man—to acknowledge him.

"Brian often wondered why your father never communicated with us, and it made him act out at times. He has a short fuse. Always did. When he played football and wrestled, it was turned to his advantage, but it did and still does amaze me just how strong a genetic link can be." I nodded in agreement, not because I knew that Brian had my father's temper; I had never witnessed this, but because the genetic link Rosa was referring to was true for me as well.

"I have a temper too, but I learned to control it at a very young age. I had to. My childhood was all about protecting and defending myself against his words and backhand. Instead of acting out physically, I learned to hate. I guess that was my defense mechanism. Harboring anger. It must be one of the things we *both* inherited from him."

Talking with Rosa was exhilarating. Each word that came out of my mouth made me feel lighter. More physically fit. Mind less cluttered. Almost like confessing to a priest. *Now* I knew what the buzz was about—the reason why the holy rollers ran to confession boxes—it made them feel more human. They were able to explain to someone the awful ways they felt about people they were supposed to love. Rosa was the first therapist I trusted to say the one thing that I had wanted to say to someone for the longest time, "*I love them. But I really have a hard time liking them.*" And the best thing was, she didn't tell me to forgive and forget.

Rosa's phone jingled and mine vibrated. It was Scott alerting us that he was on his way.

"Ben, you better jump in the shower. Scott will be here soon."

I took a quick shower, and threw my clothes back on again. My contacts were still a bit fuzzy, even though I used the saline solution in Rosa's cabinet. I could hear talking from the kitchen.

"Hey Unc. You ready to roll?" He was sitting next to Rosa on the couch; the lids of her eyes were pink, so I could see that she had cried a bit while I showered. My eyes must have looked the same.

"Yeah, ready. Listen, can you make a quick stop back at my motel? I need to change out these contacts, especially if we are going to be gone for a while."

"Sure." He got up and gave Rosa a hug. She got up and walked over to me. We looked at each other and smiled. She walked up to me, and we embraced. We held it for a few seconds.

"Thank you." I whispered in her ear. She moved her head back and looked at me. At first, she seemed puzzled, but then she understood me. She placed her hands on the sides of my face. Her palms were warm. Therapeutic.

"You're welcome."

I felt forgiven.

CHAPTER SIXTEEN

◆

"CARMELLA QUINN, please report to customer service. Carmella Quinn, please report to customer service *immediately*."

The announcement echoed and crackled through the entire store, including her hideout. Although she had only been in the bathroom for about fifteen minutes after hearing Sean's footsteps descend the stairwell, it felt like an hour. She was scared that he was still lurking around, waiting for her to come out; as she slowly opened the door, her colleague Virginia came running in.

"Carmella! God, there you are! Everyone was freaking out looking for you. Get your ass downstairs!" She grabbed Carmella's hand, practically pulling her from the bathroom doorway. Carmella dropped her make-up bag, and it spilled out on the floor. As she bent down to pick up her things, she realized she was missing something.

"Wait, I have to get my...where's my pocketbook? Oh God! He has my pocketbook! Is he down there? I don't want to go down there if he is still here!"

"No, he left, but he was throwing shit, and yelling as he left the store. Carmella, he drove off with your car. We called the police—come on, you need to hurry up."

For about an hour, Carmella sat on the bench outside with two police officers, answering questions about Sean and filling out a report for her stolen car. Curious shoppers and concerned colleagues glanced through the large windows. She felt like she was on display. Her life had become an open book for all to read.

Ten years earlier, it was her keys and shoes—now her means of transportation. Sean always found a way to make her vulnerable—having to rely on others. The officers drove her home, and Carmella explained to her parents and sister what had transpired.

No one was surprised. It was just another control tactic added to Sean's twisted list of deceit. One more nail in his coffin—proving to Connie, Josephine and Pellegrino that Carmella needed to make this divorce happen as quickly as possible—not just for her, but for me as well.

The next morning, Carmella used Connie's car to go to work. Carmella didn't want to put her sister in another awkward situation, but she couldn't miss another day of work; besides Connie had the day off and didn't need to use it. Carmella had used up almost all of her sick, family and personal days, and she would be docked pay if it continued. Money was tight, and Sean was not helping her, although the courts ordered him to pay her a certain amount each week. She had already begun receiving state assistance, so rather than communicate with Sean; she relied on that to help us get by.

When Carmella showed up for work the following day, she was asked to man the express line. It was closest to the exit of the store and the customer service department, so the manager strategically placed her there in case Sean was to show up again. Two police officers were sent to scour the parking lot throughout the day, and Carmella was allowed to use one of the handicapped parking spots so that she could be quickly escorted in and out of the store.

Everyone felt more at ease, except Carmella. She knew what Sean was capable of, and not many knew that he had threatened her life. For the first half of the day, Carmella worked with one eye on the register, and the other on the entrance to the store. She felt guilty knowing that she was putting her colleagues in jeopardy.

Although our lives were less than *normal*, Carmella desired some level of privacy at her workplace and my school. She had grown tired of explaining her situation to everyone, and she could tell when people knew her personal business by the way they looked at her and gazed at me. For this reason, she took each knockout as it came, not allowing anyone to know she was expecting another round. And then, just as Carmella had expected, Sean arrived.

In an instant, Sean had transformed the front end of a peaceful supermarket to a mess of frantic customers, fearful of leaving the store. Sean parked Carmella's car parallel to the bay windows so everyone could see him. He was wearing sunglasses, like a movie star on the big screen. He was getting the attention he wanted. The once shiny brown Buick Century that Sean had given her years earlier now looked the way she felt. Banged up, scratched and abused. He parked and revved the engine. Sean cranked down the window, and began his tirade.

"CARMELLA! You think you can leave me? HUH? DO YOU HEAR ME, BITCH!! I will make your life miserable—DO YOU HEAR ME, CARMELLA?"

Then he sped off. Everybody watched as Sean smashed into two shopping carts, flinging them into parked cars, as he exited the parking lot. Carmella hadn't moved an inch. People were running around her finding a safe place, not knowing who the lunatic was, or what he was capable of. Just as she was about to walk out from behind her workstation, she saw her car entering the park lot again. Sean drove head on into the driver's side of Connie's car replacing the sound of customers screaming with glass shattering, metal twisting and bending, then backed up and drove off. As quickly as it began, it was over.

The next five months of my young life were riddled with horrific episodes such as this. Sean randomly trying to snatch me from the bus loop, listening to him threaten teachers and administrators while I was being whisked away to a safe place. Waking up in the middle of the night to him screaming obscenities about my mother, grandparents and Aunt Connie from the street below. Strangers from CPS showing up at school or my grandparent's house, questioning and terrifying me, like I had done something wrong. Graffiti. Slashed tires. Broken windows. Phone calls at all hours. Courtrooms. Therapists. Deepening my fear; creating paranoia. Sleepless nights and daydreams about being someone else's child. I desired another family and grew jealous of the normalcy those around me seemed to have.

Those tumultuous months extinguished the last flicker of childhood within me. My father was insane. My mother was broken, and emotionally detached. I felt alone. I wished they would *both* go away, and leave me with my Nana, Poppa and Aunt Connie.

They could protect me. Unfortunately, I was not that lucky. What was to come would shock everyone, and disable my ability to trust the ones I loved the most.

———————◆———————

Although I was only ten years old, I had matured early in order to hold my own. Because of this, I had the ability to recognize when something was "off" about someone. When you see them evolving from one emotional state to another. For about two weeks, I noticed that *everyone* was off. Especially my Aunt Connie—or DeDe, pronounced Dee-Dee, as I would call her. My Aunt Connie *acted* happy, but I could tell she wasn't. Something was different, and she often became "unavailable" when Carmella needed her for something, like babysitting me. Connie would tell her she was coming home late, or staying with a friend. The tension between them became palpable.

I adored my "DeDe." The only fond memories I can muster up from those traumatic early years of my young life are with her. She was my guardian angel. The one who bandaged the emotional wounds others overlooked. She figured out how to help me express them; not repress them. DeDe could see that that her godson was on a one-way road to self-destruction, and so, she did everything in her power to battle each surmounting negative experience with a positive one. Each day after school, I looked forward to going downstairs when she got home from work and spending some time with her. It didn't matter if I had anything constructive to do. Sitting in her presence was perfect enough.

Connie was beautiful. She had escaped the prison of her childhood home, as she had silently promised herself when she watched her sister suffer years earlier. She found herself. Her entire childhood was a step-by-step training video on "*How to Make Your Youngest Daughter into Your Caretaker.*" She knew where her life was headed and decided to take control before it was too late. For this very reason, she became my role model. She was outspoken, confident and independent. She also had a fierce sense of style, which to this day, is the reason why I take such pride in the way I look.

As a child, I would sit for an entire hour watching her apply make-up. Pencils, brushes, lipsticks, you name it. I found it calming. She was very feminine, and watching her made me think of what my own mother used to look like before Sean stripped the beauty from her face. Carmella still had it, but she didn't take the time to make herself look as good as she could. Her beauty was hidden under all her layers.

My Aunt would talk to me about my day as she got ready for her evening out, and even though I am sure she could have used some down time after having worked all day—she made sure to include me. Overnight trips to Astoria, Queens to visit my cousins, Rockefeller Center to see the tree followed by the Christmas Spectacular. Jumbo sized, warm, salty pretzels and hot chocolate. The smell of her Jovan Musk would linger on my winter coat and scarf for weeks, and it made me feel like she was with me at all times. She made me feel important. Her soul reached out to mine when I was at my lowest. The change I could *feel* from her alarmed me; it was almost as if she were pulling away.

Josephine and Pellegrino were different too. Whenever I came home from school, I would find them talking with each other over coffee at the dining room table, but their usual loud conversations and bickering sessions about nothing important had turned into whisperings, which made it difficult for me to hear. They had secrets I was not allowed to know. I was only ten feet away from them watching cartoons, and when I would glance over, they were often staring at me—trying to smile, but finding it difficult to. Only when I take the time to think about my past do I realize why everyone was acting strange. They were all *worried* for me. They all felt useless. Their hands were tied.

Carmella had been going out every night after I fell asleep. And she looked different. Transformed, like Connie. Instead of a quick hairbrush and some eye shadow to look *decent,* the bathroom was cluttered with all sorts of things a woman uses to make herself desirable. A curling iron, hairclips, and her large, clear makeup bag that I recalled her using when we lived down the block. And perfume—to go with the new figure that I had no idea she had again. Fitted jeans, high heel clogs, and brightly colored silky shirts replaced the humdrum housedresses that made her look twenty years older. She would come in and give me a kiss on my forehead as I lay there with my eyes closed. I would hear her down the hall, keys jingling in her hand. Although her perfume lingered, it was not like my Aunt's.

I heard the door close. She was gone. Like every night for the past two weeks, I got up and walked out into the dimly lit living room. My Poppa was sitting in his leather recliner. My Nana sat in the kitchen, waiting for me to come in. They knew that I was scared and suspicious, but they never spoke a word. My Nana would give me a kiss, and I would fall asleep in my Poppa's lap. Every morning I would wake up sleeping between the two of them—nestled with my guards.

Good memories. To this day I still find myself crying for them.

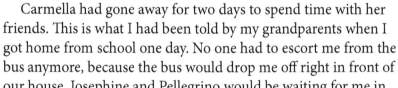

Carmella had gone away for two days to spend time with her friends. This is what I had been told by my grandparents when I got home from school one day. No one had to escort me from the bus anymore, because the bus would drop me off right in front of our house. Josephine and Pellegrino would be waiting for me in the driveway—sitting in their favorite lawn chairs, whenever the weather permitted.

Carmella did not tell me herself, she just went and left me for her family to take care of. Probably because she didn't want to lie to my face. Even though she had been in and out quite frequently, none of her *friends* ever came over. I wasn't really sure what friends my grandparents were referring to, but like any other ten year old child, I believed it. Maybe that was why she looked so beautiful again. *Believing* my mother was still an option, and up to this point, she had not given me any reason to think otherwise.

As usual, my Nana, Poppa and Aunt kept me busy. They took me to the diner for a cheeseburger and fries, and Carvel for a chocolate flying saucer. DeDe Connie took me to the movies, and she let me listen to her new *Olivia Newton-John* album. Connie loved music and went out dancing with her friends all the time. I actually *knew* all of my Aunt Connie's friends. She often took me with her when she visited them. Being kept so busy made me easily forget that my mother was gone.

◆

"Benny! Come here for a minute!" Josephine summoned me from down the hall. After coming home from one of our outings, I went to my room to play with the two large boxes of Lego's Santa had brought me. Once again, I began building another house. This one had windows with little red shutters that could open and close, large green pine trees that you could snap onto the flat green *lawn*. It was a single level, blue and white house with a red roof and a chimney. For hours, I would meticulously construct them, destroy them and start all over again. Each house was different—as if I were trying to design my own perfect home for my pretend happy family. But none of them ever satisfied me--like I knew the perfect family didn't exist. I stepped on my happy home, annihilating it into a hundred pieces, then casually walked down the hall, following the glorious smell that filled the entire top level of the house.

Nana was standing at the stove cooking. Josephine always cooked more than she needed to, and everyone who knew her loved everything she made. Today she was frying meatballs in a large pan, next to a colossal saucepot that seemed to scream *"It's Sunday! It's Sunday!"* When I walked in, she scooped one of the meatballs out onto a paper plate and put some sauce on top of it. I knew it was for me. She always did that just for me.

"Come baby, come sit down." She placed the meatball on the table and sat down next to me.

"Who's coming to dinner today, Nan?"

"No one is coming today. I am going to freeze this for another day." She was back at the stove ladling. Her massive arm swaying to and fro with the motions. With sixty plus years of stirring, ladling and pan scrubbing, you'd expect her biceps to be firm and toned. She filled up three large recycled ricotta cheese containers, wrapped them in old supermarket plastic bags and summoned Pellegrino to put them in the enormous industrial sized freezer in the garage.

"What are we going to do for dinner then? When is DeDe coming home?" She had finished ladling and was washing the pot in the sink. I finished my meatball and threw out my paper plate. I walked over to her and looked up.

"Aunt Connie is going out with her friend Rita."

"Oh. What are we doing? Can we go and get pizza?" I continued to look up at her, but she wouldn't look down—instead she looked away. I tugged on the side of her sauce smock, trying to get her full attention.

"Nan? Can we get pizza?" She turned to me, crying.

"Poppa and I are going to our friends' house today."

"Are we bringing pastries?" I loved going to the pastry store with them. They would buy me rainbow cookies.

"You're not coming with us Benny."

"Why can't I come?"

"Hey! Let's go outside for a bit." Josephine placed the clean pot in the dish rack, took off her smock and walked into the living room to get her sweater. "Go get your jacket."

I ran down the hall, stepping over my demolished home and opened the closet to get my jacket.

Empty.

A worn out, red jacket with baseball patches remained.

I knew why we were going outside.

Empty.

A worn out child about to be abandoned.

I knew why Sunday dinner was cancelled.

Empty.

I was Carmella—staring into a closet void of shoes.

Betrayed.

CHAPTER SEVENTEEN

◆

"DO YOU LIKE *FRANK SINATRA*? *Michael Buble*? God. I love to sing while I am driving!" Scott blasted the radio, singing at the top of his lungs, apologizing when his voice cracked, or he jumbled the words. I was impressed with the way someone so young could appreciate a legend such as Sinatra, and his ability to carry a tune. Just as I began to join in, he switched to another song, then another and yet another—eventually turning off the radio to talk instead.

Scott's conversation was youthful and erratic, talking and pointing incessantly as he drove me to his favorite coffee shop. This was his favorite place to eat sushi. That was the thrift store he loved to find cool clothes in. There was the mall that he wanted to take me to later. His voice was a smooth tenor, but it got a bit higher when he laughed. I recognized his range from my years of competitive singing during middle and high school. We had a verbal likeness.

He drove a small, tan Honda, given to him by his aunt. I learned this in one of his many mini-lessons. We turned onto a main highway, and the car swerved on the thin layer of ice beneath us. The snow made the roads slick, and although I was not nervous about his "multi-tasking," I made sure to mentally brace myself for a fender bender.

"You ok Unc? I can handle it! Honestly, this little car is nothing— very easy to control. I really want a truck though, a truck would be awesome." I nodded my head and smiled, realizing that I actually was a bit nervous, especially since he looked directly at me the entire time he spoke; not the icy road. I wondered how many cups of coffee my young nephew had before he picked me up.

"Here we are. I can't wait to get a cup of coffee—we didn't have any back at the house." This surprised me. This high energy was *natural*, just multiplied by nervousness. I would have to keep up. I made sure to order the boldest blend in the largest cup available. I even considered asking the barista for a side of grounds to munch on.

He pulled a crumpled ten dollar bill out of the front pocket of his fashionable baggy jeans to pay for the coffee, just as I pulled a crisp twenty out of my wallet. I found his offer endearing, but I insisted. He was beginning to deflate a bit now that we were in a larger setting with people around us. I followed Scott as he walked towards the sitting area.

"Let's sit here. It's the best spot. You can watch people as they come and go. Do you like to watch people?" After we settled into the two large espresso-colored leather chairs, he began tapping his finger on the armrest. I was shaking my foot. I noticed Brian tapping his foot the night before. Sean tapped his fingers *and* shook his feet when he was nervous. Our genetics were beginning to reveal themselves.

"Yeah, I watch people all the time," I laughed. "Probably too much."

"Nah, you can never get enough people watching. It's fun as hell, especially at the mall. You want to go there later? You like to shop, right?" I wasn't sure what he meant by that. Was he genuinely asking if I enjoyed shopping, or was he trying to placate the stereotype?

"Hell yeah!" I raised my voice, acting as gay and sarcastic as I could. He looked at me and laughed. So did I. Both of our voices going up one octave. He could see that I wasn't uptight, and I wanted him to feel comfortable knowing that I was okay with him asking whatever he wanted to know.

Scott was well versed and intelligent. He was a straight-A student, and he was planning to graduate high school with honors and become an orthopedic surgeon. At first I thought him handsome, but as I sat there and got to know him on a deeper level, stunning seemed a better fit. His facial characteristics were an interesting combination of chiseled features and softer lines. The corners of his mouth naturally curved up, which lent a permanent devilish smirk. But his eyes were intense, a mixture of greens and browns, and when he spoke to you, he looked right through you. His eyes had a story to tell, and by the way he looked through me, I knew he was interested in mine.

Although he pretended to be rough around the edges, acting as if he had a tough as nails personality, the rough and toughness wasn't physical, but emotional, and after two hours and several cups of coffee, I could see that his cocky personality masked vulnerability and pain. Someone important did something bad. It had affected him. I could sense his pain almost immediately.

"I'm done here. Let's see if the mall is open. You down?" The coffee shop had gotten quite busy, and people were standing around waiting for a table to open. We ignored piercing stares from those waiting. We had hogged the best chairs in the place for far too long.

"Sure thing."

The first hour or so at the mall was enjoyable. Scott and I shared a love of hats, so we made that our mission when we first got there. After getting more coffee at the mall kiosk, I thought a pair of aviators and a navy blue wool bomber jacket from Abercrombie & Fitch suited Scott well. I loved the store, but my shoulders and thighs were too muscular to wear their clothes. I always looked like a middle-aged man trying too hard.

I enjoyed spending a small fortune on him. It made me feel "uncle-ish," which was something I had always desired growing up, but sadly knew I would never become. I was an only child, and Max had a fraternal twin brother, also gay, who had no interest in being a father. Max's brother was my last hope, until finding out I had a brother and two nephews two years earlier.

The idea of actually being someone's uncle was exciting and terrifying. I had no idea how to be an uncle, and I had become comfortable, knowing that I would never be one. Now the big question was *could* I be one? Scott and Collin were teenagers with strong personalities. They were far from impressionable. How do you just walk into someone's life and say, "*Hi. I'm your long lost Uncle from New York.*" I allowed things to just unravel on their own.

They would teach me.

As the day slowly passed, Scott had become quite comfortable talking about his hopes for the future, his family, and the things that he enjoyed. He was equally and genuinely interested in my family, although unconventional, and the things that interested me. Our conversations flowed naturally and freely, and as he became more comfortable, the questions became more direct.

"How did you know when you were gay?"

"How did you feel when you found out about Dad? Us?"

I answered each question without hesitation, waiting for the next to follow. Scott needed to know about these things. The grandfather he didn't know was the beginning of his lineage. He was a curious teenager, and I wanted to be able to help him understand me. Us. How I got here, and why it took me so long. My guilt weighed heavy on my soul.

I had let two years go by before I made any effort to meet my extended family. I had betrayed all of them the way my parents had betrayed me. The opportunity was there, and I chose to ignore it. I wasn't any better than them, but I needed to be.

"Do you like your mom?" I heard him, but I kept walking, not realizing that Scott had stopped.

"Hey, Unc!" I turned and saw him about fifteen feet away. I walked up to him.

"So, do you? Like your mother?"

Our eyes connected. Both of our stares were intense and curious. The question blindsided me, like a slap across the face. Scott was curious to know what my answer was. I was curious to know why he asked me. My eyes challenged him.

"I love my mother." I could feel my cheeks getting warm. I was anxious, uncomfortable, yet calm and intrigued.

"That's not what I asked." Scott didn't seem to blink, but his cheeks were flush too. He was chewing on the side of his mouth.

"I'm not sure exactly what you mean, Scott."

"It's easy Unc. Do you *like* your mom?"

My mouth got dry. No one had ever asked me that question before. Not even the multitudes of therapists I pissed all over during my youth. Maybe it was the fact that I hadn't mentioned a word about my mother since my arrival that sparked his curiosity.

Maybe it was the stories about Carmella, Sean and his grand-mother, passed down over four decades that made him wonder. Fact was—Scott's question was a reality check. Something that I never allowed myself to ponder. He was challenging me to dig deep and realize something that I hadn't allowed myself to.

"Well, I love her, but I don't *like* what she did to me. So, I guess my answer is no. But I am trying to learn how to." He looked at me and smiled.

"Me too."

In that moment, he knew me. It was then that I realized he hadn't spoken a word about his mother either.

The past was erased. Replaced with a crisp off-white cottage-style design, with brushed bronze pulls.

Just like my lightly starched dress shirts.

CHAPTER EIGHTEEN

◆

THEY DID IT FOR ME.

Or at least that was the reason Carmella and Sean gave me.

As an adult and father of two, I think back to my own child-hood, and wonder why people use this excuse when they know all too well that getting back together is NOT the best decision for their offspring. I believe it's because they think they are too weak to make it on their own. They cannot live alone. It is too difficult to go out and find another mate, so getting back together for their "children" seems like the most logical thing to do. Husbands and wives continue to live volatile lives, allowing their children to be the rope in their cyclical tug-o-wars, ultimately making life a living hell for their kids.

Carmella and Sean told me they wanted a fresh start as a family. It was for me. I would have a better life because they were secretly going to couples' therapy, and now they finally had their shit together. I was scared, but I believed them. Why wouldn't I? I was ten. My parents were doing this for *me*. I now realize it was a selfish decision for *them*.

Carmella had not gone away with friends. She was with Sean, making their damaged and bruised house of shame, back into an appropriate home for their child. Holes were spackled, walls were re-painted and my bedroom organized—ready for a smooth transition. It was picture perfect on the outside, but when you took the time and looked really close at the details, you could easily find reminders of what transpired while Carmella and I were gone. Especially the kitchen cabinets.

Sean, in fits of rage, had taken a large butcher knife and carved out chunks of the cabinets. All of them. And even though he had wood puttied, sanded and stained them, you could still see the gouges. Every time I needed a bowl or glass, those marks would stare back at me. I would see my father's face, and I would have to close my eyes to find a better place. Eventually, Carmella and Sean had the cabinets refaced.

The past was erased. Replaced with a crisp off-white cottage-style design, with brushed bronze pulls. Just like my lightly starched dress shirts. A shell masking what I knew was still inside—a beat-up, darkly stained past.

After settling back into my freshly decorated *normal* routine, Carmella and Sean did their very best to help me move past the horrific memories, and reignite the spark that should be in every child's eyes. They took me on family vacations to the Catskills, and Pennsylvania Dutch Country. We went out to dinner, to the movies, played Yahtzee, and nestled back into the pattern of overeating every Sunday with the extended family.

I loved all of it. What child wouldn't? My mother looked and felt better than ever, walking with her head held high. She had won round two of the game show, *Got My Husband Back,* and my father was now working the day shift at his new job. She controlled where he was at all times, and he was fine with being the submissive of the two. But as the years passed, there was one teeny, tiny hairline crack in the "perfect family plan" that slowly crept across their windshield—the only thing they had in common was *me.*

Both, equally, provided me with all the things a broken child needed—clothing, shelter and attention, and they tried desperately to make sure some unconditional love was in the mix. I recognized the challenge, but appreciated the effort. But…they forgot about themselves in the process.

Maybe they did actually do it for me.

As a teenager, I did whatever I could to be away from them. Not because I didn't love them. Every child loves their parents to some extent, but I didn't *like* them very much—and that feeling was beginning to worsen. Their entire windshield collapsed in by the time I was fourteen, and although the battles were not physical and violent, they were verbal and caustic—like battery acid being poured on living flesh. I often found myself being pulled into their arguments, standing there like a judge, trying to understand each point of view, but being overwhelmed because they stated their sides simultaneously.

I was nervous to take a side. Guilt was my mother's new form of ammunition, and if she saw that I agreed with my father—she'd lay it on thick. Sean was coated in guilt, and I saw how hard it was to chip away the layers. Just as he freed himself of some, Carmella made sure to lay it on even thicker. I did not want this to happen to me. When I saw the dark clouds rolling in, I sought shelter from the storm.

It didn't matter if I were sitting in my bedroom studying, sitting on the sofa between the two of them, or eating dinner in the kitchen. When something triggered Carmella, she went right for his jugular. Nothing Sean did was good enough. Everything he did annoyed her, and at times I think she was angry with him for breathing the same air. She would belittle him in front of anyone watching.

"Look at you! You couldn't even take the time to comb your hair before everyone came over for dinner!"

"Look at that shirt. It hardly fits! All you do is sit around and eat!"

"Stay home by yourself. We will all go out and enjoy ourselves."

"Get up and do something! Don't just sit there."

He always gave up without a fight, having no authority, and no opportunity to offer suggestions. She ruled him, and he was scared she would leave. I could hear the defeat in his voice, and even though he had caused me so much pain, it broke my heart.

She had completely emasculated him, and over the years he physically transformed from a handsomely rugged man, to an overweight slob, who cared very little about himself.

I found myself lying to my friends, making sure they rarely came over to my house to hang out. I wanted to keep it all a secret. For this very reason, I joined every before and after school activity I could. I even went to extra help, though I was a straight-A student. But what pulled me in the most was acting.

I was already honing my acting skills every day at home. Staring at my parents as they spoke about their day, pretending to care, offering up *genuine, heartfelt* hugs before bedtime, and acting like the kitchen cabinets didn't bother me every time my friends would ask what happened to them. Although I kept quiet about the chaos, I still needed to be heard. My parents were making it difficult for me to feel confident and secure in myself. What they had together had not been a positive model for me, and it clouded my own judgments. What exactly should I be looking for? Who should I become? I aspired to be perfect, and acting would teach me how to appear confident. That confidence would make me appear polished and well-rounded. This became my lifelong goal.

Acting became an addiction, both on and off the stage. Just like I had hoped, I evolved into an outgoing, confident, entertaining, fun loving and *completely authentic liar,* to all those around me. They all actually thought I had my shit together. Just like real actors on the red carpet, who looked so put together for everyone in public. When they got home, they peeled off their fancy clothes and expensive jewelry, and then they proceeded to crumble. It was time consuming and exhausting, but it was the only thing about myself I could control.

Carmella and Sean were good actors too. It amazed me. She would rip him into tiny pieces. He would sulk in his oversized chair. An hour later we would be at church and they would hold hands, kiss on the lips and say "Peace be with you." It turned my stomach. I always wanted to look at them and scream *"PEACE? Really? Peace for WHOM?"* But a good actor never breaks character.

In spite of all the acting, and as difficult as it was to admit, I truly loved them both—*separately.* They each had good qualities— genuine ones, but while I was trying to forgive and like them, their disharmony overpowered those qualities and smothered me.

◆

Montana was a word I recognized but had not heard in a long time. Also, I never understood what it represented. The thing I knew for sure was that "Montana" surfaced during some of Carmella's thrashings. When I heard the word, I knew to disappear.

Years earlier, when we lived with my grandparents, I overheard *Montana* in conversations between The Three Cheeses, but I never knew who she was. As a child, it sounded like they were talking about a person, a woman, and by the tones in their voices, they were not very fond of her. As a teenager, I realized it was a place. It made more sense, *but little did I know, it was a place AND a woman.*

Montana was a place that Carmella hated. It was evident. During the times I overhead her screaming at him for something he did or didn't do, she would bring that place up, and it brought out a level of anger in her similar to what I feared in Sean as a child. I often ran into the fire, expecting to find her holding one of Sean's hunting rifles in his mouth. But there was one thing I did notice—my father never brought that topic up, and he never retaliated when she used it against him. This sparked my curiosity, but I knew to never go there.

"HERE! Take the phone, Sean. CALL HER! Call her up. Go back to Montana, where you belong!"

"Why don't you just get in your car and DRIVE back to Montana!"

"GO BACK TO MONTANA, SEAN! You BELONG in the woods!"

It was evident that something in Montana caused her great pain, but I never knew what happened there, until my cousin Emma felt it was necessary to share the secrets she knew about my family. Josephine and Pellegrino had many grandchildren by the time I was in my early to mid-teens, and Emma was just one who envied my relationship with them.

Emma was my first cousin, the daughter of Carmella's brother, Vito. We would see them on occasion, and I always looked forward to spending time with her. Emma knew everything about everyone, because her mother was one of those typical family gossips and shit-stirrers that everyone avoided at weddings, birthday parties and funerals. We all pretended to like her, just so we could see Uncle Vito.

Emma knew all about my parents and the mystery behind Montana. She had overhead some of the facts discussed between her parents at home. Obviously, the original plan to keep the Montana secrets hidden from "those" family members had leaks, and unfortunately, Emma's mother was one of them.

"Your mother left your father in Montana because he was having an affair with someone. Her name was Rosa. She drove all the way home from Montana by herself with her cat. Your mother had a miscarriage when she got home, THANK GOD, because she wanted to divorce him. But now they are together. They really shouldn't be though. My mother told me they have a bad marriage and fight a lot. Do they?"

Emma went on and on, almost *happy* to be sharing such awful details about the dawn of my parent's marriage. I zoned out during most of the conversation, watching her poisonous lips spew venom. My mind had shifted, and my wheels were turning.

Therapists always say that something triggers you to spiral. As an adult, I heard this and ignored it numerous times while lying on *"the couch,"* but as a teenager, I had no idea what a trigger was. But in an instant, as Emma's words came out, all the dirty laundry Sean had given me, which I had stuffed away in my closet, all came tumbling out. The door couldn't hold it all back. My mind had become clouded—full of voices—arguing with each other.

Hate him! Love her!
Help her! Curse him!
Sacrifice him! Idolize her!

Everything made sense. The way my mother treated my father made *complete* sense. Montana, Heather, and having to commit a mortal sin! Why hadn't I defended her? How could I allow her to take him back? Why did he *deserve* to have us back?

I adopted the emotional baggage from Carmella's Montana experiences, and piled them on top of my own. I wanted to suffer with her. For her. My father became "Sean," the enemy. I needed to protect my mother. What if he did this to us again?

It became two against one. Unbalanced. Unfair. And destructive.

It lasted well into my thirties.

Sean didn't even have a chance.

———————◆———————

Carmella's car pulled up promptly at four-thirty in the morning, just as we had all planned several days earlier. I was already on guard, shaking my foot with anticipation, as I sat on the new beige microfiber sofa, staring out the front window. The grey 1988 Buick LeSabre, which belonged to her father before he died a decade earlier, turned the corner—leaving a trail of exhaust vapor behind it. It was the end of November, and Mother Nature was beginning to give everyone a sneak peak of the impending winter. Although I was not into layers, even I had to give in. I quickly put on my thick black pea-coat, and the fingerless gloves and grey plaid scarf Max had gotten me for our anniversary one month prior. I inhaled the lingering smell of burnt cedar from the fire we made the night before. It calmed my nerves.

After grabbing my extra-large Dunkin' Donuts travel-mug, I carefully opened up our freshly painted, bright-red, *Elizabeth Arden* style front door. I didn't want to make too much noise. Max was still asleep, and he had to go to work in a few hours. I made my way outside onto the front porch of our new home and approached my mother's car. She and my Aunt Connie got out of the Buick and opened up the trunk. I hugged my mother and winked at my Aunt, but I didn't speak a word. We had a schedule to keep, and the clock was ticking. I opened up the trunk to my white Maxima and transferred the luggage. Other travelers would think that Carmella packed excessively for her trip, but my Aunt and I knew why. We were part of the process.

Carmella had tried her best to compact her life into five mis-matched suitcases. Thirty-six years of marriage in five suitcases. The small pile made me sad. It only took twelve minutes to unpack, reload, and be back on the road. My mother sat next to me, read-ing her bible. Tired, weathered, and broken. My Aunt sat in the back with her eyes closed, pretending to sleep. I could tell by the way her eyes moved under her lids that she wasn't. As I drove to LaGuardia Airport, I thought of my wonderful life with Max. I dreamed of being a father. I filled my mind with everything good. I needed to. My Aunt was doing the same.

Our home was beautiful. More than we had hoped for. Max and I saved for five years to buy our first house. In a total of seven years, we had moved six times, wasting our money on rent. The only good thing about moving so much was that we purged each time we did. By the time we moved into our new home, we had exactly what we needed, and just enough money to purchase the things we desired. As the closing date approached, we enjoyed buying new furnishings, window shades, wall paint, and stylish light fixtures to replace those contractor-grade light fixtures that looked like boobs.

It was a new, three bedroom, two bath Victorian with a front wraparound porch, and just enough yard to landscape without feeling overwhelmed. Within a year, we had added a back deck off the kitchen and dining room, surrounding a semi-in ground pool, perfect for entertaining. It also had a small fireplace, which was something we always wanted, but we were unsure we could afford in our first home. We were ecstatic about being genuine home-owners, but what we were most excited about was starting a family in it.

Once settled in, we immediately began the process. Our home was filled with the positive energy that I longed for growing up, and it was time for us to bring new life into it. This was my personal accomplishment. To live in a home free of battle scars. Void of bad memories, and shaky futures. Our home was perfect.

———————◆———————

Max and I muddled through *our* usual Saturday morning routine. We were still recovering, aimlessly walking around the house trying to do our household chores, ignoring the pounding headaches from too much wine the night before. Then the mail came.

Female.
Mother of four.
39 Y.O.A
4 months.
Pennsylvania

This one stuck out. It spoke to us. We put the postcard on our refrigerator.

Since officially signing with the adoption agency from Vermont, we had received numerous postcards like this one. Each time a woman called and our profile was sent to her, we got a brief outline of her. We had learned not to become too excited, since we were told that most inquiries never transpired into adoptions. Plus, many of them were from very young women who were in their first trimester. But this one seemed special to both of us. She was older, and she already had children. She knew this was the right choice, and she was actively seeking a couple. It was the first postcard that made us feel like we had "*conceived.*" Even though it wasn't definite, it gave us hope. It snapped us out of our hangovers and made doing the household chores a bit more tolerable.

The phone rang. I looked at the caller ID and decided not to answer it. It was my father's cell phone. My parents were probably on their way somewhere, checking in. They did not leave a message. My dull headache immediately returned.

"Who was it?" Max walked back into the kitchen. He had just finished smoking a cigarette on the back deck while attempting to rake the leaves off the top of the pool liner. His ability to multi task with a cigarette in his mouth reminded me of my father when I was young. I couldn't do it. Smoke always got in my eyes or nose.

"My parents." I continued to Comet the kitchen sink. I hated when coffee made the stainless steel look dirty. "They did not leave a message."

"Hey, do you want me to make a few calls, and see if anyone wants to come over tonight? We can play poker." Max was trying to bring me back from the dead. Whenever Carmella and Sean called, I often felt torn to answer the phone. When I did pick up, they usually bickered with one another on the other end, and it ruined my day. But when I didn't pick up, I felt guilty. Carmella had continued to lay on the guilt through my young adulthood, and even as a thirty something, it worked.

Why haven't you called?
Why didn't you call back?
What do you mean you can't come over for dinner?
Were you busy last weekend? We could've used your help with the leaves.
What do you mean you can't spend the holidays with us?

Most of the time, I picked up the phone based on my mood. I had to. I had a lot of resentment towards my father, and even though I cherished my mother, I had even more for her. If I had had a bad day, or something was bothering me, it was in everyone's best interest that I not answer, or call back at all.

"Sure. Let's do it! I am totally up for a good night of poker!" Max and I had become an updated version of Carmella and Sean. Good poker, party throwers, but without a big, black guy named Spades. Max left the room with his cell phone, and began making calls to our close friends. I had stopped collecting people when I met Max. Our group was small, tight, dedicated and genuine. They were my family.

My cell phone rang. It was a restricted number, but I knew that when the adoption agency called our cell phones, it came up restricted. Letting those calls go straight to voicemail was never an option. It could be "*that call.*"

"Hello?" I always answered cheery and hopeful. No one responded, but I could hear someone. I repeated myself.

"Benny?" It was my mother. It was hard to hear her. It sounded like she was talking through a wind tunnel. I couldn't tell if she was crying, or if the background noise was making it difficult to understand her, "Benny? Can you hear me?"

"MA?" I was yelling into the phone.

"Ben, let me pull over and call you right back. I wanted to make sure you were home." She was driving. The wind noise made sense, but now I could tell that she was panicked and upset. Fifteen minutes passed, and she never called, but my father tried calling me from his cell phone three times, leaving no messages. They were trying to communicate with me separately. I knew it couldn't be good, and as I walked up the stairs to alert Max of the impending storm, someone began banging on the front door. It was my mother. I could see the top of her head through the glass, and her car was parked in the driveway.

"Benny? Max? Open up! It's Mom!" I quickly ran down the stairs, and opened up the door. She rushed in and headed to the kitchen. Max came down.

"THANK GOD! Did he try calling here?"

"Who, Dad?" I followed her in.

"Yes! Lock the door!"

"What's going on? Mom, are you okay?" Max walked towards her, and put his hand on her shoulder. He was more concerned about her. I was more concerned about my father showing up.

"Why? WHAT THE HELL, MA?!" I locked the front door and turned the bolt. I walked over to the window and looked outside. "He tried calling a few times from his cell. Is he coming? What the hell happened, and why do I need to lock my fucking door?"

"I'm scared, Benny. He got angry with me. He ripped the phone out of the wall, and he came at me with the telephone cord." As she continued to sob, I became the little boy staring in the window, watching my father overpower my mother. But I didn't need to run for help this time.

"Jesus! Ben, what do you want me to do?" Max said, walking around the kitchen, unsure of how to react. He had heard the stories, but never truly understood them until now. Max loved my father. He knew a different side of him. He paced, trying to understand how quickly our house had been transformed into a battleground.

"Mom, calm down. Did you call DeDe?"

"No, not yet. I'm scared."

"Max, do me a favor. Call my Aunt; see if we can come over now."

"What do you want me to tell her?"

"Just tell her that my parents are having trouble again. That my father has become violent. Again." Max headed upstairs where it was quiet, and called.

"I am so scared that he is going to hurt me, Benny." She was sobbing and digging through her purse for tissues. Her hands shaking the same way they did when Sean would harass us when I was a small child. I began to tear up. I held her hand, and we looked into each other's eyes. We were *there* again. But this time, I was stronger than he was.

———————◆———————

Carmella wanted to run. But again, she didn't know how. All she knew was that Sean lost his temper, became violent, threatened her life, and showed the side of him that she feared the most. Just as Lilly helped her devise a plan of escape 36 years earlier, this time, she allowed my Aunt and I to take full control. My mother wanted out. She wanted to leave, and go somewhere far away from my father. Carmella talked divorce. To move on, and make a new life for herself. We didn't blame her. This would be the third time Connie helped her sister, and she was not sure if Carmella would actually be strong enough to move on, and start a new life. She doubted her sister's ability to be strong and independent. *If she couldn't do it when she was so much younger, why would Carmella do it now, when she was retired and financially comfortable?*

But Connie knew the right thing to do was to help her again, hoping this time Carmella would see that her life didn't need to be filled with so much negative energy. I, on the other hand, *did* believe my mother had what it took to begin a healthier, more self-sufficient and positive life. Even though she was much older, it was possible.

The three of us sat around Aunt Connie's dining room table, and devised a plan. Carmella was going to practically reenact the escape from Montana all over again. But the first thing that she needed to do was pretend. Go home and pretend that she was okay from the incident. Forgive his actions. Act and treat him the same way she had for years. Lying and surviving for a few days, then escape when he went to work. It was a game that ALL of us had to play, and Connie and I were willing to do it for her.

My father had frantically called all our cell phones, leaving numerous messages on my phone, and his wife's. Most messages reeked of anger. Only a few had subtle hints of compassion and concern. However, his main concern was not for her. He just feared being alone again.

Where is my wife? I want to talk with my wife!

She better not be leaving me!

Where is your mother, Ben? You need to call me back and tell me!

I'm sorry, Carmella. I won't do it again.

Eventually, my mother turned hers off. My Aunt and I agreed that her emotions were too transparent to speak with him yet. It was better that she hold off until she was composed. That left my Aunt and me. One of us was going to have to eventually answer his call. Sean wasn't stupid. He knew that she fled to one of us. It was only a matter of time before he began searching for her, so when my cell phone began to ring again, I decided to answer.

"What?" I answered the phone with a sharp irritability.

"What do you mean, *what*?" He was irritable too, and everyone knew that the two of us could not be in each other's company when we were on the same wavelength.

"How the hell do you expect me to answer the phone, Dad? What the fuck did you do now?"

"Ya know what, Ben—shut the FUCK UP and put your mother on the phone!"

I hung up. Not because I didn't want to continue the fight— I was totally up for it, but because this was something I enjoyed doing to people when they got on my last nerve. Although it was a terrible tactic, if I changed the way I reacted to him, he would know something was up. I sat down, and waited for him to call again. I knew he would. Since I was old enough to hold my own and battle with him, I either cursed him out, or hung up on him, and he *always* called back.

"Dad, what do you want?"

"I want to talk to my wife!"

"No. You can't. You hurt her again. Did you try and choke her?"

After a long paused, he answered, "I wouldn't have."

"But you thought about it. Dad, this is a problem. You cannot act this way and get away with it! She is scared of you!" Whenever I mentioned her being scared of him or fearing him, it would trigger his anger.

"She has nothing to be scared of! What the fuck?! I wasn't going to do anything!"

"Like rip the phone off the wall again? Dad, you need help." I hated saying those words. Even though it was true, I hated saying it, because so many people had thrown that in my face as I tried to cope with my past. People who look at you and say, *"You should see someone,"* or *"You really need to get help,"* and a light bulb fucking appears above your head, like it was something you already didn't know.

"Your mother pushes me, Ben! She won't shut up! She just keeps pushing me until I snap." He was right. I knew he was. My heart wanted to reach out to him and say, *"Dad, listen. I understand. I've been witnessing you getting belittled for years. I think Mom needs to get some help. I think you BOTH need to get some help."*

But, I never expressed my true feelings. My mind told me something different. *"Ben. It is too dangerous. Connie and Carmella will chew you up and spit you out. You'll become the enemy too."* So I answered the only way I felt comfortable.

"You have no right to be angry with her after all she has put up with over the years! Get your shit together! I will call you in a bit. Give her some space for now, she is still upset."

I hung up and we made a plan.

———————◆———————

Carmella went home the next day. She walked into the house with her normal "chip on the shoulder" attitude, making Sean think she was pissed off and "hurt." This was her normal attitude when Sean did things that made her angry, so he fell for her act. She kept her distance from Sean, keeping busy with church, the food pantry, and going to the gym. She followed each step of the plan my Aunt and I laid out for her perfectly. She was quite the actress, impressing me immensely, especially since acting had been something that helped me so much. Each day, she packed one bag of basics, and put it in her trunk. Carmella did not blink an eye each time she snuck around and lied to Sean about her plans for the day.

"I'm going to the gym for a while." *Meant: "I'm heading to the bank, and emptying out the safety deposit box full of my jewelry and dropping it off at Benny's, along with all of my life insurance policies, of which Benny is the beneficiary now."*

"They need me at the food pantry for a few hours extra today." *Meant: "Benny is taking me to the bank to help me transfer our money from the joint accounts into my personal account. Then, I am paying him back for the one-way airline ticket he bought me."*

"Connie and I are going out for lunch." *Meant: "I am going over to my sister's, and spending a few hours on the phone, taking my name off all the household bills."*

"I'm going to read in the backroom for a while." *Meant: "I am writing my farewell letter to you, sealing it in an envelope with my rings, and going over my last minute list of things to do before I leave you tomorrow."*

At four in the morning, Sean left for work, and Carmella did just that.

CHAPTER NINETEEN

◆

I WAS WEARING THE NEW SUIT I had purchased from Country
Road of Australia two weeks prior. It was tailored to fit like a
glove, and I felt like a million bucks. My equally polished and confident colleagues were sitting around the large conference table with
me—waiting for other ad execs to arrive. As I initiated some small
talk with my neighbor, my phone began to vibrate. Caller unknown.

"Hello?" I got up out of my ergonomically structured chair and
walked away from my colleagues, answering the unknown number as quietly as possible. I had to. Our adoption agency called the
day before to inform us that the "postcard" woman, named Karen,
wanted to speak with Max and I on the phone that evening. My
heart sank, thinking that maybe Karen had a change of heart, and
they were calling to let us know just that. Max and I couldn't deal
with any more stress, especially with everything that had recently
went down with my parents.

"Hello. May I speak with Benjamin Quinn please?" Her voice
was almost poetic. Smooth, airy, and professional.

"This is he."

"Hello Mr. Quinn. My name is Sarah Wilkins. I am your father's
psychiatrist here at Hartwell Memorial Hospital. Do you have a
moment?" I could picture her in her white coat, sitting behind her
cluttered desk of client folders, full of juicy, fucked up personal
information. She had a pencil tucked behind one ear, and she sat
back in her leather chair with the receiver to her ear. Her lipstick
was perfect, and her legs were crossed. Her chocolate colored croc-
odile pumps were sexy.

"Oh, hi Dr. Wilkins, how are you? Sure. I am at work, and
a meeting is starting soon. Will this take long?" I was shocked
to hear from her. As a matter of fact, I had no idea that my

father even had a psychiatrist specifically assigned to him after being admitted.

"Yes. Your father has come a long way in the last few days."

"Really? How?"

"I cannot disclose any information about our sessions; however, he has asked me to invite you to come in today. He has something very important to share with you."

"Well, I am at work in the city, but I guess I can leave after the meeting. Would five-ish work?"

"That would be fine. This will be an important step for Sean. I will let him know, and put you down on the visitor list. Just have your driver's license with you when you arrive."

"Will do."

When I hung up, I had a pit in my stomach. I texted Max to keep him in the loop, then turned off my phone, returning to the conference room. The meeting ended up feeling twice as long, and I could hardly concentrate through it. I no longer felt like a million bucks, and my suit felt constricting, like I was being suffocated. I wasn't sure if it was the phone call that bothered me, or the fact that this would be the first time I saw my father, after calling the cops, and having him committed.

◆

Carmella was already half way across the country before Sean came home from work. It was like déjà-vu, only this time, Carmella was heading back in the same direction that she escaped from decades earlier. Carmella left a note behind, explaining everything she had felt for decades. Her inability to ever completely trust him. The constant fear that anything could trigger him to spiral into someone violent and uncontrollable. Unhappiness. Loneliness. You name it. The one thing Carmella *did not* include in her letter were apologies.

Apologizing for not allowing him the chance to prove he was trustworthy. Realizing that when she took him back the second time, she established a dictatorship rather than a marriage. Understanding that by emasculating and belittling him, she was one of the main reasons why he spiraled. Her letter blamed Sean for everything that had gone wrong. Ever. I was the innocent bystander, who whole-heartedly disagreed.

Sean would find her letter the moment he placed his blue Igloo thermos and keys on the kitchen table. His initial reaction was typical and expected. He threw things, smashed things, and then called me. I knew he got home at around 3:30 in the afternoon, so when the phone rang at slightly before four, I knew it would be him.

"Hello?"

"Benny. It's Dad. Your mother left me." He was eerily calm. To the point, as if he surmised this would happen.

"*What?* What do you mean she *left* you?" I was supposed to act shocked. It was part of the plan. To pretend that I had no idea of what transpired, and no clue as to where she could be.

"You don't know anything?" Sean was suspicious. He knew that Carmella and I were a team, but the one thing he didn't realize was that I was slowly breaking away from her side. Again, I wanted to tell him everything, but I feared the consequences.

"Dad, listen. I know nothing about her leaving you. All I know is what you did to her last week, and that she was really upset and nervous. It brought back lot of memories for her. Did you call DeDe?"

"I called, but she didn't answer. She knows where your mother is. Connie is the one that put her up to this! I know she did!"

"How do you know she left you? Are her things gone?"

"She left me a note, and her rings. She left me instructions on how to write checks, and all this other bullshit! It's all spread out on the kitchen table. She said she changed her cell phone number too, so I have no way to find her." My father began crying on the other end of the phone.

"Ok, listen. Let me change, and I will be over in about a half hour."

"Ok. Can you grab me a coffee on the way?"

"Sure."

On the way to my father's, I tried calling my Aunt on both her home and cell phone. She did not answer, so I left a message on each, telling her that Sean was well aware of her sister leaving, and that I was heading over to make sure he was ok. I also called my mother to see how her flight was, and I left her a message. She had a layover in Denver, so I figured she'd call me when she landed. I didn't hear from either of them that day. As a matter of fact, I didn't hear from either of them for three days.

When I arrived at my childhood home, which again reeked of tragedy and despair, Sean was sitting in his sulking chair, as my mother would call it. That was hardly ever the case, but it was appropriate *this time* because that was exactly what he was doing. He had the letter in his hand, and he allowed me to read it. I read it twice. It was cold. Harsh. Final. He had her engagement ring, and the three-diamond wedding band he gave her when they renewed their vows after twenty-five years of marriage. The words in her letter did not seem to make sense as I looked at that ring. She said she had never been happy. Carmella expressed that she wanted a better life for herself. *So then why did she renew her vows?*

Accepting that ring almost seemed hypocritical. Why reaffirm vows that you regretted taking in the first place? I took the letter from him and tore it up. At first he got agitated, but I explained to him that sitting around rereading it would make him sick, and that he needed to focus on trying to pull himself together now that she had left.

"Do you think she will come back? She'll come back, right? Maybe she just needs time alone. Do you think she is staying with your Aunt? Maybe I should go to the food pantry and ask around." He was trying to convince himself that it was just a phase.

"I think you need to consider that she is NOT coming back. Did you look around the house and see what's gone?"

"Most of her clothes are gone. Her jewelry box is gone. I have no idea what else could be."

Over the next few days, Sean tried to keep it under wraps. Although he had found out Carmella cleaned out their bank accounts and safety deposit box, he still did not want to truly believe she was gone for good. He did not tell anyone at work, and he did not mention anything to the neighbors, although some began to suspect something was wrong. Carmella was usually in and out of their home all day long, chatting with the neighbors when they happened to be outside at the same time. Day after day, Sean began to fall into a deep depression, and by the time she had been gone for a little over two weeks, he had begun to call in sick. I would stop over and check in on him. Chinese food containers, pizza boxes, and empty soda cans cluttered the kitchen—everything he was not supposed to eat because of his health issues. High cholesterol, diabetes and heart issues no longer seemed to matter.

He was dirty, unshaven and unloved.

I was ashamed of myself.

"Hello?"

"Hi Benny? Oh thank goodness! It's Peggy. Your parent's neighbor." She was uptight and sounded desperate.

"Hey Peg. What's wrong?"

"Have you heard from your father?"

"I spoke with him yesterday. Why? Is everything ok?"

"Benny—you need to get here right away! I went over to give your dad something to eat, and he is not answering the door. He is in there, we can hear him. Something is not right!"

"What do you mean *something is not right*?"

"Steve tried looking through the shades. He can see your dad sitting in the dark. He has one of his hunting knives in his hand, and there are pill bottles next to him. We can hear him opening and closing the knife. You want me to call the police?"

"I'll be right there!"

On the way over, I called his cell phone. No answer. I tried the house phone. Again, no answer. My heart raced, and I couldn't help but think that I would arrive to find him dead and bloody on the living room floor. I drove as fast as I could—it only took me fifteen minutes to arrive. By the time I did, Peggy and Steve had already called the cops. They began to arrive a few minutes after I got there. I began to bang on the front door, calling out to my father.

"Dad? Dad!! Open up the door! What are you doing?" I thought about breaking the kitchen window, but I was scared that it would be the *push* that made him slice his wrists.

"DAD! OPEN UP THE DOOR!" I continued to bang on it as hard as I could, but as I tried looking in the two rectangular leaded glass panes, his shadowed silhouette remained motionless. There was no longer the sound of him opening and closing the switchblade. I feared he had already accomplished what he set out to do that day. I fell to the stoop and began to sob, just as the cops came up to the door. They moved me out of the way and broke in the door. He was still alive, but already dead inside. He couldn't respond. The Coumadin bottle was empty. The knife sat upon the wedding picture he had in his wallet.

"Sir, are you his son?"

"Yes," I said. My father's head continued to hang low.

"Since your father is unable to communicate with us and we fear for his safety, we need your consent to take him to the hospital."

"Yes."

In a foggy daze, I collected some clothes and toiletries and put them in a bag, handing it to the EMTs. They made sure I had not included any razors or objects my father could harm himself with. Unable to use words, all I could do was nod in agreement. I sat on the front porch, and watched the ambulance take my father away.

I called my mother. No answer.

I called my Aunt. She picked up the phone for the first time in over a week. Finally, someone that could help me. Someone who could allow me to express the pain I was going through. I felt alone. Abandoned. My mother had escaped, but she had also left me with her broken pieces to put back together. My Aunt had decided now that her sister had fled, anything associated with Sean was not worth her time, including me. As I sobbed into the phone, explaining what had happened—looking for the love and support I desperately needed, she said,

"You should have let him kill himself." I hung up. Her words were like daggers in my eyes, distorting the way I would look at her for a very long time. The moment Carmella got on that plane, I was officially in this alone. Connie's hatred for Sean, and my mother's dissatisfactions with her marriage had become *my* burdens to bear.

They were free.

I helped them to be.

But neither of them factored me into the equation.

On the train ride, and the entire time I drove to the hospital, I kept repeating in my head what Dr. Wilkins had said on the phone, *"Your father has something very important he'd like to share with you."* I couldn't for the life of me, figure out what it could be. By now, I thought myself the expert in both my mother and father's lives; however, I did have some ideas.

Did he have another affair I didn't know about?

Did he know what happened to me during his affair with Heather? That Donna had done more than help me pick out seashells?

Did he meet someone new in the looney bin?

I got myself a large coffee at the hospital cafeteria, along with a small decaf for my father. He was only allowed decaffeinated coffee. No stimulants, especially since he had begun a new medication to reduce his anxiety and even his demeanor. As I walked up to the entrance of my father's temporary home, I followed the instructions on the sign, and rang the doorbell. Within seconds, a large female guard approached the door, speaking into the monitor next to her.

"May I help you?"

I leaned into the monitor on my side and pressed the button. "Uh, yes. I am here to see Sean Quinn. I am his son."

"Do you have an appointment?" She looked at me as if I had *suspect* written across my forehead. I didn't recall being branded that as a child. I couldn't stand guards who took their job too seriously. As if I were going to go in and throw my three hundred pound father over my shoulder, and smuggle him out. I wanted to be my normal sarcastic self, but I decided it was probably not the best place to showcase my talents.

"Yes. Dr. Wilkins called earlier today and set it up."

"Ok, one moment." She walked back and disappeared into a room. Moments later, a homely woman, with darker hair interwoven with coarse, kinky white ones, approached the door. As she got closer, her name tag read: *Sarah Wilkins.* She didn't have the medical suffix she earned at the end of her name, and it was nice to see that some doctors didn't feel the need to brag.

Over the years I had encountered several uncomfortable situations when I forgot to address doctors or lawyers the "right" way, and I was hastily corrected. She was not what I had envisioned, but nonetheless, she was helping my father, so that helped buffer my initial fantasy. I passed my license through the tiny opening, and I was buzzed in.

She introduced herself as Sarah. This made me feel at ease, especially knowing that my father did not really believe in psychiatrists, or psychologists. He always felt they made people feel worse about themselves than they really were. She was *normal.* No clipboard in hand, no pamphlet rack in her waiting room or office, and no affectations whatsoever. Nothing shocked or amazed her—which was exactly what Sean needed. Someone who would not judge him for the poor decisions, violent outbursts, or infidelities he had. However, Dr. Wilkins wanted to make sure I knew this was her style.

"Mr. Quinn."

I interrupted. "Please call me Ben"

"Sure. Ben. Please understand that your father is going through a lot of mixed emotions right now. Guilt, anger, frustration, confusion, betrayal, you name it. He blames himself for a lot of what has transpired in his life. Do you understand?"

"I do. I have lived it alongside him."

"Well, yes you have, but not really. He probably views things that have happened in his life much differently than you may have. I need to make sure that this session is not going to be one based on discussing feelings and regrets."

"I don't quite understand."

"Your father is learning to let go of things he has been punishing himself over. He needs this time to grow, which means this is a no-judgment zone. The way you may or may not feel about the things he has done is not the reason why you are here today. Also, the way your mother may or may not feel about him in general, is not something we need to delve into."

"I completely understand what you are saying Dr. Wilkins."

"Please, call me Sarah."

"Ok."

"Your father is in the general meeting room, where we hold group sessions. He has come a long way, and I must say, *he really loves you*. He genuinely loves you. He brags about you all the time."

Hearing her say those words made my bottom lip begin to shake. For years, I had wanted to open my heart up and accept those words from him, but I never allowed him to say them. I had covered my ears with duct tape every time he tried to express himself. I would turn and walk away. Allowing myself to realize he loved me made me feel like I was betraying my mother. Knowing she was not around made it easier for me to see him with fresh eyes. Sarah could see that my eyes were watery, and she offered up a tissue from the box on her desk, cluttered with files.

She guided me down the hallway, past a common area where patients were watching television, and there was a cafeteria with snack and beverage vending machines. We walked into the group session room and there he was, sitting at the therapeutic, calming-blue, round Formica table. He was doing the daily crypto-quote in his newspaper. As a child, I loved when he taught me how to solve the crypto quotes—telling me to search for the double letter patterns first and common three letter words that could be *"the"* or *"and."* By the time I was thirteen, I could finish crypto quotes faster than he could. I smiled as I quietly observed him finishing the one he was focused on. It was the first good memory of my father that I had allowed myself to enjoy in a very long time.

"Ah! Done!" He looked up. His face was so relaxed. Calm. The deep angry wrinkle between his brows seemed shallower and kinder.

"What does it say?" I asked.

"The key is to keep company only with people who uplift you, whose presence calls forth your best. Epictetus"

"Hmm. Good one. Here's some decaf. I thought you'd like some." I walked over, and he got up. We hugged. He smelled like Old Spice, which was really nice. Dr. Wilkins stepped forward to garner our attention.

"Ok, I am going to leave the two of you alone for a while. Sean, if you need anything just let me know. Ben, would you like anything? Water? Diet cola?"

"No thank you. I am fine. I have my coffee." Dr. Wilkins walked out. I felt nervous, because I knew that I had sent him to this place. A place where I had to prove to some stranger behind a padlocked door that I was worthy of visiting him. The thing was, I wasn't sure if I was worthy. I had lied to him. I had watched him crumble, knowing very well where she was, and how wrong I felt about what I had done. My brain was scrambling for the right words to begin a sentence. One that would not offend him or make him feel bad. He must have sensed my anxiety.

"Hey, listen, I am not mad at you. I just wanted you to know that. You did what you had to do. I wasn't the best father to you, and I am sorry." Sean's eyes wandered around the room, trying not to focus on me too long. He was also nervous. He was rolling his fingers from pinky to index over and over again. This was another hint of deep thought. What he wanted to *share* was on the tip of his tongue. I could tell, just as he could tell earlier that I needed him to start the conversation.

"Dad. I know you have something that you want to tell me. If it is that important to you, then I want to know. I won't judge you, or get upset anymore. The past is the past, I can't relive it anymore." As the words came out of my mouth, I felt a sense of release. I separated my life from that of my mother's. My pain from hers. Looking at my father, and knowing that I was forgiving him for what he had done to me, and not Carmella, gave me the freedom to feel empathy towards him. I allowed myself to understand that he was not unlike the rest of us—someone who made mistakes and wanted to be forgiven for them, not eternally punished.

"I am scared to tell you. I am scared because I don't want to push you any farther away than I already have."

"Don't be."

"Well, you know that when Mommy and I got married, we moved to Montana, right?"

There it was...Montana. It was not a surprise that it came up. As a matter of fact, I was glad it had. Finally, I would be hearing the truth about Montana from someone other than my cousin Emma.

"I know all about Montana, Dad." I tried to shrug it off as old news so that he would feel less anxious about having to introduce me to all that happened there decades earlier.

"No, you don't." He got serious. I paid attention.

"Ok."

"When you mother left me, I fell in love with someone else."

"Were you having an affair?"

"At first it was a one night stand. But when your mother left me, I had a relationship with her."

"Who?"

"Her name was Rosa."

"Dad. I already knew that you had an affair and Mommy left you, and then you both got back together. Rosa is not something you need to share with me, I already knew."

"It's not just that Ben. When I left, she was pregnant."

"Who was? Mommy?" I was confused. Somewhere in the conversation I had gotten confused about who he was talking about. I knew my mother found out she was pregnant when she left Montana, so it must have been her he was talking of. But Carmella was already gone.

"*Your* mother wasn't pregnant!" He got serious. Father serious. He had no idea I knew about my mother's abortion. After all that had happened between them, he was still protecting her. He still loved her.

"Dad, what the hell? I am so confused."

"Ben, you have a brother or sister in Montana. When I left Montana to get back with Mom, Rosa was pregnant. There, I said it." He sat back, and put both hands on the table. He had anted up. It was all on the table. Completely dumbfounded, I sat back and stared at him, not really knowing what to say. I tried to collect my thoughts and stay calm. I was here to support him in his personal journey without judgment. He wanted to share something very important with me, and he did. I needed to allow him this opportunity, no matter how hard this was going to be to swallow.

"Um…Ok. So let me get this straight. You left Rosa for Mom when she was pregnant and then you never contacted her again? What the fuck, Dad?"

"I know! Don't get upset. I have been keeping this secret forever, and I can't handle it anymore. It is eating me alive."

"Wait…you don't know if you have a son or daughter?"

"No."

"What do you know?"

"Your brother or sister was born in December 1971."

I took a deep breath in and exhaled.

"I am the same age as my brother or sister?"

"Four months apart."

The room began to spin. My heart began to race, so I stood up. Everything was a whirlwind, and I could not collect my feelings or thoughts. I began to rummage through my pockets for some change, then I walked to the next room to get water from the vending machine. My life as an only child had changed in one short conversation. I had a sibling. The brother or sister that I had wished for my entire childhood. Someone that would keep me company, and I could grow close with and cling to when times got difficult. Now, I had one—somewhere. Dr. Wilkins told me I was not allowed to judge him. How couldn't I? He abandoned Rosa when she was pregnant. He allowed one child to grow up a bastard, while he raised another among lies, betrayal and violence. I walked back into the room angry, but I did my best to refrain from feeding into it. I sat back down across from him. He was nervous.

"Dad. Thanks for sharing this with me, but I have to say, I am unsure what you want me to do. Does Mom know?"

"No! You can't tell her."

"Why? What's the big deal now? You aren't even together anymore."

"Um…" He stopped himself.

"What?"

"Nothing. Forget it."

"What Dad! What is it? Is there another child?" It made me laugh. I often laughed when I felt uncomfortable in a situation. The laughter made it less tense. It relaxed the conversation a bit.

"I know what I am about to ask you is a lot, but I hope you can understand. For the last forty years, I have lived with this, Benny. Your whole life I have watched you grow up, knowing that I have another child growing up in Montana too. This burden is way too hard to bear anymore. I can't keep this to myself anymore. Can you try and find them?" *How could I say no? What type of person would I be to refuse helping someone find the child they left behind? What type of person would I be, if I didn't try and find my own sibling?* I leaned over and ripped off a piece of newspaper and took his pencil. I sat up and smiled at my father. I needed to do this for him. I wanted to do this for me.

"Fine. Give me names. All the names you can remember."

Two hours later, Max and I spoke with Karen. She chose us to adopt her unborn daughter.

Four hours later, I found my brother Brian.

An hour after that, I told my dad he had a son and two grandchildren.

In one day, I had become a father, brother, uncle and savior.

CHAPTER TWENTY

◆

SEAN SPENT TWO FULL WEEKS at the hospital finding himself, and learning why he acted the way he did. After the first three days of mandatory observation, he could have put all of his things in a plastic bag and walked right out the door. He had every right to. But he didn't. This was a huge step. My father had never really taken care of himself emotionally, nor did he ever consider it an option—he was always *told* that he was fucked up, so after a while he just believed it. I guess that is common for many people. At least I know that it was that way for me. For so many years, I had created a wall around myself, masking my pain, making others perceive me as vain, self-centered and sarcastic. It was easy to allow myself to adopt these traits. During my visits at the hospital, I actually listened to my father for the first time. I learned who he really was—under all that guilt, anger, and frustration. As a result, I also realized my own shortcomings.

With the help of Dr. Wilkins, and the other patients he met during group sessions, he finally thought about his life, and freed himself from the decades of guilt he had carried and took out on everyone he loved. He forgave himself, and grieved his mistakes. But the biggest obstacle was coming to terms with that fact that Carmella had left him again. He was going home to an empty house. Even though it would be difficult, he knew he had to try and figure out how to move forward. I had exactly what he needed. The day I went to pick him up, I gave him my gift.

"Hey! You ready?" He was already sitting in the waiting room, ready for me to take him home. We hugged, and I took his bag.

"Hell yeah! First thing I am going to do is shave." He scratched his beard. I couldn't believe how white it was. Sean always had a mustache, with hints of white and red, but his Santa beard and glasses made him look fifteen years older.

"Do you want to hit a diner on the way home?"

"Nah. I just want to go home, watch real TV, and sit in my chair. These two women watched nothing but talk shows, and the cushions on the chairs were awful. I did a lot of reading." My father loved to read. He would read a novel a week, usually during the last two or three hours before bed.

"OK." We got in the car, and headed home.

"Have you heard from your mother?" His question alarmed me. We had just left the hospital, and he was already asking. I turned to him.

"Not really."

"Oh. Is everything okay? Is she okay?"

"I guess. We haven't really spoken much." I had no desire to talk about her. Her, or my Aunt. Neither of them had reached out to see if everything was okay with my father, and neither of them had asked me how I was doing through all the recent bullshit. Max had to talk me off my own ledge on numerous occasions, since being emotionally abandoned by them weeks earlier.

"Honestly Dad, I really don't want to talk about them. Let's get home. I have something for you."

"Oh, okay. I didn't mean to upset you. What do you have for me?"

"It's a surprise." I was excited to tell him more about the child he had left behind forty years earlier. Happy to share with him the things Brian and I spoke about. My brother. His son. I had never given anyone a gift more profound, and I was glad I was giving it to him.

After getting Dad settled in, I gave him the pile of important mail I had collected for him. I had created a list of bills to be paid by date, company and phone number. He put it on the table alongside his chair, along with his books, hunting and fishing magazines, gum, glasses case, and toe nail clippers.

A few days earlier, I had taken the opportunity to remove the pile of pictures Sean cried over two weeks earlier, and replaced them with a "Welcome Home" card I had bought him. For about a half hour, it remained unnoticed, leaning against the green and gold lamp right next to him. I was anxious for him to open it, but I was having fun. I enjoyed laughing with him as he shared more stories about the staff, the food, and how fucked up the other patients were compared to him. Then he saw it.

"What's this?" He reached over, and took the bright blue envelope into his hands.

"It's from me." My heart began to speed up as he tore it open.

It was a cheesy, mushy card. One of those water colored tall ones explaining how proud I was of him. Blah, blah, blah. Usually a parent was giving one of these to their child, but it seemed fitting. I watched his eyes move back and forth across the calligraphy. Then he opened it up, and stared at what I had written inside. *"Dad. This is my gift to you. I love you. I am here for you. Only you can make your life better. The phone numbers are in your wallet. – Your son, Ben"*

Under the message was a list of names.

Rosa.

Brian, your son.

Scott & Collin, your grandchildren.

He looked up at me with tears in his eyes, unable to speak. I smiled at him.

"You're welcome."

My mother wanted to move on. I helped her go.

My father needed to move on; I helped push him in the right direction.

———————◆———————

Being alone with Brian was something that I really looked forward to. Up until now, most of my four-day visit was spent gallivanting with Scott, and getting to know everyone that I now referred to as my extended family. I needed face-to-face time with my brother, with no one else listening to the words we exchanged or examining our body language.

Although I appreciated the quality time I had spent with Rosa and my nephews, Scott and Collin, connecting with my brother before I left was imperative. It had been two years since that first phone call, and I knew it was something we both wanted and needed. Since my flight was leaving at 1:30 the following day, we decided to get in our quality time over a few drinks at one of the local sports bars in town. I had come up with the idea, and although I could sense some anxiety from my brother, he politely agreed.

Brian hardly went out to socialize in public. Rosa had shared that with me. Since becoming a father, he had become extremely reserved and very private. Crowded bars, alcohol, and rowdy people were no longer a part of his life. I found this to be very interesting. In the limited amount of communication we had over the last two years, one thing that Brian had shared with me was his passion for football, wrestling and photography. He was an all-star football player, and an amazing wrestler all through school—and star athletes were known for being some of the most rowdy and outgoing of all high school students. I knew there was a history behind his choices to remain private, and I wanted to know why. Rosa's tidbits of information about Brian made his initial apprehension to go out for drinks make sense, and it amazed me how similar he was to *our* father. Sean hated large crowds, and this lack of desire to attend large functions caused many a fight between him and Carmella. Then again, what didn't?

In the early evening, Brian and I went out for burgers and fries with the boys then dropped them off at Rosa's before hitting Champions. Champions was your typical loud, man-sporty, beer-pounding bar, just like the ones I had frequented every Thursday through Saturday night, during my entire four years of undergraduate work in Washington D.C. It was already crowded, and full of high energy. I loved it. The atmosphere brought me back to my youth, but by the look on Brian's face, I could tell he had no desire to revisit his. Luckily, we found the one remaining pub table with two chairs, tucked away from most of the already tipsy twenty something's who had come directly from work. This put Brian at ease. Before we even had a chance to get our jackets off, our waitress came over.

"What would you boys like?" She was barely legal, overly bubbly, and perky. And her perkiness had nothing to do with her personality. Claire had a push up bra that made her two tiny tits look like they were part of her neck. Her hard nipples poked right through her white *un-buttoned* down shirt, which was conveniently tied in a knot just above her navel.

"I'd like a Guinness." I kept my eyes on Claire, but I could see Brian through the corner of my eye. His eyes were not looking in the same spot as mine. He had a shit eating grin on his face and I could tell by the way his eyes were squinted and focused, he was doing something that I did all the time—giving her a story.

"Okey dokey! And you sir?" I looked over at Brian. Our eyes connected, and I couldn't control myself. He had rolled his eyes when she said "okey-dokey," and it was all it took for me not to piss myself.

"I'll have the same."

"You guys want any apps? They sure are *tasty*." We looked at each other again, and this time we let the laughter just flow. We both looked away and tried to compose ourselves to answer, but by the time we looked back, confused Claire had gone to fetch our drinks.

"Let's call her Tasty Nips," he said. Her nickname came so easily from his lips. Accurate and effortless. It was unbelievable. It was as if he plucked her nickname right from my brain. Although so physically different, we were obviously made from the same mold.

"Indeed."

The first two hours were both easy and enlightening. Tasty Nips made sure to keep the drinks flowing, and we even enjoyed a few appetizers. We elaborated on the basic things we knew about each other from our few emails and phone conversations. I explained the adoption process, and how, although gay marriage was not legalized yet, Max and I had a commitment ceremony a decade earlier. At first I wasn't sure how far the conversations would go, especially with him being a hunter-gatherer, and I, the shopper-decorator. Brian seemed genuinely interested, asking probing questions about the details of both. I enjoyed sharing these *happy* parts of my life with him.

Listening to my brother tell his story was fascinating. Brian had fallen in love with the wrong girl and started his family too young. He was *way* too young, only 22—still not ready to let go of his wild days of partying, football and wrestling. He also had a short fuse, which when mixed with alcohol, often led him to search for trouble. Brian's temper, along with his spontaneity, led him to make decisions that were less than desirable. By the time he realized he needed to be a responsible father and husband for his family, his wife had left him. She relinquished her rights, and gave him full custody. His life changed in an instant, but unlike his biological father, Brian chose to be a man, and not run away from his responsibilities.

"It gave me the motivation to become the father I never had."

I called over Tasty Nips. It was time for another round.

◆

Brian and I had become quite comfortable joking around with each other during my stay in Billings. He teased me, making funny remarks about being sexually attracted to men, and being physically fit. *"You guys are hotties. You have to be for each other."* He made me laugh, and I loved the fact that we felt so comfortable acting that way with each other. Brian teased everyone around him, but he did it in the way only people who cared about each other did. This made me feel included. Like a *genuine* brother. And although Brian was rough around the edges, being well over six feet tall and three hundred fifty pounds, he was the emotionally softest of all. I wasn't sure how the next part of our conversation would go. And before that day, I had no idea what my perfect brother would be. But now that I had met Brian. I realized—that he fit the bill.

Claire came back with two more Guinness, placed them on the table, and left. We had pretty much ignored her throughout the evening, not participating in her quirky, bubbly remarks, obviously driven by the desire for a big tip—so like many other passive-aggressive waitresses, she left our table cluttered with empty glasses and appetizer plates. Both of us could care less. Neither of us liked women who played games.

I dove into my beer as Brian dove into the murky waters of my childhood.

"So, how was it growing up with a Dad? Was he a good father?"

Two very loaded questions in one fluid breath. I wasn't quite sure how to answer without seeming inconsiderate, and unappreciative of having grown up with one. I was the brother *blessed* with the father, so I wanted to make sure my answer was sensitive, which would not be easy. Sean had ruined my childhood in so many ways, but now that I was an adult, I had organized everything so neatly. Explaining my childhood to Brian meant I would have to open up the closet door to relive it. I didn't want to become a twisted pile again, but I owed it to him. Brian was a twisted pile himself, and by answering the questions he had carried for decades, I could help him get everything organized, folded, and put away.

"Well, he wasn't a very good father growing up." It was short enough to satisfy both questions. I wasn't sure how much to offer up without sounding like a crybaby.

"How so?"

"He was abusive."

"He hit you?"

"Yes. He was physical at times, but mostly emotional abuse." Even though I was trying to be strong, I could feel myself becoming wrinkled. The alcohol had softened my hard exterior.

"Hmm. Ma had told me some about him. She said that he had a temper."

"That is an understatement." My glass was already half empty.

"Bad, huh?"

"Very. It really fucked me up for a very long time. Still does on occasion."

"Is he a better father now?"

"Oh yeah, most definitely. But the way he would lose himself in fury and become so violent…it still makes me look at him in a way I wish I didn't anymore. It disappears for a while, but sometimes it resurfaces and brings me back."

"I have a really bad temper too. Funny thing is, I sound like him. Growing up, I often wondered why I didn't have a dad. It was hard.

By the time I became a teenager, I was getting in fights all the time, actually looking for them. People feared me. When I look back, I regret a lot of my behavior."

"I totally get the fear factor. My mother and I feared Dad for a very long time."

"That sucks man. I'm sorry."

I didn't want Brian to be sorry. It made me feel weak and vulnerable again. And as I spoke about Sean and relived the disgusting things I had to endure as a child, I wanted Brian to celebrate the fact that he *didn't* have him around as a child. *He* was the lucky one. Thinking that made me feel ashamed. I wanted to make sure that my brother understood the entire scenario—that Sean was not the only problem. Our father had grown into someone good, and capable of loving unconditionally, but Carmella now dictated who he was allowed to love that way.

"Listen Brian, I don't want to sit here and make Dad seem like just a horrific asshole, because he isn't anymore. It wasn't just him. My parents are just not good for each other. Never have been. Honestly, I think he should have stayed in Montana after my mother left him."

"Really? I think it is good that he left. I don't think my mom and him would have been a good fit. She doesn't take anyone's shit. And if he had ever tried to lay a hand on her, my grandmother would have killed him."

"I think she wanted to! Didn't she hold a gun up to him?"

"Yeah, Mom told me that story!"

We both began to laugh.

"Did you ever try and find Dad?"

"I did, but I figured that if he really wanted to have me in his life, he would have tried to find me."

"He wanted to. In the hospital, Dad told me he thought about you throughout my entire childhood. I think he acted the way he did, and did the things he did, because of just that. I couldn't image living my entire adult life knowing I had a child that I abandoned. He mistreated me, because he felt guilty about you."

"I know. He told me some of those things when we spoke on the phone. He seems like a really nice guy. I enjoyed talking with him those few months. The boys really like talking with him too. I wish our talks didn't have to end."

"I'm sorry."

"Ya know, I wasn't looking for a father, but I would've liked having him as a friend."

"He really enjoyed those talks."

"Thanks man. Hearing you say that means a lot."

We sat there for a few minutes absorbing it all. Sorting out all the laundry, and placing it where it belonged. We lifted up our glasses.

"To Sean."

"Yes. To Sean."

We toasted him.

He wasn't a good father.

But he inspired us to be great ones.

...I could smell his presence.

His Old Spice lingered on our sofa, the hand towel in the powder room off the kitchen, and on Ava.

I never asked. She never confessed.

CHAPTER TWENTY ONE

◆

JUST SHORTLY AFTER her 63rd birthday, Carmella decided to come home. It was inevitable. She had only taken five small suitcases, so when the phone rang, and it was her on the other end, asking me to book her another one-way ticket, I wasn't surprised. On several occasions, I hoped she would request that all of her belongings be shipped to the west coast, but being so far away from my Aunt and I was too difficult for her—and now that Max and I were only a few weeks away from the birth of our first child, she knew she needed to come back. She was going to become a Nona, and when I came out to my parents, she had written off the chances of ever being able to call herself that. Her jealousy swelled, knowing that Sean would be the one closest to me when our baby arrived.

Carmella had been gone almost five months. So much had changed. Once she settled into Connie's spare bedroom, she planned on finding a small apartment. Although I was happy to be seeing her, and I was glad she had found the strength to come home and continue her new life back on Long Island, I was also concerned that she wouldn't be able to handle what she was coming home to. There were no more secrets to tell, but there were new family dynamics, some shocking. Connie may have been calling Carmella to check in and see how *she* was doing; however, she left out that we had stopped communicating with each other. The two who helped her leave and who she was looking so forward to seeing again had grown extremely far apart. Also, unbeknownst to Connie or Carmella, the relationship between my father and I had grown stronger. She was not the only one who had moved on. We all had.

◆

Several months earlier, days after I found out I had a brother in Montana, I made sure to keep things truthful, honest and transparent with everyone. Although this made Sean nervous, I explained to him that he no longer needed to keep secrets from Carmella. Their marriage was over. Both of them needed to know everything in order to have closure, and I refused to be their secret-keeper anymore. I had carried way too many secrets from the age of nine, and I was tired. Besides, now that I had helped everyone reveal their secrets, I needed to focus on the one that ate me up inside. The secret I dragged alongside me since that dreadful day on the beach—like the cross Jesus dragged to his crucifixion, heavy and undeserved.

In the quest to open up my father's closet, which was not only full, but covered in 40 years of dust, I chose to call my Aunt Connie first. I knew it would be a quick, uneventful conversation. She and I had grown apart very quickly since her callous comment months earlier. Connie felt no need to call and check in, not even to find out about the adoption. She had her own family now, and she didn't want any sour Quinn brew to leak into her happy home.

As expected, she expressed herself, telling me that my father was a piece of shit, and that she was glad my mother would find out. It would be the nugget of information Carmella needed. It would "set her free." Again, she did not ask how I was, or how it was affecting me. When my mother left, she not only washed her hands of Sean, but me as well. She was one of the few people in my life I had learned to trust, and she showed no concern. My wall for her grew the thickest, not because I didn't love her, but because I expected more from her.

Calling my mother to tell her the news did not bother me in the least. She had become cocky and short with me—as if she and Connie had morphed into one person. I called this Carmella's "*independent tone.*" It was the one I watched her use on my father for years. Only this time it was my turn.

"*You sound so irritable. Are you starving yourself again?*"

"*You should go back to church.*"

"*I'm surprised you answered. I know you screen your phone calls.*"

"Have you called your Aunt lately, or are you too busy with your father?"

Whenever she wanted others to think she was strong and capable, she held her head high, and became short and cocky with her words. And I knew why she had taken this tone with me—I had stopped talking about my father with her. When she first left, I was still angry with Sean for the things he had done, but my views were changing, and I was no longer interested in bashing talks, or explaining all the things he was doing. She recognized the shift. Carmella was on guard. She realized she wasn't the only one being rescued. *Did my mother actually think I would kick my father to the curb, and let him wither and die alone?* This realization caused her to withdraw. It was probably the same reason why Connie did too.

"Hello, my son!" This was Carmella's new way of answering the phone when I called. Exaggerated and transparent.

"Hey, Ma. How's it going?"

"Oh, *very* good. Keeping busy with my cousins. I got involved with a small church group here too." We had cousins all over the West Coast, so it was easy to find Carmella the refuge she needed when she wanted to leave.

"Ah, that's great. How is everyone?"

"Great! It is so good to be spending time with them. So much reminiscing and laughing. How's Max?"

"He's fine." He wasn't. Max was angry, and fed up. My history shocked him, and he had no tolerance for it repeating itself. He disliked the fact that my mother and Aunt had not stepped forward to recognize how hard all of this was on me. He grew up in a divorced family that had kept secrets and chose the path of least resistance. He was much better at politely stepping around the elephant in the room, rather than confronting things straight on. He was on overload.

"That's good. I have been keeping a journal, like you told me to. And I am reading all the articles you copied for me. Thanks, Hun. You're right; keeping a journal helps. You learn a lot about yourself when you reread it." I had never kept one. It was advice I had gotten from a colleague and passed off as my own to help keep her busy.

"Oh, good. Listen Ma, I'm calling for a specific reason. I have something to tell you."

"I know you do." Her independent voice turned on.

"What?"

"Your Aunt called me."

"She did? What did she tell you?"

"That you were going to call me."

"She called you to tell you I was going to call? Why? What the fuck is she, your informant? God. She's such a shit-stirrer."

"She's my sister!"

"I could care less who she is! She has nothing to do with this conversation. I don't feel like fighting with you about her."

"Fine." Short. Cold. She had transformed into a Quinn and didn't even know it.

"Listen. Dad told me something, and I have to share it with you."

Silence.

"Ma?"

"Yes. I am here."

"He has a son."

Silence again.

"Ma?" No answer. "He has another son. He is only four months older than me. He's been carrying this secret for decades. I thought you should know."

"Rosa." The genuine Carmella returned. She couldn't use her independent voice when she went weak—she wasn't as good of an actor as I.

"Yes."

"When did he tell you? I can't believe this. How could he do this to me?"

"Mom, you need—"

She interrupted. "I had a feeling. Montana! I should have left him there!"

"But you did."

"I should have never taken him back! My life would have been so much better if I had divorced him the first time! Nothing good came of this marriage!"

She continued to dump her anger through the phone and into my ear. Part of me felt sorry for her—finding out that her husband who had betrayed her more than once fathered another child decades earlier. But listening to her say that nothing good came of her marriage, compounded by the fact that she, again, did not ask me how I was handling the news, made my insides burn with hatred.

Did she actually think that everything I experienced only affected her?

Could she be that clueless? That blind?

Didn't that fucking journal teach her anything important about herself? Her shortcomings? Or was she only writing things in it about everyone else?

For a few more minutes I allowed her to scream her frustrations and cry her woes, consoling her like the selfless son I once was. I was slowly realizing that I could no longer be. After she told me that she was going to take my father for all he was worth, she told me *"You can take care of him!"* and hung up. Like *he* was my burden. It was as if she were angry with *me* for finding out I had a brother.

———————◆———————

I decided not to tell my father that Carmella was living with her sister two towns over. For now, I thought it best he still believe that she was far away somewhere. He never really knew where she went, but the one thing he did know was that she couldn't be found. This was good, because he never actually wasted time searching for her once he got home from the hospital. I knew she would eventually begin to show up at church and other places they had both gone to as a couple, so it was only a matter of time before they crossed paths. Besides, Sean was busy with his own life—back at work, keeping the house in order, and spending more time with his mother.

Sean had also begun to make new friendships. The day after I gave him my gift, he began to use it. The first person he called was Rosa. When I found out, I was glad. He had taken my advice. He called me the morning he planned on reaching out to his past.

"Benny. It's Dad. How's Max?"

"Good. How are you?"

"Good. Keeping busy. Listen, you got a minute?"

"Sure. What's up?"

"I want to call your brother today, but I am nervous as hell. What do I say?"

"Well, he knows you're going to call. I told him it would happen eventually, once you were ready. But can I give you some advice first?"

"Yeah."

"Call Rosa." I heard him exhale on the other end. I knew that sound. He knew I was right, but he needed to hear it.

"I should, right?"

"Yeah Dad, you should. She deserves the call. What you two did to Mommy was wrong, but that was so long ago. What you need to do is focus on what you did to her. You need to try and make things right. How can you possibly have a relationship with the son you never even looked for, when you haven't tried to make amends with his mother?"

"Ok."

"Good luck. I'll call you later."

Rosa was very angry with his initial call, expressing her distaste, and cursing him for neglecting to acknowledge her son all those years. When he shared this, I was glad to hear that she cursed him. To go all those years without closure must have been hell, and now it was *her* opportunity to make him listen. Sean felt bad that he had stirred up old painful emotions for her and backed off, leaving it up to her to call him if she desired to. He was fine with this. Sean's apologies were forty years overdue, and now that he had all this free time, he decided to be patient and make things right. It took some time, but eventually Rosa called, and pretty soon they were talking for hours every day, like old friends. She was able to share her motherly memories of Brian as he grew up, and he enjoyed hearing about how much his son was just like him—even though he wasn't around. One day, while they were talking, Rosa passed the phone over to Brian. It was the first time they spoke. I enjoyed listening to my dad talk about it.

Sean was forgiven.
Reborn.
He appeared younger.
I booked him a round trip ticket.
He was free to be a father to both sons.
Free for three whole months.

———————◆———————

Our daughter, Ava, was born in April. We got the call from one of Karen's friends at around three o'clock in the morning. We already had a bag packed—like expectant mothers— knowing their water was going to break any day now. Karen lived in Pennsylvania, so Max and I had a five-hour drive ahead of us, but luckily we made it just as she was crowning. We were both elated and scared. Six hours earlier, we were fast asleep, expecting our daughter to be born at least 3-4 weeks later, so when we cut the umbilical cord and were handed our tiny little angel, we were still in shock. I called my mother on the way to give her the update. Her bags were also packed and ready, waiting for the phone call that would change her title.

Nona would be moving in with us. Although Max and I were apprehensive at first, we decided that having her around would be a great help, especially for the first couple of weeks. She was still edgy and abrupt with me at times, but since moving in with my Aunt Connie, they both seemed less distant. My Aunt began calling again to see how we were and express her excitement for us. With all the anxiety and stress Max and I were going through as Ava's arrival got closer, I had no desire to express my concerns. I went ahead and played their game, knowing all too well that Connie's excitement was more for her sister rather than us.

After Ava was released from the hospital, she, Max and I stayed in a hotel on the Pennsylvania/New Jersey border for a couple of days. This was the New York State adoption policy. We enjoyed this time together. Max and I were able to take turns getting up several times throughout the night to feed her and change her doll-size diapers. During those couple of days, Carmella moved into the guest bedroom, directly next to Ava's, and helped get our house in order with the things we needed for Ava's arrival. Many of our close friends helped, so by the time we got home, we didn't want for anything.

By the third day, everyone in our immediate families had expressed their desires to meet the new addition to our family—especially Max's mother and brother, as well as Carmella and Sean. By this time, Carmella and Sean had been to our home, in each other's company, to discuss things they wanted to do for us for Ava's impending birth. On several occasions, they had individually expressed their desires to help us. Each wanted to buy furniture and clothes for the baby's nursery. I could sense the competitiveness, and I had no desire to play favorites, or be a referee.

To avoid either of them spending too much money separately, I asked them to come over, so we could all communicate about it, and come to some sort of agreement. Each meeting went well, and both of them were considerate of us, and civil to one another. After a few minutes of small talk, I would quickly get down to business, telling them what we would appreciate from them, and allowing them to divvy up the list. I began to trust that they had both emotionally moved on, and they could now celebrate their new grandchild in each other's company without making anyone else uncomfortable. I wanted only positive energy in my home, and I made it clear to them at our first meeting that if either of them made any waves, they would be asked to leave. I also explained to them that I did not want to be their telephone operator, giving messages to either of them from the other. They would need to discuss things directly, leaving me out of it. My own fatherly instincts came into play, and I knew I would never allow their negativity to infect my children the way it had infected me.

Two days before we got approval to leave Pennsylvania, the phone rang early in the morning.

"Hello?" I could hardly communicate. Max and I had been up most of the night, not because Ava kept us up, but because like all new parents, we couldn't sleep. For hours, we sat there and watched her breathe, making sure her tiny chest kept moving. The hospital had made us watch several videos, one of which was on SIDS. Go figure.

"Benny? It's Mom. How are you feeling honey?"

"Exhausted."

"Awww. It will get easier. Believe me, I've been there."

"Yup."

"Listen. Is it okay if we come and see you today? I'm dying to hold my grandbaby!"

"Sure. Bring whatever you want to eat, we only have the basics here. What time are you expecting to arrive?" She covered the phone, and I could hear her talking to someone.

"Around noon. Is that okay?"

"Sure. I have tea bags for you and DeDe, so you don't need to stop for it before you come." Max and I had stocked up on caffeinated tea bags, and instant coffee pods and cups from the continental breakfasts we had dragged ourselves to since we checked in.

"Who? Aunt Connie's not coming."

"Oh, I'm so exhausted, I misunderstood you. I thought someone was coming with you."

"Dad is driving." She said it as if she was surprised I was confused.

"Oh. Ok. I wasn't *expecting* that." Max could hear the shift in my voice, and he was waving to get my attention. We were both wide awake now. I covered the phone and mouthed the update. He raised one brow and walked into the bathroom.

"Why not? *You* told us that you wanted us to be able to get along for our grandchild." She was defensive, which immediately made me defensive.

"Getting along and driving together are two completely different things, Ma! Don't get attitude with me because I am surprised about this. Honestly, I am not in the mood to be concerned either. We will see you around noon."

"Fine." She hung up.

They drove together and spent several hours with us. I observed the way they communicated with each other. Neither of them seemed emotionally distant, and my mother did not use the tone of voice with my father that I had become accustomed to my entire life.

Maybe they were acting to keep the visit peaceful.

Maybe they realized that they needed to act like adults for Ava, Max, and me.

Maybe they improved so much separately that being around each other didn't matter.

For a very brief moment in time, my beautiful daughter blinded me from the obvious, and Max kept his concerns to himself to alleviate some of my anxiety—but all along I knew it was too soon for them to be in each other's company. I shouldn't have used my daughter as an excuse for them to "get along," but rather have them spend time with us separately. Now when I think back to that day, and I rehash every moment in my mind with a fine-toothed comb, I realize I missed the most obvious thing. Subtle to others perhaps, but from experience, it should have been obvious to me.

Carmella called to let us know they were coming.

Carmella called when they got home.

Carmella commanded most during their visit.

Even days after that visit, when Max and I got home and settled in with Ava, I didn't recognize the obvious. By the time I actually did, I feared it was too late.

———————◆———————

A few months were all I could handle. In the recent weeks of chaotic fatherhood transition, Carmella proved extremely helpful with Ava—waking up at night to let us catch up on lost sleep, offering to change her diapers, feed her, or take her on walks in our neighborhood so she would take a nap in the stroller. She also did her best to give us our space, but no matter how hard she tried to be useful, after the initial dust had settled, what should have been obvious to me weeks earlier finally became apparent. It enraged me to the core. And it wasn't just her. Sean enraged me too.

Even though I never caught them together, I could tell when my father had been over, or they had been in each other's company. I had taken time off from work to be home with Ava full-time, so my mother would often say *"Why don't you go out for a few hours and have some time alone. You need it Benny!"* This was great, but when I got home, I could smell his presence. His Old Spice lingered on our sofa, the hand towel in the powder room off the kitchen, and on Ava. I never asked. She never confessed. Neither did he. They were sneaking around like when I was a young boy, living with my grandparents—"dating" again. Enjoying their *newness*. However, I was not a little boy looking into an empty closet this time; I was an adult becoming more and more disgusted with their secretiveness.

I had my own secret weapon. I wasn't sure if I would have to use it, but before I did, I needed to make sure. I played along with Carmella and Sean, playing deaf, dumb and blind, hoping whatever was happening between them would run its course, then fizzle out. Each time Sean came over for dinner, they sat far apart from each other and engaged in small talk. No prolonged eye contact, no hugs, or kisses hello. He never mentioned "stopping by," and I never spoke of his smell. We all played our roles in our tragic and twisted play.

They pretended not to want each other, and I pretended to tolerate the awkwardness between them. I knew what they were doing would certainly fracture the bones that had finally mended. Eventually, the game became too much for me to handle, and for Max to tolerate. When I came home from the gym one day, I noticed a Dunkin' Donuts coffee cup in the trash. He left evidence behind. Carmella's back was to me. She was washing all the annoying parts of Ava's Dr. Brown's baby bottles.

"Hey Ma. Has Ava been sleeping long?"

"No. She just went down about fifteen minutes ago. My God! There are so many parts to these things!" Carmella seemed jumpy and unsettled, and even with the steam from the hot water billowing around her, she did not turn around to face me. I walked over and put my hand on her shoulder.

"Just let them soak, Ma. I'll take care if that later." She shook her head, and kept washing the inserts. "Did she have a hard time falling asleep? I expected her to go down for her nap over an hour ago."

"Yeah. She was fussy."

"Oh. I hope it's not the formula. It will be our third one."

"Nah, probably just antsy. You were like that sometimes. So, how was the gym?"

She changed the subject. I knew why. I made some tea and decided to change the topic myself.

"You want some tea?"

"No thanks. I had some earlier." She was still keeping herself busy, wiping up the water around the sink with the bright yellow dishtowel.

"Ma, listen. I want to talk to you while Ava is asleep. Come sit." I walked into our dining room and sat down at the large oval table. We had recently purchased distressed black furniture to match the hutch I had refinished. It belonged to my Nana and Poppa, and as a child I would open up the bottom doors and hide inside it. I wanted Ava to do the same. It was my new favorite room, and it reminded me of them.

"What about?" Carmella sat down. Now I had her full attention. I could tell by the serious indent between her brows.

"About you and Dad."

"What about us?" Although the tone of her independent voice hadn't made an appearance, I could see she was deciding if it should.

"Well, lately you seem different. Like something is on your mind." I wanted to still play my part right. The concerned son—making sure his Mommy was okay. Dangling some bait. Seeing if she would bite.

"Not really. I have been a bit *lonely*, but other than that, nothing."

"Lonely? How? You are in so many clubs, and you're always going on bus trips and stuff."

"I know. But that's different."

"How?" She looked at me and sighed, knowing that I was not going to stop probing.

"Benny, you may not understand this because you are so young, but after you have been married for as long as your father and I have been, you get used to having a companion. I am lonely for a companion." As she spoke, I understood what she was saying. It made sense. It was heartfelt and true. I felt bad for her.

"Mom, I totally understand and I can see that you are lonely. Let's do something about it! Why not go to a single's dance for older people?" She still hadn't given me what I was looking for. I wanted her to tell me that Sean had been sneaking in visits. That they had been to the movies and dinner and God knows where else. I needed her to tell me that they were "dating."

"Nah! That's not for me. I'm too old for that." She nervously laughed it off, as if she was senile and frail, ready for a nursing home. Like it could never be an option. She was on to me. I could tell. Either my acting skills were slipping, or I was looking to be caught. Whatever the case, I *did not* want them back together.

Whether they were secretly dating or not, something wasn't right about the whole situation. *Why would she be hiding this from me? What did Sean do that made her forget about everything that he had ever done, especially the news about his other son?* Then it made complete sense.

In recent weeks, Sean had not updated me on his phone talks with Rosa, Brian, or his grandsons, Scott and Collin. He had dodged the topic and often changed the subject when I brought it up. Although Carmella knew about his son in Montana, she was unaware of his long distant communications. He had kept it a secret. Carmella would *never* be sneaking around with Sean, starting a new beginning with him, if she knew. They were beginning a new relationship, already built on secrets and lies. Just the thought of possibly reliving another round of the Carmella and Sean saga made me nauseous.

I needed to stop it.

I wanted to sabotage it.

I thought my plan would work, and make everyone happy.

I was wrong.

◆

A few months before Carmella left Sean, I talked them into getting cell phones. Up until now, neither of them wanted cell phones, or an answering machine, but since they were getting older, I felt it necessary in case of emergencies. For Mother's and Father's Day, I surprised them with cell phones by adding them to my own plan. Knowing they could reach me gave me peace of mind—but now, being able to pull up Sean's records gave me the ammo I needed to stop what was going on between them.

I let them secretly date for another full week, each day printing out Sean's phone records that I would eventually give to my mother. As I highlighted each phone call to Montana, it made me happy to see that he was still communicating with everyone, including Rosa. But as I highlighted each late-night two hour phone call, I noticed a pattern. During the day, he would spend time with my mother, then as soon as he got home, he would call Rosa. Sean did this every single day. Not only was he keeping this secret from Carmella, he obviously hadn't told Rosa he was seeing his estranged wife again. Sean was digging his own grave, and I knew that if I didn't act fast, it would all blow up in his face, and I would end up having to be the one picking up everyone's pieces.

Max knew my plan. Max strategically made plans to spend the whole day visiting his childhood friend, Sarah, who also had a child around the same age as Ava. He knew I needed an entire day—time to not only present Carmella with my findings, but for her volcano to explode. Ultimately, I hoped it would wake her up and set her free. But it wasn't all just about her. It would set Sean free too. I wanted to free him from the web he was allowing himself to get tangled up in again. The web I had rescued him from.

After Max left for the day, I made myself a pot of coffee. Carmella had just gotten out of the shower, and I could hear her tinkering with her make-up in the guest bathroom. It was late morning, and I knew the only plan she had was to help out at the food pantry. She had made friends there, and I knew it would be a good place for her to go after I dropped the bomb.

A bright red folder sat upon the black dining room table, like one of those emergency fire alarms on any school wall—just screaming to be touched. Inside were all of Sean's new secrets. Weeks of them. Organized, and highlighted in neon yellow. It was for her. I had made copies for myself. I knew she would want her own copies to throw in Sean's face, the same way she threw Heather's phone records at him when I was a child. When she finally came down, I was ready, sitting at the table with my favorite red mug, full of black coffee.

"Hey honey. Did Max leave already?" My mother was in a good mood. Almost chipper. She had taken extra time on her hair and makeup, something she normally didn't do when helping out at the food pantry. She was wearing a fitted plum colored sweater, with dark gray slacks. She looked beautiful, and for a brief moment, I felt bad knowing that the red folder would change that.

"Good morning. You look nice."

"Thank you. I am going out for lunch with the girls after helping out. I just bought this outfit yesterday at *Kohl's*, along with some other things. Everything else is too big."

From the time she left New York to now, Carmella had once again lost a considerable amount of weight, and she was happy to show off her figure. But I could tell that her new outfit was *not* meant for her lady friends. She also had on some of her best jewelry—her diamond stud earrings and pendant, the watch my father had given her years earlier, and the large, emerald cut, Amethyst ring I had given her when I was younger. *Who spent an hour creating the perfect smoky eye and wore fine jewelry to hand out food to the needy?*

"Ah. Well, you look beautiful." I got up and gave her a kiss on her cheek, then I refilled my mug.

"You want tea?"

"No. So, what are your plans for the day?"

"Not really sure. I might take a long walk on the beach, then hit the gym." I sat down at the table again. "Ma, come sit. I need to ask you something." I spoke, as nonchalant as possible. I did not want to alarm her.

"Sure, honey," she sat down across from me. "What is it? Is something wrong?"

"Yes. Something is wrong. I have something important to ask you, and I need you to be honest with me." As I spoke, I moved the red folder in front of me.

"What's that?" Her focus shifted to the folder.

"I'll get to this in a minute. But I need to ask you something first."

Like a school girl, Carmella straightened her posture, put her arms on the table, and crossed her hands. "OK. What?"

"I need you to be honest about this. And it's hard for me to ask. But...are you and Dad seeing each other again?"

My mouth went dry as the words came out of my mouth. Her posture stiffened, and her face went rigid.

"That is none of your business!" Her nasty tone excited me.

"What? What do you mean *none of my business*?"

"If your father and I are trying to work things out, it is *our* business! I don't get involved in your and Max's business, do I?" She spoke to me as if I were a child, asking something inappropriate for my age.

I slammed my hands against the table and got up. Carmella was bringing out the worst in me. The part that I kept locked up and tried so hard to control my entire life. The part of me that Carmella and Sean had created. Anger.

"What the fuck do Max and I have to do with any of this? You have not answered my question, Mom! Are you guys getting back together?"

Carmella got up, and walked over to the coffee table. She grabbed her jacket and purse. "Mind your business! I don't want to talk about it. I'm leaving. I don't need to be around you when you are like this." She was running, again. Except this time, she was running from me.

"Wait! Before you go. I have something for you." I walked over and grabbed the folder. I was happy to give it to her now—happy to the point of being sadistic. Although not a physical person, I wanted to slap her across the face. Unlike the way she spoke to me, she deserved these papers. I had saved her time and time again, wasting my entire life protecting her, and here I was, being spit in the face. I held out his lies, and she walked over to take it.

"I don't have time for this shit! What is it?" She grabbed it with attitude.

I didn't answer. I sat on the sofa and watched her open it. Her smoky eyes scanned the first page, only looking up at me for an instant. She dropped her purse and jacket on the floor and walked over to the table. My mother force fed herself each page—chewing on it—trying her best to swallow it all. It was pleasurable to watch. For weeks, I had degraded myself. Cheapened my own identity. I had volunteered myself to get wrapped up in their drama again. Now, I was finally releasing myself from it all.

Finally she spoke. "I don't understand. What is all this?"

"You figure it out." It was all I could say. I got up, and went upstairs. The level of anger brewing inside my gut made it impossible for me to speak. Carmella had made it clear that their relationship was none of my business. And the more I thought about that, I realized she was right. It wasn't. As a matter of fact, most of what they did to each other my entire life should have been none of my business. *They were the ones who made it my business.* I took her advice. And for my own sanity, I promised myself to keep it that way for the rest of my life.

Carmella was downstairs crying, weak, broken, and confused. This time I didn't have the energy in me to care.

———————◆———————

Three days later, Carmella moved out. Actually, I told her to. At some point after I left her at the dining room table, crying over the phone records, she left. I heard her come back very late that night, and for the next few days she avoided me by leaving before I got up, and coming home after she knew I went to bed.

I never went back downstairs after leaving her with Sean's lie. I stayed upstairs until Max got home. I was too angry to. Too scared of what I may do if she was still down there.

Would I rip a phone off the wall?

Would I get physical?

Would I berate her until she fell to the floor begging for mercy?

Had my time come? Was it my time to transform into them?

New anger piled on top of all the old anger I had stored in my closet. It became too much to handle. It weighed my head down like an anchor. My eyes became too heavy to open. I had hit my breaking point, and many would say they were surprised it didn't happen sooner. My anger was pure. Genuine. Toxic.

I was angry for everything my parents had done to each other for the past 40 years.

I was angry for all the shit they had put me through, and were still throwing my way.

I was angry for saving her way too many times, then being taken for granted.

I was angry for being touched, and treated like an adult when I was a child.

I was angry for allowing my cowardly father to give my brother and nephews false hope.

I was angry for being expected to always forgive and forget.

I was angry for being used like a personal therapist while trying to stay sane.

More importantly, I was angry for being masochistic, because obviously, I was.

Carmella and Sean were officially back together—take them, or leave them. It was a slow process for many, but over time, everything fell back into place the way it had so many times before. They went to church, and hung out with the friends they had taken a hiatus from. They "grew" as a couple through counseling, learning how to communicate better, and be more understanding of each other. They finally had the relationship they had wanted from the very beginning. Everyone learned to be happy for them again. I was indifferent. I played along for two years, hoping that someday I would be able to look at them and not be angry. Holidays. Birthdays. Anniversaries. *They* celebrated being a family, and I was acting again, longing to reach out to the family that Sean was forced to abandon once more—that I had now abandoned too. Everyone had moved forward, but I had regressed.

It was simple. There was no room in *her* life for *his* son and grandchildren.

In the end, Carmella won. Sean caved to Carmella; Brian, Scott, Collin and I lost.

After two long years, I gave up on Carmella and Sean the way they had given up on me many times throughout my life.

I needed to find peace again. Without them.

Letting them go was easier than I thought, and the best thing I would ever do.

CHAPTER TWENTY TWO

◆

THE ENTICING SMELL of freshly brewed coffee woke me. Groggy and confused, I sat up on the edge of the bed. It was still dark outside, and at first I thought I was home, expecting Max to walk in with a cup, telling me it was time to start the day. Then I realized where I was. Down the hall, I could hear Rosa emptying the dishwasher. I would be leaving my Montana family in a few hours, and for the first time, the thought of drinking a cup made me sick to my stomach. Although I missed Max and the girls tremendously, four days just didn't seem like enough time, especially after waiting two long years. The day before, Rosa had offered for me to check out of the motel and stay in her guestroom, so we could all have some last minute quality time before I had to leave.

I dreaded opening the bedroom door and walking down the hall. Saying "goodbye for now," was going to be much harder than I initially thought. It was going to be hard for everyone. The night before, we all had dinner together, laughing and joking around, as if we had been in each others' company our entire lives, but in the back of our minds we all knew that would end the next day. No one said it, but that feeling was evident the entire time. The visit, although short and intense, had significantly changed each of us. We were stronger. We had closure. We were family.

I turned on the light, folded the clothes I had scattered around the room, and packed them in the large red duffle bag I traveled with. I picked up my wrinkled jeans, and the Montana State sweatshirt Scott had taken me to buy at the mall two days earlier. Even though I had worn them the night before, I shook them out, placed them on the bed, and decided to wear them again. Besides, I hadn't shaved during my entire visit, and the growth on my face seemed to match my disheveled clothes perfectly. I looked in the mirror and liked what I saw. Rather than a corporate polished mannequin in a starchy suit, I saw a content, relaxed guy, comfortable in his skin.

After a quick shower, I finally made my way down the hall. Rosa was sitting in the living room drinking a cup of coffee, and reading the new book she had bought the day we met at *Barnes and Noble*.

"Well good morning. Coffee is made, so help yourself."

"Thanks. I'm going to need it. Lots of it. After my flight lands and I get out of long term parking, I have about an hour drive." My flight was landing at 10:30 at night, so without traffic, I was hoping to make it home by midnight at the latest. "How's the new book?"

"It's good! I couldn't sleep very well last night, so I am already half way through it. How'd you sleep?"

"Ok, I guess. It took me awhile to fall asleep, and I tossed and turned a bit."

We both had told each other "This is going to suck!" without actually saying it.

"The guys will be here shortly. I am going to make breakfast for all of us before they take you to the airport. You okay with eggs and sausage?"

"Sure. Thanks."

Rosa got up, put her book down on the coffee table, and walked into the kitchen. After she placed the dishes and silverware on the kitchen table, she stopped and sat down. She was staring out the window, and I could see she was crying. She took off her glasses and wiped her eyes. I wanted to look away. Pretend that I didn't see her sadness. But I couldn't. I got up and walked over to the table, sitting down right across from her. We both sat staring out the window, watching the snow fall for a few minutes, tears gently rolling down our faces. The silence between us was comforting. We were getting ready to say goodbye.

"I am so glad you came, Ben. I really am."

"So am I."

"You have given me so much. More than you know. Thank you." Rosa reached out her hand. I held it.

"No, thank you. You have no idea how much coming here has changed my life, and I am sorry for everything that my father has done to you."

"That doesn't matter anymore."

"No, it doesn't."

We both got up and hugged. It was a genuine hug—like the ones I saw between her and Scott. I felt honored. I didn't want to let go.

A few minutes later, Brian, Scott and Collin arrived. We sat around, ate breakfast, and laughed about some of the things we had said and done during the visit. After about an hour, it was time to head to the airport. Rosa walked over to me, and put her hands on my shoulders. She looked at me and smiled.

"I'm going to miss you, Ben."

Rosa and I already had our moment. Our moment of closure. I wanted to keep that between us. "Damn straight you will!"

She let go, laughed, and threw her hands up in the air. "Oh Lord! Sarcastic. Just like Brian! You two must get that from your Dad."

Sean was *our* Dad. No longer taboo to say. No longer shameful to admit.

◆

The drive to the airport only took about twenty minutes. Scott and Collin sat in the back of the truck and did most of the talking. Brian and I couldn't. Our visit had come to an end, and we were both too sad to speak. Although Brian was the epitome of rugged masculinity, his heart was softer than mine. He had no defensive shell. The two of us kept looking straight ahead, avoiding eye contact, trying to hold back what we were both feeling. It was the first sign of true brotherhood. We were trying to protect each other from feeling pain. When we passed the spot where Sean had taken the very first picture of Carmella in Montana, I looked over at my brother.

"Brian, why don't you just drop me off in front of the terminal? I have to check in and go through security. You all don't need to come in and wait while I do that." I was giving him an out. Rather than suffering through a prolonged goodbye, I could exit the truck quickly, making it more casual and less dramatic. I could see the relief in his eyes.

"Are you sure, bro?" He had Sean's smile.

"Yup."

"Cool. I am not one for weepy goodbyes anyway."

"Neither am I."

"Ha! Of course you are. You gay guys are all so sensitive."

We both laughed. Not because of Brian's levity in our moment of sadness, but because we both understood how sensitive we both were.

As we pulled up to the terminal entrance and Brian parked alongside the curb, Scott leaned in.

"Hey Unc. I have this for you." He handed me his copy of *The Four Agreements*. "It's a quick read. Read it on the way home. It's way better than GQ."

"Thanks. I will."

"It's not a *gift*. I'm lending it to you. Bring it back the next time you come and visit."

"Sounds like a plan."

I hopped out of the truck, and grabbed my bag from the back seat. Brian opened up the passenger window.

"Ok Bro. I love ya man."

"Love you too."

I stepped back and waved goodbye as they drove off.

Although our goodbye was quick, it was not final.

It was just for now.

───────────── ◆ ─────────────

Once again, the tiny airport in Billings was practically empty. Within twenty minutes I had checked in, walked through security, and found my way to the *only* coffee shop in the entire place. It was refreshing to have only one option rather than fifty, like in New York. The simplicity of Billings appealed to me now. It put things in perspective.

How many minutes had I spent in my life figuring out which coffee shop to enter?

How many hours had I wasted trying to find the right pair of jeans in my messy walk-in closet just to go grocery shopping?

How many years did I waste time and energy being angry for the things I couldn't control or fix?

My time in Montana did more than just bond me with my brother and nephews—it had changed the way I viewed life and myself. However, it *did not* change my desire to read magazines, or turn my back to strangers sitting next to me on planes. Some things were just too engraved into me to buff away. But isn't that true for anyone?

Although the book Scott lent me was screaming my name, and burning a hole in my backpack, I still needed my trivial, shallow reading material and crossword puzzle. By the time I actually got to Gate 2 (there were only three at Billings Airport), I had an array of them to keep me entertained and make me appear busy to those around me during my flights home. By the time I reached my layover in Denver, I found it difficult to focus on new fashion trends and exercise tips for killer biceps. I kept thinking about Scott's book, and how similar we were. How I felt like I was looking at myself before the decades of pain had stripped me of my softness. If someone so young, and so similar to me, had found a self-help book so rewarding, eye opening, and poignant—then there was a reason why he wanted me to read it.

I quickly checked in with Max to let him know that I had safely landed in Denver, and I told the girls I would give them kisses when I got home, even though they would be sleeping. After hanging up, I immediately sat down and dove into my borrowed, *"Practical Guide to Personal Freedom."* By the time we were ready to board, I was already halfway through the 138 page miracle read. I was amazed that a book finally grabbed me. I had made it past the first ten pages, and I didn't want to put it down. For years, I wandered through book stores, waiting for the right one to call me. To help me. To heal me. To make the anger go away. But all along it was sitting on my nephew's shelf in Montana—the state that Sean and Carmella had run from so many decades earlier. I couldn't wait to run back.

Kate was the stewardess for this portion of my trip. She was not as interesting or attractive as Nancy. She didn't seem to enjoy her job, and I could tell she was pissed at her prettier colleague who got to work First Class. I watched her for a few minutes, dragging herself about the cabin, giving evil eyes to her nemesis. It was far too easy. Kate's story could have evolved through my imaginative mind without effort, but this time, I had more important things to do. I had to finish helping myself.

Don't Take Anything Personally. This was the second of the "Four Agreements." It was the perfect part to read, *then re-read*, as I got closer to New York. The philosophy behind this chapter spoke volumes to me.

Throughout our lives, we learn to suffer at the hands of others because we take the things they do personally. This was the main difference between my found family, and the family I was born into. In Montana, no one seemed to blame anyone for anything. No one harbored anger. Rosa didn't blame Sean for leaving when she was pregnant and never turning back. She didn't harbor resentment towards him for not stepping forward. Brian never showed anger towards Sean for coming into his life so suddenly, then dropping out again so abruptly. None of them took things personally. They didn't allow the poor decisions of others to negatively impact their own.

I had.

I had taken everything Carmella and Sean did to *each other* personally. But it was always all about them. Yes, I was affected, but who wouldn't be? I realized it was time to let go. The anger was never mine to have. It was something I decided to take. Something I chose to store away.

I felt regret. Regret for creating an exoskeleton to protect myself from harm. Even though it protected me, it also trapped my anger inside, not allowing forgiveness to permeate. Each time someone told me to forgive and forget, I took it as a personal attack. Like they were telling me the anger I felt wasn't important enough to hold on to. Really, they were trying to tell me it was not worth it. It never was.

But I finally listened. My found family gave me the gift. The gift of forgiveness. A chance to finally heal.

To purge the anger.

To find the ability to love Mom and Dad as they were.

To no longer take their actions personally.

After leaving Montana, I was free.

THANK YOU

I want to thank Ida and Frank Bellissimo—Your loud, proud unconditional love flowed effortlessly during your time here on Earth. I can easily feel you around me every day.

I also want to thank *and* apologize to all my genuine friends, both old and new, for withstanding stormy Whaley's process with a simple smile. I owe each of you an umbrella.

◆

ABOUT THOMAS

THOMAS WHALEY was born in 1972 and has lived on Long Island his entire life. He has been an elementary school teacher since 1999 and has had a passion for writing since childhood. He earned his B.A. in Communications from Marymount University in Arlington, Virginia and his M.A. in Elementary Education from Dowling University on Long Island. After his debut novel, Leaving Montana, Thomas plans to focus more time on a second novel and publishing his children's books.

Thomas currently lives in Shoreham, New York with his husband Carl, their two sons Andrew and Luke and their loyal dogs Jake and Sam.

◆

47179948R00125

Made in the USA
Lexington, KY
29 November 2015